Raven

Dressed to Kill

By:

Kris Butler

First Edition: April 2023

Published by: Incognito Scribe Productions LLC

Kris Butler

Proofreading: © 2023 by Owlsome Author Services

Formatting: © 2023 Incognito Scribe Productions LLC

Cover Design: © 2023 Jodielocks Designs.

❀ Created with Vellum

Raven

KRIS BUTLER

CONTENTS

BLURB

Being an assassin could be lonely at times.

To pass the time, I did three things: talked to myself, created chemical formulas to use on marks, and watched my favorite medical drama. Oh, and yeah, that other thing where I healthily stalked my favorite thief group.

That was a thing, right? Favorite thief groups? If it wasn't, it should be. Everything about the Loxley Crew sent my heart into a flutter. They stole from the rich and gave to the poor, like a modern day Robin Hood. I caught sightings of them at times before or after a job, but we never ran into one another while working.

Not that I'd know what to say if I did. Awkward girl alert.

My current mission included three names—the last of a corrupt pharmaceutical company that I had a score to settle with. It should've been a piece of cake. Mmm, cake.

Except, nothing was simple when murder was involved and I stumbled into the Loxley Crew—all four of them. Now that they'd found me, they insisted on following me, and making my once hollow heart full.

But assassins didn't get happy endings.

This is a standalone multi-love interest book with violence and explicit scenes and ends in a HEA. Check the foreward for more information to decide if this book is the right fit for you.

FOREWORD

This book is about assassins, and therefore does contain some violence. Raven's method of killing is medical (death by embolism).

The main characters have all experienced traumatic pasts that deal with drug abuse, physical abuse, emotional abuse, sexual abuse, and murder of loved ones. This mostly takes place off screen with just a few recollections. That being said, this book is more gray than dark, with loving and obsessive men who love to dote on their girl. It's a med-high burn with love at first sight. There are explicit sexual scenes and language. This book does not have other women drama or cheating. It's low angst with the love interests and ends in a HEA.

TRIGGERS

- Death
- Violence
- Past abuse (sexual, physical, emotional, substance)
- Witnessing death/murder
- Medical conditions (seizures)

TROPES

- Identical Twins
- Female Assassin
- Thief group (Robin Hood-esque)
- Obsessive men
- Doting caring men on female (feeding, carrying, brushing hair)
- Curvy FMC who likes to eat and embraces her body

THINGS YOU'LL FIND

- Sensory play
- All the guys have tattoos
- Size differences

- Men comfortable with each other both in affection and in the bedroom, but no sword crossing
- Dirty Talk
- Toys
- Anal sex
- Group Scenes
- "It will fit"
- Praise "good girl/good boy"
- Female switch
- Twin sandwich
- "You'll break first" bet
- Road head

*To being accepted and cherished for all the parts of you
from the awkward flirt, kind heart, to the darkness.*

*To being able to take care of yourself and handle your
business, but also enjoy being pampered and loved on by a
group of men who think you hung the moon.*

*To discovering your sexual desire in a safe relationship and
not being afraid to learn and experiment, or ask for what
you need.*

To first loves and friends who never give up.

*Now go and eat that piece of cake and then sit on a face
afterward—you deserve both the cake and the orgasm
without shame.*

TWENTY YEARS AGO

My feet slapped against the pavement as I ran, my worn and battered shoes doing nothing to keep the cold from seeping up my legs. My breath fanned out in front of me in the cold night air; my running was the only thing keeping me warm.

I zoomed past darkened doorsteps and storefronts as I raced to my hiding spot, knowing the way by heart. This area of town didn't have a single streetlight to assist me in my escape as I blended with the shadows. The shadows were my friends, hiding me away from the bad people.

All the scary stuff happened in the daylight. That was when I was truly afraid.

Taking the last corner, I fought the urge to glance back, too scared they'd be right on me. No, it was better to pretend I was safe.

Ducking beneath the tarp covering my hiding spot,

I stopped and listened for the sound of footfalls. When I heard nothing, I peeked out, exhaling when it was clear. I'd rather risk capture here than lead them to our spot.

Crawling the rest of the way, I ducked under the stacks of boxes and railings before climbing the ladder to the attic in the old theater. It was filled with mannequins, outdated costumes, and set designs. I hadn't known what they were, but Otto did, and he'd told me how they were used to bring a story to life.

Late at night, when everyone slept, we'd put on shows by dressing up and making our own stories. My favorites were when I got to vanquish my enemies and then live happily ever after with Otto. He insisted that all of our stories end in a happily ever after so we'd have something to look forward to. I didn't understand the importance, but I trusted Otto. All I cared about was being with him. I'd be happy as long as we were together.

"That you, Little Bird?" he whispered, coughing, his whole body shaking with the effort.

"Otto! I got you some medicine. It'll make you better. I promise," I said, rushing over to him with determination.

He'd huddled under the king's robe, the heaviest thing I'd been able to find. Despite the layers, his body shook and his teeth chattered. His brown hair stuck to his forehead, and his face was bright red, matching the king's robe. I placed my hand carefully against his skin as my momma had done. I instantly jerked back at his warmth.

"Oh, Otto," I whimpered, tears forming. "Here, this will make you better." I opened the bottle I'd stolen, pouring some red cough syrup into the little cup. Tilting it into his mouth, I watched as he struggled to swallow it. Eventually, he got it all down and I sighed in relief.

"Thanks, Little Bird. Did you have any trouble?" he whispered, his voice hoarse.

I shook my head, tears streaming down my face as I watched my best friend. He lifted his hand, taking mine in his. I placed my other cold hand against his forehead, hoping to cool him off.

"How's that?" I asked, sniffling.

"No more crying. I'm going to be okay."

I shook my head, not believing him. "Are you hungry? I can run out and get you something," I said, mad at myself for not thinking about it earlier.

"I'm good, Doctor."

I giggled, shaking my head at his joke. "I'm not a doctor, Otto."

"You're the best doctor I've ever had," he said earnestly, his gray eyes opening and meeting mine. "Tell me a story, Little Bird. Make it a happy one."

Sitting back against the wall, I pulled his head into my lap, combing my fingers through his soft hair. He smelled of the peppermints he always carried in his pocket; his familiar scent calmed my racing heart. Watching his face, I retold him one of my favorites.

"... and then Robin Hood punished all the rich for not sharing what they had in abundance, killing them in their beds while they slept."

"I don't remember that part," he whispered, a smile on his face. He'd closed his eyes while I'd been talking, just listening to me.

"Shh, it's not over," I said, waiting until he quieted. "The best thing was after Robin killed all the rich baddies and gave the money to the poor, he pulled off his hood and shocked everyone when they realized that Robin was a girl!"

"I can believe it. You'd be a fierce Robin Hood, Little Bird." He coughed, his whole body shaking. When he finished, he rolled over. "What did Robin do next? What's her happy ending?"

"Robin takes her share of the money and builds a giant treehouse where she can live with all her friends. That way, Robin is never alone again."

"But of course. Robin is very popular after saving everyone. She'll need a lot of friends to keep the bad people away," Otto added.

"And these friends, they're the best kind of friends. They never get mad at one another, help each other with their chores, and share everything; that way, no one is ever left out." I nodded, picturing how nice it would be to be surrounded by friends.

"It sounds perfect, Little Bird. I like your version. I get to live in the treehouse, too, right?" he asked, opening his eyes.

"Of course, silly goose. You're my best friend. Your room will be next to mine so we can fight the nightmares together and tell each other stories at bedtime."

"It's perfect, Little Bird. Just like you."

I smiled, my face flushing at his praise. "Thanks, Otto."

He closed his eyes again, the smile staying on his lips as he fell asleep. I watched him, wishing I knew how to make him feel better. I didn't like it when people were sick or injured. It made me feel helpless and alone.

The last memory of my parents surfaced, and I squeezed my eyes shut to block it out, but it was no use. Now that I'd thought about it, it pushed forward, not letting me hide.

Someone pounded on the door, shaking the thin walls of our home. My mom jumped up, looking everywhere for something. She and Daddy had been on the couch when they took the special medicine that made them feel better. They didn't look sick, but they always seemed better afterward. Mommy would hold me and tell me how much she loved me, and Daddy would dance and sing, laughing until he fell asleep.

I hated it when the medicine wore off, and they went back to ignoring me, forgetting I was there most days. During those times, I had to feed myself, finding what I could in the fridge. I was so lonely when they were out of their special medicine. It hadn't always been this way, but loneliness had become the norm for so long, it pushed away the good memories.

Stepping out of my room, I looked to the front door and my mom as she bit her nails. Maybe I could help make them happy.

"Mommy?" I asked, snagging her attention. Her eyes went wide as she stared at me, like she'd forgotten I was there.

"Open up, George. You're overdue, and I'm past kindness. If I have to bust in, you're not going to like it," a man yelled, slamming his fists against the door.

I'd heard him before and knew he wasn't a nice man. Mom always made me hide in the closet when he was here, saying he didn't like little girls. Her lip quivered as the man spoke, and she rushed over, pushing me into the closet and pulling the coats in front of me.

"Whatever you do, don't make a sound, and stay here until I get you. Can you do that for Mommy? It will be like a game of hide and seek. I'll get you a new toy if you win."

"Okay, Mommy." I nodded, and she kissed my fore-

head, stepping back with tears on her face. I didn't understand why she was crying. The game was fun, not sad.

Peeking through the crack, I watched Mom hurry to the door, opening it as she smiled wide. My dad stayed on the couch, his hands on his knees. The angry man rushed in, pushing Mommy to the ground. Covering my mouth, I held my gasp in, wanting to win and not be found.

"Where's the money, George? You haven't been holding up your end of the bargain, so I want it back," he demanded, walking into my father's space and staring down at him.

"It's been a little tight this month, Carlos. I'll get you double next month. Promise. These new pills make it hard to get out of bed. Maybe we can have some of the other stuff instead?" my father asked, hope brimming in his eyes as he licked his lips.

The big man gritted his teeth, shaking his head. "No. I'm done listening to your excuses. Let your death warn the other lowlifes who think they can steal from me."

My young mind got stuck on his words, trying to understand what he meant. We hadn't stolen anything. And what did he mean by death?

The next few seconds happened too fast for me to react. The man lifted a gun and pulled the trigger, shooting my father in the head. Mommy screamed, her tears falling fast as she stared at Daddy, his body limp on the couch, a red puddle forming around him.

Carlos turned, the gun in his hand sounding again as he aimed at my mommy on the floor. Her screams stopped, and the air in the trailer shifted as he stomped toward the door, the sound of the TV the only thing I could hear in the background now. Carlos paused, his hand squeezing the wood of the doorframe, making it splinter. I blinked past my tears, my body shaking as I watched, not wanting him to find me.

"I know you're in here, Cindy. One day we'll meet again, and I'll end your life just like I did your parents. When, is the price you pay, never knowing when I'll be around the corner waiting for you. Bye... for now, Cindy."

The door slammed shut, and I sat frozen in that closet, too scared to leave, afraid he'd open the door and take me. When it got dark, I finally crawled out and approached my dad first. His body was cold, but I got his medicine where he kept it, pushing it into his mouth.

"Wake up, Daddy. I have your meds. Please, Daddy."

My hands became covered in blood, the slipperiness not deterring me from trying to get him to respond. Giving up on him, I crawled over to my mom. Blood covered the ground, soaking my jeans and socks. From the light of the window, I could see the hole in her head, the top not looking right. Frantically, I scooped up the pieces, trying to shove them back inside.

My tears continued to pour, and snot dripped down my face as I tried to save my parents. Wiping my nose, I smeared blood on my face; the rust smell infiltrated my nostrils, making it all I could notice. I kept working on putting the pieces back in until my hands shook too much for me to do anymore.

When they wouldn't wake up, I curled into a ball and laid next to my mommy, hoping she'd wake soon.

A car door slamming woke me, the sun beginning to peek through the window. Sitting up, I wiped my eyes, my face feeling funny. Blinking down at my hands, all I could see was red. My clothes were stained red, my hands and even my hair were tinged red.

Scooting back, I kicked the hard object in front of me before realizing it was my mom. The tears fell again, the horrors of yesterday returning. Noise from outside sounded again, footsteps approaching. The angry man's, Carlos, words repeated in my head, and I knew he'd returned to finish the job.

Scampering up, I ran to my bedroom and locked the door as the front door banged open. Grabbing the back-pack I kept under the bed, the one filled with snacks, clothes, and my favorite stories, I slung it over my back as I climbed onto the bed and shifted the window open, just like Mommy had made me practice. Jumping out, I took off, not looking back as I ran through the trailer park.

I made it to the park where Mommy took me on days she felt good. The blood coating me itched, and I knew I needed to get it off before people noticed. Climbing through the open window of the locker room, I sat against the tiled wall, catching my breath and listening to see if the bad man had followed.

The longer I stared at the blood covering me, the more my panic grew, the memory of how Carlos had pointed his gun at my parents and vowed to come after me, too.

My breath quickened, my vision blurry as I replayed how the blood covered the floor and me over and over. I stood, my legs wobbly as I raced to the shower, barely turning the knob before I fell over. I gripped the wall and used it to support myself as I stood under the spray, and my body shook as the cold water ran over me. Once I no longer feared I'd fall, I scrubbed at my skin as I shed all my clothes, ensuring I washed every trace of the red stickiness away.

When no more blood remained, I turned off the water; my naked body shivered in the cold air. Squeezing my eyes closed, I picked up the bloody clothes and shoved them into the trash can. I couldn't look at them without remembering what had happened and sending myself into a panic. I didn't have any time to waste; I had to keep going, or he'd find me.

With trembling fingers, I redressed into clean clothes and left the locker room, spotting a school bus up ahead. Climbing onto it, I ignored all the kids' stares, sitting in the back. I didn't care where it went. It was away from here, and that was all that mattered.

Fingers wiped my tears, bringing me back to the present. Opening my eyes, I spotted Otto below me.

"No more tears, Little Bird."

"I know. I was just remembering..." I didn't need to say anything else. The only time I normally cried was when I remembered my parents. Though Otto might fall into that category soon, too.

"He's not going to find you. I'll protect you until you can protect yourself," he vowed how only an eight-year-old could—with his whole heart.

"And I'll protect you. Together forever," I whispered, holding my pinky finger before him. He lifted his, wrapping it around mine. It was weak, and my heart worried now for a different reason.

"Running into you was the best day of my life," he said, shocking me.

"It was?" I asked, wiping the rest of my tears away.

"Yeah. Because I found a friend, I didn't have to do it alone anymore."

I smiled, nodding. He was right. Our lives hadn't been the greatest, but we'd found one another and were surviving together. We might be homeless and always hungry, but we had each other and our imaginations to entertain us.

We'd even given each other new names, leaving our pasts behind us.

"Tell me another story, Little Bird." His voice sounded weaker, so I nodded, willing to do anything he asked.

"There was a ship of pirates who sailed the seas, looking for treasure..."

"You know, all your stories are about taking from the rich and punishing the bad," he said when I'd almost finished.

"Those are the best kind!"

He gave a small chuckle, bringing a smile to my face, and I believed he'd be okay. But a second later, his body shook hard as foam formed around his mouth.

Panicking, I jumped up, running out of the attic through the main part of the building as I screamed for help, breaking our promise never to reveal our secret location. But I was too scared to worry about the consequences, wanting Otto to be okay. I couldn't lose another person. A woman and man hurried out of an office, halting in their tracks at the sight of me.

"Where did you come from? What are you doing here?"

"Please, help. Something is wrong!" I cried, not stopping to explain. I turned on my heels and raced back to where we'd been hidden for months now.

Otto wasn't shaking anymore when I got back to him, but his face was redder, and he wasn't responding. The woman dropped beside me, placing her hand against his forehead.

"Call 911!" she shouted, bending down to gather Otto into her arms.

"Wait, you can't take him!" I screamed, fear that I'd never see him again racing through me.

"He needs a doctor," she said, not pausing as she rushed out of the room and down the stairs. I hurried after her, promising to stay with him so he wouldn't be alone.

The paramedics met us at the front, taking Otto's small form from the woman and placing him on a bed. They started to hook things up to him, and I watched in amazement as they worked, praying they'd be able to save him. They wheeled him away, and I ran, ignoring the woman's pleas, and climbed onto the bed, wrapping my arms around his legs.

"Um, what should we do?" one of the paramedics asked the other.

"Leave her. There's no time."

The door closed, and I relaxed as the ambulance took off, knowing I hadn't lost him yet. When one of the machines beeped, the EMT pulled me off, explaining they needed the space to keep him alive. Nodding, I watched as they worked, inserting a tube down his throat and an IV in his arm.

Tears fell effortlessly as I watched them, praying that my family wouldn't be taken from me this time. When his heart started again, beeping a steady rhythm, I knew this was what I wanted to do. I wanted the skills to save people so I wouldn't lose someone again.

Once we arrived at the hospital, a flurry of activity occurred as they rolled Otto into a room, directing me to sit outside. I wrapped my arms around my legs as I watched nurses and doctors entering, saying a lot of words I didn't understand. At some point, I fell asleep, the day's exhaustion catching up to me.

"Hello, dear, are you Birdie?" a kind voice asked, pulling me from sleep. I sat up, rubbing my eyes as I looked around, trying to remember what had happened.

"Birdie?" she asked again, and I turned to her, nodding. She smiled, pointing to a curtain. "Your friend is asking for you." I immediately jumped off the chair and raced to the curtain, vaulting myself into his bed.

"Ouch, Little Bird. Careful," Otto said, making fresh tears return to my eyelids.

"You're alive," I whispered, my hand hovering over his arm, scared to touch him.

"I am. Thanks to you. You saved me, Little Bird." The tears I'd been holding escaped, rolling down my cheeks earnestly.

"Hey, no tears. I'm on the mend. We'll be back to making stories in no time." Nodding, I wiped my face, falling into his arms when he opened them.

Unfortunately, our tale did not end in happiness, as the hospital was not keen on allowing two kids without parents or guardians to leave on their own. I screamed and kicked, hissing and chomping my teeth at anyone who neared.

"If you don't come on your own, we'll have to get the cops involved," one tired nurse said, dropping her arms.

"Go, Little Bird. It's okay. I promise I'll find you. Together forever, remember?"

I shook my head no, not wanting to leave him, but in the end, I didn't get a choice. I'd gone to get some food with one of the nurses, returning to find his bed empty and a lady with a badge waiting for me.

The first moment I could escape, I did, running from my appointed babysitter. But after a few blocks, I slowed, realizing I had no clue where they'd taken Otto, and was unfamiliar with this side of town.

Sitting on the curb in defeat, I debated my options as my stomach rumbled. A sleek black car pulled up a bit later, and I jumped up, ready to flee as the door opened, a man's voice stopping me.

"Wait. I have an offer you might want to hear. If you don't, I'll help you go wherever you want. All I ask is for you to listen to my proposal."

The man didn't look like any of the social workers I'd seen before. He was dressed in nice clothes, and while he didn't appear friendly, he wasn't scary either. His beard was trimmed, and his eyebrows resembled caterpillars, making me like him for some reason. He held out a paper bag, and the smell of food reached me, and I grabbed it.

"What if I told you I could help you become strong, to learn skills you could use to make bad people suffer?"

"Why would you do that?" I asked between bites.

"Does it matter why?"

I thought about it and realized it didn't. I shrugged, shoving the burger in my mouth. "No, I guess not. What do I have to do?"

"I'll give you a nice place to live, clothes, food, and your own room. I'll offer you whatever education you want and train you to fight bad guys. Once you're ready, you'll take on the jobs I give you, earning money for yourself."

My mouth hung open, and I turned around to look for the joke. When no one jumped out, I scrutinized him closer. I couldn't detect any lies. He stood still, letting me observe him. Despite this man being a stranger, he didn't set off my danger signals like Carlos had.

"So, if I come to live with you, you'll give me whatever I want and train me to kill bad guys?"

"Yes. Several girls like you will be training alongside you."

The idea of others training with me captured my attention even more. Looking down at my dirty clothes, I faced the facts. I had little to no resources left in order to survive, much less find Otto.

"I have a friend who was taken. Will you help me find him?" I asked.

"If you wish." He nodded, and it felt like he was giving me his word.

"Okay then." I shoved the last of the food into my mouth and stood, tossing the trash into the garbage next to a bench.

"Wonderful. What's your name, little one?" he asked. He didn't particularly smile, but he wasn't angry either. I kind of liked the fact he didn't pretend like most adults.

I shrugged, not wanting to give my real one. Cindy Hopevale needed to stay dead. "I don't have one, but my friend calls me Little Bird."

He smiled, reaching to shake my hand and directing me to open the car door.

"Welcome to the Belladonnas, Raven."

Raven

PRESENT DAY

"You're going to sever the artery," I cursed, squeezing my eyes shut tight to avoid the blood squirting; my heart raced as it pounded in my ears, my vision blurring.

A second later, the patient's vitals dropped, their heart flatlining as the machines went haywire. I could hear the nurses and doctors scurrying around to repair the tear before the poor man bled out. Through it all, I kept my eyes closed and focused on what I could hear. Finally, the patient's heart rate returned, and he was no longer in peril.

I peeked through my fingers when it sounded safe, not trusting that the danger was over. I'd been fooled a time too many by *Phoenix Hospital*—my favorite medical soap opera—to trust it was completely safe. Spotting no blood on the screen, I exhaled and dropped my hands, bringing some popcorn to my mouth as I watched the doctors make out on screen.

"About time you gave in, Rebecca. Hottie McGruff over there has been crushing on you for ages. He's no Dr. Romano, but he'll do," I sighed, talking to the characters like they could hear me. "Oh, yes, get it, girl! Chase that post-opt adrenaline high!" Giggling, I continued to eat my popcorn, enthralled by the episode. *Would someone ever kiss me like that?*

When the credits rolled, I sighed blissfully, already jonesing for the next one. Despite my aversion to blood, I never missed an episode of *Phoenix Hospital*. I couldn't help it. It fascinated me and had everything I loved about the medical field, with hot doctors to boot! And in a way, I got to live vicariously through the characters.

My obsession with the medical field had started early, a need to take care of those around me and gain control. Or at least that was what one tutor had told me. Since the day Man had picked me up, I'd learned everything I could about the body and how to heal others. I'd taken enough classes to earn a Ph.D. and an MD; there was just that one hold up—the whole blood thing. I could do without the blood.

Every time I saw blood, I was transported back to the night my parents died and how it had coated me as I lay in my mother's remains. I'd inevitably pass out, which made it challenging to doctor people when you fainted at the sight of blood—real or fake.

It was my one flaw in life. Le sigh.

Okay, maybe not my *one* flaw, considering I had several, but it was the one I hated the most. The others I'd learned to accept.

"Yo, Rav, we need your assistance!" one of the girls shouted, banging on my door.

Dropping my head back, my blue and black hair fell over the arm of the chair as I stared at the wall upside down. My vintage Tardis tee rode up my stomach, my police box skirt fell to the sides, and my short legs dangled over the other side as I kicked my stockinged feet.

"What?" I shouted, not wanting to get up if it was something stupid like when Darcy used her latest drone to glitter-bomb everyone the second they opened their door. I'd cleaned out pink glitter dicks in crevices I hadn't known existed for weeks. That crap had taken forever to clean up.

"Karma burned her hand," Naomi said, activating my mother-hen tendencies.

"On it!" I placed my hands down on the carpet and kicked my feet off the other arm, flipping my body over and landing on my feet. Jumping up, I grabbed my medical kit and rushed to the door, letting Karma in.

"Sorry, Raven, I know your show's on," Karma

said, her brow creasing as she held her hand to her chest.

"It just ended, but you know I'd stop it to help you. Did you bake me anything good?" I asked to distract her as I peered at the burn.

"Some double chocolate chip cookies." I could hear the pride and happiness in her voice. Karma loved to bake, and I loved to eat what she baked. It was a perfect relationship.

"Yes!" I threw my fist in the air, excited. Karma's desserts were the best in the entire world. We all fought over her treats, wanting them all for ourselves.

Once I had her burn cleaned and bandaged, I sent her on her way, promising to stop by for some cookies later once they'd cooled.

Flopping onto my bed, I pulled my laptop closer, clicking on the search bot Man had one of the older girls set up for me after I'd moved here. I couldn't help but check it every day, even if the criteria was long outdated—gray eyes, brown hair, smells of peppermint, cute smile. Yeah, not the most specific keywords to locate a missing person from twenty years ago.

No results found.

"Where are you, Otto?" I mumbled, stroking the computer screen.

Despite all the years that passed, I hadn't given up

trying to find Otto, my first friend. It might be stupid to hold on to a childish promise, but I believed him when he said he'd find me one day. So, I wouldn't quit or give up hope either.

Rolling onto my back, I crossed my legs, the blue stockings rubbing against one another in the process. As I stared at my ceiling, I tried to remember what Otto looked like, but just as I'd grab onto his image, it would float away back to my memories.

I'd been so upset the first time I couldn't recall him until an older Belladonna had sat me down and told me that "memories fade, not the person." My younger self had taken that to heart, believing as long as I remembered *him*, then he existed out in the world. Possibly searching for me just as hard as I was for him. At least, that was what I told myself.

My life in the mansion had been everything Man had promised. I had my own room, all the clothes and food I could hope for, and a family of other girls living and training alongside me. Perhaps my favorite part of becoming a Belladonna was the ability to learn anything I desired. Unbeknownst to me, I'd been a child prodigy with a genius-level IQ. Of course, with my parents addicted to drugs, it was no wonder that fact had slipped under the radar.

I'd mastered several languages, completed multiple doctorates, and knew numerous ways to kill a person. Though, my personal favorite was death by embolism. Mainly because it was the least bloody; my condition was well-known in the house, which had led to some unfortunate incidents growing up. My method worked for the marks that needed to appear to have died from natural causes, either due to their position of power, family, or misdeeds.

And because of my knowledge and past, most of my jobs revolved around the medical field and pharmaceuticals—legal and illegal ones. That was when Man would call me in.

"I wonder what my favorite thieves are up to," I mused, rolling back over, a smile stretching across my face in anticipation.

Oh, yeah, one of those flaws I accepted about myself? Having out loud conversations like it was normal. I'd done it since I was a child, often left alone to my own devices while my parents got high, and I didn't realize it wasn't "normal" until my second year here when one of the girls asked who I was talking to in my room every night.

Clicking on the other search bot I had set up—this one only known to Darcy—I smiled when this one populated with a new story. Sitting up, I pulled the laptop into my lap, settling against the pillows to read about my group of thieves. I knew they weren't mine technically, but I'd claimed them long ago when I'd first heard of their exploits.

My love for Robin Hood and treasure hunts hadn't

diminished, and while I often redirected funds and goods to those less fortunate, I was nowhere near the level the Loxley Crew was.

"Loxley Crew hit another heavy hitter tonight, stealing millions in jewels from a Brazilian crime lord, giving most of the proceeds to the villagers, making them all instant millionaires overnight. Just who is behind Loxley Crew, and who will they target next? Drop your suspicions below."

I read through the comments, chuckling as I grabbed a package of peanut M&M's off my nightstand. Flaw number three for anyone counting, I constantly snacked. It was a comfort thing now from going without food during those developmental years.

User123: I heard they're secretly a pop band, using their influence to sneak in.
User456: No, they're the sons of criminals, banding together to take out foes.
User789: Why can't they be both?
User198: I've seen their call sign around town —the wings and arrows. I think their home base is in NYC.
User267: You're not the first one to claim that. Could be some merit to it.

User365: How do you hire them? I have someone they could rob.

User489: Unless it's a corrupt wealthy person, you're out of luck, kid. They're honorable thieves—only stealing from dishonest crooks.

User521: Do you think they're single? I bet they're handsome. I'd let them take my jewel. IYKYK.

Shaking my head, I tossed the M&M's into my mouth, crunching on the salty-sweet goodness. My obsession with the Loxley Crew had started a few years ago when I crossed paths with them on a job. They hadn't seen me, but I'd been intrigued as I watched the two guys interact. When I learned afterward that they gave most of their treasure to the poor in the area, I'd been shocked and immediately started stalking them.

You know, in a healthy way.

I justified it because I wanted to keep tabs on them in case they needed to be dealt with at some point. I'd done a deep dive and discovered they had a whole network called PROP. But it was all I could find even with Selena and Darcy's help.

But even without knowing where their home base was, their names, or how many of them there actually were, it didn't matter. I was obsessed. I watched them just as much as *Phoenix Hospital*. While I knew there were at least two guys, I felt like that wasn't their entire team. It was hard to judge since they covered their heads.

Sometimes they'd appear after I was finished, and other times they were there first. It had become a little game I played, wondering if they'd be at my next mark and if I could remain undetected. I wasn't even sure they didn't know about me, but for sanity's sake, I pretended like they didn't.

Despite never having talked to them, I felt a connection, like we were kindred spirits. Intellectually, I knew it probably had more to do with my childhood obsession with Robin Hood and its relation to Otto, but it didn't make it any less real. I'd been trying to find the perfect way to introduce myself, but my awkward self hadn't gotten past, *"Hi, so you like to rob bad people? Cool bro, I kill them."*

Sighing, I closed the laptop and rolled off the bed, my chemistry lab calling me. Whenever I was too in my head, I'd focus on the chemical components and create something for myself or my fellow Belladonnas. Currently, I was tweaking a combination I called Knockout that put others to sleep. On the rare occasions I bumped into my mark, it worked to knock them out quickly.

Royal had asked for some tranquilizer darts before she left on her mission and it got me wondering what other compounds I could add to darts. The idea of making a laughing one struck, and I began to work.

Humming to myself, I added the chemicals to the beaker, mixing in a floral signature scent, and spun it around. The tricky part with this one was testing it. Not many of the girls volunteered to let me try my most recent formula because it left them potentially vulnerable for an unpredictable amount of time. Wimps.

When the liquid turned pink, I poured it into the bottle and pocketed it for the perfect opportunity to test it. Like next time I got glitter-bombed. Then who'd be winning our prank war, Darcy?

"Me. That's who." I cackled, faintly worried I'd inhaled some of the mist.

A soft knock sounded on my door, and I walked over, figuring it was Karma reminding me about the cookies.

"Yeah?" I asked, peeking out the crack, still not trusting it wasn't another prank.

Tabitha smirked, showing her hands were empty. "You've been summoned." She turned and left, and I quickly grabbed my shoes to head to the basement.

The hallway was empty; the other girls on this floor were either out or training somewhere in the mansion. Even after twenty years of living here, I still couldn't get over how luxurious the place was. My hand trailed down the large banister as I descended the two flights of stairs and made my way through the halls to the sitting room. I waved at a few people but didn't linger, knowing Man would expect punctuality.

Accessing the hidden stairs, I raced down the last flight into the training room, the vaulted ceilings and pristine floor taking my breath away. Darcy was in one corner kicking a dummy, and Naomi was in the armory, surveying the wall of weapons as I continued to Man's office.

The door was ajar as I approached, so I entered the masculine and elegant space with a knock. My eyes took in the heavy drapes and the bookshelf before falling to Man. He didn't look up, his salt and pepper head bent over a document on his large desk. Taking the seat in the chair across from him, I waited for him to finish, knowing he'd tell me what I needed to do when he was ready.

I tried to tell if any of the items on his desk had been moved, knowing Harlow and Royal disagreed on the proper placement of things in the house, shifting things half an inch to their preferred liking. But as much as I stared at the things on Man's desk, I couldn't determine if any of them were in a different spot than before.

A few seconds later, Man closed the file he was reading and met my eyes. Once we'd arrived at the mansion, Man had left me in the care of others, not speaking to me outside of a few words. I hadn't minded it, knowing if he needed to say something, he would. His blue eyes held respect as he stared, and I had to stop myself from squirming under his praise.

"Sir," I said in greeting. He nodded in response, sliding his customary envelope across the desk. Without any words, he returned to his files, leaving me to my task. Gripping the thick envelope, I hurried back to my room, eager to learn who my next mark was.

It was time for my killer side to come out and play.

Raven

THREE NAMES WERE WRITTEN ON THE PAPER. THREE NAMES I'd been hired to kill. Three names that required *my* skills.

I'd been called several names over the years in the few times my presence didn't go unnoticed—from the Needle Assassin to Peppermint Killer and Doctor Death. And I hated them all. They were boring, and quite frankly, I wanted something more badass.

For one, I didn't even use peppermint to kill, so that was false advertising. I just left one on their bedside table. A little "get well soon" gift and an ode to the boy I couldn't forget.

The other two had taken zero creativity, and I had better luck using an assassin generator than whoever decided Needle Assassin and Doctor Death were cool. But it felt even lamer to name yourself, so I casually tried to drop my approved monikers and hoped they'd catch on.

Sounded easy enough, right?

Nope. It had been three years, and Peppermint Killer still made the headlines.

Anyway, back to the three names who required my skills.

Millicent Winters. John Mathis. Jerome Fulton.

The last three remaining members from the board of Good Meds Pharma, thanks to me. I'd hunted them down one by one over the years. Their company had done atrocious things, like keeping important medications from those in need, hiking up the costs on life-saving drugs, and creating drugs that made false promises.

Most recently, they'd been in the news for Artevac. A medication advertised as a miracle drug for addictions, targeting receptors to block signals in the brain. They promised relief for addicts, offering them a solution to break out of the addiction cycle.

Artevac had worked, at least at first, dramatically changing people's lives.

However, the studies on the side effects had been grossly under-reported, hiding that while the addiction part of the brain was shut off, depression and suicidal thoughts increased tenfold. In the six months it was on the market, thousands of deaths were reported.

Good Meds Pharma couldn't escape the fallout this

time and folded; the board members went into hiding and left the mess for investors to handle. They'd thought they could hide behind their fortunes and avoid any accountability. It might've been the chemists that created the drug, but it was the board that had pushed it to market before it was ready, fully aware they were hiding the side effects.

And now we had found the last three, the president of the board included. These three were at the top of Good Pharma Meds and had known what was coming well before anyone. They could've stopped production or even taken responsibility for their greediness. Instead, they took all the evidence with them, so the families affected couldn't even file a lawsuit. They changed their names and sequestered themselves away before the news broke. These three selfishly saved themselves, not even sharing the information with their fellow board members.

"Your days are numbered," I whispered, excitement spreading through me at finally uncovering their aliases and locations.

Glancing at the clock, I calculated I had roughly twenty-four hours to prepare. Spreading out the blueprints, I reviewed the three buildings' layouts, noting the entrances and exits and identified the best places to sneak in for each hit. Once I felt confident in my basic knowledge of the structures, I studied everything

I could about all three marks' habits, schedules, likes, and dislikes, so I could exploit them to my advantage.

Eventually, my neck cramped and eyes blurred as my muscles protested from sitting in one position for hours. Stretching my arms, I closed the laptop and hopped off the bed to change. I had to practice rappelling and balancing in case I needed to use either skill to escape. With the layout of one of the buildings, it was a likely possibility.

When I entered the training room, it was quiet; most of the house was asleep at this hour. I didn't let it deter me, walking to the section I needed and hooking on the necessary safety equipment. Climbing up the rock wall, I practiced my balance as I crossed the thin beam from one corner to the other while twenty feet in the air. The muscles in my legs shook at the halfway point, sweat dripping down my face and I focused on not looking down.

Keeping my eyes on the wall before me, I stretched my arms out to my sides to help steady myself. A door slammed below me, and I cursed, jerking to the right and grabbing the cord holding me up as I swayed.

"Blue cheese!" I shouted, causing whoever was below me to laugh.

"Sorry, Raven," Naomi yelled back. "Continue. You got this."

It took a few minutes for my legs to quit shaking,

my heart to return to normal, and my breathing to even out. When I felt stable, I focused on the wall and moved one foot in front of the other. Slowly, inch by inch, I crept closer to the other side. My head spun toward the end, but I kept my gaze locked.

The last few inches came into view, and I jumped, sliding down to the flat surface as I caught my breath. Naomi and Karma clapped below, reminding me they were there. I waved once I could move my arms again. It was another twenty minutes before my muscles allowed me to budge from my spot, and I rappelled down the wall, eager to touch down on the solid ground again.

"Ravioli, that never gets easier," I mumbled as I unhooked the harness.

"Just imagine if you were taller. The ground would be further away," Karma teased.

"Ha! My shortness is good for something."

"You headed out?" Karma asked as they stretched, her brown hair touching the ground.

"Yep. Might be a while. It's a three-in-one."

"Nice. Catch ya later, Raven." Naomi and Karma waved as they exited, and I collapsed against the wall, wiping the sweat from my face as I debated crawling back to my room or inventing a flying disk that could carry me.

My watch beeped, alerting me to how much time I

had left. Groaning, I rolled over to the ground and pushed up, my thighs screaming at me. I'd need to stretch later, or I wouldn't be doing any climbing any time soon.

Each step up was torturous, my body yelling as I ascended the nine million flights. People were up and bustling around the house, but they left me to my grumblings and nonsensical words. Stopping in the kitchen, I grabbed the last of Karma's cookies, a sports drink, and a banana, hoping to appease my muscles with some nutrients.

The second-floor landing came into view, and I practically wept as I shuffled down the hallway to my room. Face-planting on my bed, I groaned as I lay there, knowing I couldn't waste too much time. Rolling on my back, I peeled the banana, attempting to eat on my back without choking myself.

"Practicing how to give a blow job?" Darcy asked from the hallway. I lifted my middle finger, too tired to do anything else. She laughed but left me to my misery.

Ten minutes later, my watch beeped again, and I groaned, rolling over and pushing up with my arms. Shutting my door, I undressed and headed to the shower, the jets and hot water calling my name.

The aches lessened as the water ran over my body, and I perked up, thinking about the new job on the horizon. Twisting my hair into a bun on my head, I dressed in my standard attire of a nerdy t-shirt, skirt, and stockings with my favorite pair of Converse. I changed out my eyebrow and nose ring, going with something smaller and less conspicuous than the hoops I usually wore.

I fell into a rhythm as I packed my bag, tossing in all the things I'd need on this trip: black clothing, makeup, my chemical goodies, medical bag, computer, and surveillance gadgets. Grabbing a random passport, I glanced at the name I'd be for the trip and chuckled.

Robyn Banks.

I swear, Darcy picked names for Man to use just to mess with me. Oh well, I couldn't do much since forging an ID was not in my wheelhouse.

Double checking everything was secure and that I hadn't forgotten an item, I zipped my suitcase closed and grabbed my backpack. I peered around the room at all the things I'd collected over the years, the items I'd bought online, and the souvenirs I'd stolen as a memento of my job. I took them all in, knowing that it was always possible I wouldn't return if I failed my mission.

With a flick of the switch, the room descended into darkness, and I shut the door, hoping it wouldn't be the last time I stepped foot in there.

The mansion was livelier as I walked through, waving at the other girls as they went about their days. When it was busy like this, it made me miss the ones not here more. Royal and Harlow arguing over the best place for things, Ivory laughing with her twin, and Selena trying to one-up Darcy in the hacker department.

Stepping out the front doors, a sleek black car waited for me. Pierce, the new driver, opened the door as I neared. I placed my suitcase in first, sliding across the soft leather before the door shut and sealed me in. The space smelled of brandy, a crystal tumbler sitting next to a decanter on the drink cart, and made me curious about who was the last one in here.

I'd given up long ago on tracking everyone. Each girl had their own life and way of doing things. Our diverse skills made the Belladonnas one of the world's best and deadliest assassin guilds. While the girls had become my sisters and friends, and I'd do anything for them, they'd never fully fill that hole I had where Otto's memory lived.

Perhaps it was due to the fact I'd never let him go, so there was no space for anyone else. Or maybe because we were all orphans, plucked from the streets at a young age, and we never truly healed that initial wound. Whatever the reasoning, I still yearned for a family, one I'd make of my own someday.

"We'll be arriving at the airfield momentarily, Miss Raven," Pierce said, interrupting my thoughts. I appreciated how he didn't feel the need to chat, letting me zone out while he took the reins to ensure my safety.

"Thank you." I cleared my throat, sounding sad even to my own ears and straightening my spine. Now wasn't the time to think about needing a best friend. I had some turdnuggets to kill.

STEPPING OFF MY PLANE, I stretched my arms and twisted side to side. I waved goodbye to Phillip, my pilot. My jet had been my first big purchase. While it might seem extreme to have your own plane when you didn't leave the house a lot, it made things easier for me. I didn't drive, and avoiding highly populated places helped reduce my chance of accidentally seeing blood. So yeah, the moment I could afford it, I bought one.

Nothing beat having your own space, and the nap I'd taken while on board proved it. It was the last chance I could let my guard down until I returned. My mood had improved; my usual pep restored as I pulled my hair into a ponytail and donned some fake glasses. The small details played bigger tricks on people's minds in recognition because they weren't looking for them.

Strolling through the small office, I didn't stop to chat, knowing there would be a car for me. Man always took care of the details, allowing us to focus on the job. The wind blew my hair as I stepped through the door; the weather had changed from Colorado to Kentucky. Just one time, I'd like to be sent somewhere warm to kill someone. Hopefully, the next stop would be warmer.

Tugging on a leather jacket, I spotted the car as it neared the office. The car service tag hung from the rearview, and I eyed the driver. Typically, I'd be picked up in something nicer, but this was small-town America. Doubtful that there was much to choose from to begin with in ride-shares.

The driver jumped out, taking me by surprise as he rounded the vehicle. He was tall, probably a foot taller than me, with dark blond hair, green eyes, and the prettiest smile I'd ever seen. His whole being oozed happiness like he was filled with pure sunshine. I caught a few tattoos peeking out of the cuff on his right hand as he reached out to take my bag. His whole persona disarmed me.

"Sorry, I was a bit late," he rushed out. "I got stuck listening to my brother go on and on about his favorite show. Apparently, one of the characters finally kissed the guy she's been pining over for several seasons. You'd think he knew them personally with how he talked about them." The golden guy laughed as he loaded my bag into the trunk and opened the door for me.

My feet froze to the spot, his voice was musical and light, and I didn't want him to stop talking. His voice felt like carbonation, bubbling up in me and leaving my head fuzzy if I drank too much. I blinked when he stared at me, trying to remember what he asked.

"Shit. You're Robyn, right? Robyn Banks?" he asked, his arm flexing as he combed his fingers through his messy hair. His face looked odd without his smile, and I immediately wanted it back. This guy could cure depression with a smile like that.

"Um, yes, that's me," I squeaked, finally convincing my tongue to unstick itself. I even pointed my thumb back at myself, just in case my words hadn't been clear. He exhaled, his smile returning; it felt like I'd won something significant. My shoulders dropped, and I wanted to match his smile, his energy.

"Your parents have a funny sense of humor," he teased, his eyes twinkling at me. The green was so vivid I wanted to run through them like a meadow. We stared at one another for a few seconds, both lost in each other's eyes. Something shifted in me, my heart thumping louder in my chest.

Remembering his mission to get me into the car, the golden guy jolted into action and walked over to me, his steps practically a bounce as he took my hand, sending electricity through my entire body. He froze, glancing down at our joined fingers, his eyes wide.

"Wow." He swallowed, looking into my eyes. "Did you feel that, or was it just me?"

I nodded, words failing me. He didn't drop my hand; his thumb rubbing patterns back and forth sent jolts of heat through my body.

"I'm Porter." He smiled again, this one different. It was a little softer around the edges, one side lifting slightly higher, his eyes crinkling at the corners.

"I'm…" I stopped, suddenly remembering who I was and why I was here. For the first time since I became a Belladonna, I hated my life. I didn't want to lie to him. He deserved honesty. My face fell, my eyes dropping down to our hands.

"Robyn," he finished for me.

"Yes. Robyn." I licked my lips, my smile dimming as I nodded. "It's nice to meet you, Porter."

"Likewise." We stared at one another some more, neither of us in a hurry to move. A phone buzzed, jolting us both back to the present. Porter's smile dipped, breaking the spell fully.

"I guess I should get you to your hotel. I'm sure you have important things to do."

I blinked, nodding as he pulled me to the car and helped me into the seat, even latching my seatbelt. When his hand left mine, it felt like I'd lost a piece of myself all over again. For one second, the hole in my heart hadn't felt as empty.

Porter climbed into the driver's side, his long legs barely fitting beneath the wheel. How did he drive this all the time? His energy seemed more subdued, and I wondered if he felt the same as I had at the loss of our touch.

The drive was quiet, something I'd usually fill with talking since I rarely got to talk to strangers and enjoyed learning new things. But everything I thought to say felt dumb or like a lie, and I didn't want to create any more lies between us than what was already there.

"You here for business or pleasure?" he asked, startling me.

"Oh, um, both, I guess. You?" I asked, then realized how idiotic that sounded. "Yikes, sorry. Obviously, you live here and are currently working. Don't mind me. I don't get out much." My face heated, and I rubbed my hands on my skirt.

He chuckled, the sound soothing away some of the anxiety. "Actually, I'm just visiting and was bored, so I thought I'd see if there were any job requests. Yours was the first one I've seen all day, so I jumped on it." His green eyes met mine in the rearview.

"I did think it was odd this place had a ride-share app. Do you like your... job?" I cringed internally. Gah, I sounded so lame. I had a cute guy in front of me and no clue how to talk to him. Was he flirting?

"I don't mind driving, and I can do it anywhere. We move around a lot for my brother's job, so it's nice to meet new people this way." His hands gripped the steering wheel as he moved them. Something about his statement felt off, but I couldn't put my finger on what it was.

"That's cool. I'd be terrible at your job. I'm not the greatest with people and tend to talk about things that bore them, and I don't know how to drive."

His jaw dropped, his head turning to peer over the seat at me. "You don't know how to drive? How? Why?"

I shrugged, smiling. It hadn't been a necessary skill to learn, and a driver was always present. Besides, I often get lost in my own mind, so the thought of driving felt too dangerous. Once I got my plane, I really didn't need to learn.

"Just never wanted to."

"I couldn't wait until I could drive. It was the first taste of freedom I had. Now, I'm always the one driving my brothers around." Porter smiled, but his words sounded almost sad.

"That must be nice to have your family with you."

He nodded, turning his signal on. "Yeah. It is." He slowed to a stop in front of a hotel, and I realized our time was up. Regret filled me, knowing I'd never see him again. I gave a wobbly smile as I touched the handle.

"Well, thank you for the ride. I'm glad it was you that picked me up. I'll make sure to give you a 5-star rating."

His smile returned, and he hopped out, opening my door before I could. His big hand reached in and took mine, the tingles returning as he pulled me from the seat. My body was only an inch from his, and I had to stop myself from leaning into him. He had an aura about him that I wanted to soak in.

"I'm glad I picked you up, too. And you're not bad with people, Robyn." He bent down, his face growing closer to mine. I sucked in a breath, my eyes closing of their own free will as I waited for his lips to touch mine. It was dumb to let him, but I couldn't make myself pull away. Not even if he had a knife to my throat would I want to.

His breath fanned across my cheek, and I blinked, realizing he'd been reaching for the luggage—*not* another assassin. Of course, he wouldn't be kissing a stranger! Who did that? It wasn't *Phoenix Hospital*. I was officially going cuckoo.

"Maybe I'll see you around," he said, handing me my bag and winking.

"Yeah, maybe." I waved as I hurried inside, knowing there was not a chance in Hell he'd ever see me again. I was here for two nights, and then I'd be gone, just a memory in the wind.

Sadness washed over me at that knowledge, and I

cursed the fact I was a Belladonna. Porter was a nice guy. There was no world where the assassin got the nice guy. It just didn't work that way.

Being an assassin had never felt as lonely as it did right then.

Otto

THE MUSCLES IN MY NECK ACHED, REMINDING ME I'D BEEN poring over the blueprints for far too long. Lifting my hand, I massaged the strained area, rubbing my palm over the short, coarse hairs at the back. The texture soothed my nerves, relaxing my frayed edges.

Compared to the other jobs we'd done, this one felt more important. I didn't know why, but something inside of me lit up when it appeared. These three weren't any more criminal than the usual rich assholes we'd targeted.

Though, saying that, I knew it wasn't exactly true. They might not be mob bosses or serial killers, but they'd been greedy, entitled pricks who'd sacrificed a bunch of people's lives to get rich. So, yeah, maybe they were worse because their crimes had targeted the vulnerable, taking advantage of their desperation.

A desperation I knew all too well.

And if fate hadn't intervened, bringing me a savior

in the form of a little bird, I'd likely have been one of their numbers.

So, yeah, I guess this one was personal.

"Surveillance is set," Phoenix said, popping his head around the door. "Have you seen my brother?"

I turned my head, taking him in as I ran through my mental checklist. His dark blond hair was sticking up, probably from running his hands through it while he worked. His threadbare t-shirt had seen better days, and his gray joggers had a few orange stains from his favorite hacking snack. A sleeve of tattoos wrapped around his left arm.

His appearance, combined with the bags under his eyes, told me everything I needed to know. Phoenix had pulled an all-nighter and would need a day to recover, meaning the earliest we could strike would be tomorrow evening.

"Picked up a ride-share job. You know how he gets on the pre-planning parts. If he's not doing something, he gets bored and in the way."

"Right." Phoenix nodded, blinking, rubbing his eyes. "I vaguely remember that now. He'd gotten up after PH, and I'd zoned back into the job." He yawned, covering his mouth. "I'd honestly thought he'd gone to poop and was worried he had food poisoning or, worse, was setting up an elaborate prank."

Chuckling, I leaned back in the chair, used to the

twin's pranks on one another over the years. After my little bird had saved me, I'd been placed in a few foster homes before inevitably ending up in a group home. That was where I met Rueben and the twins a year later. The four of us had bonded, becoming a brotherhood.

At night in our bunk beds, I shared with them the stories Little Bird and I had created, helping them get through the darkness with a future to focus on. I hadn't intended for the four of us to become the modern-day Robin Hood, living Little Bird's dream. But after a handful of failed attempts to make it on the straight and narrow, it felt like the only valid option—an inevitable conclusion.

That, and I think they were all a little in love with her as well from my stories and wanted to give her the dream she had, regardless if I never found her. Knowing we were making it happen was enough for them.

But not for me. I wouldn't stop until I fulfilled my promise—together forever.

"You should get some sleep, Nix. We'll hit the first target tomorrow."

The door opened, and his wayward brother sauntered in. The grin on his face was unmistakable—he'd met a girl.

Porter was as notorious for falling in love at first

sight as he was for pulling pranks. Whereas his twin, Phoenix, tended to be more introverted and solemn, preferring to stay behind his computer for most jobs, Porter was the complete opposite. Restless with boundless energy, he couldn't stand to be cooped up and always had a smile for everyone. Porter was like a golden retriever puppy, and Phoenix a hairless cat. Both were cute to the right person.

"How did you meet someone already?" Phoenix asked, dropping his head into his hands with a groan.

Porter ignored his grouchiness, spinning around in a circle with his arms out as he fell back onto the couch. A loud sigh escaped him as he placed his hands behind his head, crossing his feet at his ankles.

"This one is different, Nix! There's just something about her."

Phoenix grumbled, frowning as he walked over and knocked his brother's legs off the cushion to sit down. He didn't get Porter's obsession with finding the perfect girl. The only relationship Phoenix entertained was with the fictional characters on his favorite television show—*Phoenix Hospital*. I had a hypothesis he only loved it because his name was in the title, but I couldn't prove it.

"Oh, yeah?" He lifted his hand, and a classic Phoenix debate loomed on the horizon. "In just the past month, there's been Luna who smelled like

cinnamon rolls but, in the end, didn't get your humor."
He dropped a finger, lifting his eyebrow as Porter
started to deny. "Then there was Jeanne who had eyes
like the sunset, whatever the fuck that meant, but
liked lemon in her water, which was a grievous error
on her part." Phoenix dumped another finger as Porter
cringed.

"But—" he started, stopping when Phoenix glared
at him.

"Cathy, whose smile made you silly but didn't
know the difference between ketchup brands."

"I think we can all agree there is only one true
ketchup," Porter interjected, raising his own finger.
Phoenix ignored him, dropping the third digit before
continuing.

"Mimi, who'd been wearing your favorite band's t-
shirt, but actually had no clue who they were, and oh,
yes, let's not forget the disaster that was Gina with her
collection of toenail clippings." He put down his last
finger, glaring at his brother, who'd gone from gleeful
to downright sad with a pillow covering his head.

I cleared my throat, grabbing Phoenix's attention
and raising a brow. Porter might be quick to love, but it
was one of the best parts about him. I knew Phoenix
was trying to protect his brother, but killing his spirit
wasn't how to do it.

His green eyes glared at me, but I refused to back
down. Being a brotherhood meant we cared about one

another's well-being. Not to mention, if Porter was distraught, it made him sloppy and reckless. We couldn't have that going into a job. But I cared about his feelings more, of course.

Phoenix dropped his eyes, his shoulders sagging as he rubbed his hair, the ends sticking in a different direction now.

"I can feel you guys talking with your eyes," Porter huffed.

Phoenix lifted the pillow off his brother's face, moving to lean against him, their shoulders pressing into one another. "What's she like?" he asked, tilting his head to Porters.

"You're right. I'll drop it," he said, his voice low.

"No. I was mean. I'm tired and cranky. But that's not your fault. So, tell me what she's like. Will I like her?" Phoenix asked, nudging his brother. Porter's head turned toward his brother, their foreheads pressing together now. They made a perfect mirror reflection of one another when they did that. Porter's smile lit back up, his shoulders dropping as he returned to his usual sunshine self.

"She's tiny, like I could fit her in my pocket, but with all these curves I wanted to touch." His body contracted as he talked with his hands, squeezing imaginary air. Porter couldn't tell a story without moving and demonstrating what he was saying. "She wore a Jurassic Park tee with a skirt. Her legging things had dinosaurs on them too, and she had on Converse. It was nerdy and relaxed but cute at the same time. She's literally my dream girl," he sighed, dropping his head back to the couch. "Her hair is long and wild with blue streaks in it. She had on these cute glasses; her eyes were the same shade of blue as the stripes in her hair."

"She sounds pretty. What else?" Phoenix asked, his voice quiet, his eyes fluttering closed. Porter didn't mind talking to him while he was sleeping. He was just happy to share with his twin. I also wasn't convinced they couldn't mind speak, so maybe Phoenix did hear him with his eyes closed.

"She was funny, a little sassy, and kind of shy. She made it out that she was awkward, but I didn't think so. Do you think she liked me?" he asked.

"Everyone likes you, Porter. I'm sure she did," Phoenix mumbled, proving my earlier point.

Standing from my chair, I left the main area and searched for our quietest member—Rueben. I passed the small kitchen and bathroom, not finding him, leaving only the two bedrooms. This town was so small the amenities hadn't been the greatest, but it was luxurious compared to some of the places we'd all grown up in.

I pushed open the door, spotting Rueben going over the equipment. He laid it out on the mattress and meticulously checked each piece to ensure it was ready and safe. He was the tallest of us at 6'4" with broad shoulders and a menacing glare that scared off most people. His brown skin was peppered with tattoos on both arms and his torso, covering his scars. His dark hair faded on the sides; the top kept close to his scalp. His beard was just as dark and full, covering most of his face. His black shirt and pants were his usual attire, contrasting against the twins and their ever-changing wardrobe.

"How's it going?" I asked, leaning against the wall.

"Good," he replied, his voice deep and thick. He wasn't a man of many words, his past not being kind in that regard.

"Phoenix has the surveillance done, and I've reviewed the blueprints. I've identified the weak points and best places for entry once Phoenix disarms the alarm."

Rueben nodded, continuing on his mission. We'd discovered our unique skill sets early in our time at the group home, allowing us to join together to create the Loxley Crew and later, PROP, our network of businesses.

Phoenix was a whiz with technology and computers and could lift a wallet from a pair of skinny jeans, with the wearer none the wiser. Both of the twins were nimble, giving them unique access to places.

Porter preferred to be active, allowing Phoenix to

stay behind if he wasn't needed. Porter had a knack for locks and could crack safes, and had an uncanny ability to escape any room he wound up in. He was a jack-of-all-trades, able to schmooze his way into any place with his charisma.

Rueben was pure muscle, using his strength to dispatch guards and shield the others from discovery. He excelled in defensive driving and knew the ins and outs of most vehicles. Most shocking, despite his size, the man was silent on his feet and could almost match Porter in the acrobatic escapes.

So what did I do? Outside of being the mastermind strategist and researching our marks, I fenced the goods and did some creative bookkeeping. My affinity for math came in handy to help the ones harmed by our marks, funneling money through PROP and our charitable foundations.

Most of our jobs consisted of Rueben and Porter going in, leaving Phoenix and me behind to monitor. Phoenix because he preferred not to interact with people unless he had to, and me because the less stress I put myself in, the better with my condition.

Each of us knew our roles, and we performed them flawlessly. We'd yet to be caught, though there were a few close calls, and had given back millions to those who deserved it more. The only thing missing was her —our little bird to share it with. The one who inspired it all.

"Porter met a new girl," I said to distract my own thoughts.

Rueben snorted, shaking his head. "Two days," he said, turning to meet my eyes.

"I'll take that bet." I grinned. As much as I wanted Porter to keep his romantic spirit, I wouldn't miss out on the chance to win a bet on when he'd fall out of love with her.

"Any news?" he asked, finishing with the last piece of equipment. He picked them up, placing them into their bags one by one in a precise order.

My attempt to discover Little Bird's whereabouts hadn't been as clever as I'd imagined. The twins didn't know I kept looking for her, but Rueben did. Mainly because the twins had had too many people leave them, and I didn't want to give them false hope. And Rueben had figured it out, his uncanny ability to suss out secrets.

Rubbing the back of my neck, those tiny hairs tingled my hand again. "No. I'm beginning to wonder if I dreamed her," I admitted.

"You didn't," Rueben said, his faith in me unwavering. He looked up, his dark eyes meeting mine. "She's..." His voice waned a little, and he swallowed, taking a second to collect himself. He typically spoke in two-word sentences, anything more caused him harm so he limited his full sentences. "She's real. Your imagination isn't that good."

Snorting, I nodded, agreeing with him. "Yeah, you're not wrong there." Crossing my arms over my chest, I let myself drift back to the day I'd first met her. The day she'd changed my life forever.

"Get the carton, boy. Don't skimp on me. If you're not back with it soon, I'm taking your dinner," my stepdad bellowed, pushing me out the door. Stumbling down the broken steps, I pulled my coat tighter around me. I was sick of my stepdad pushing me around like he was the boss of me. I wish my mom would wise up and leave him, but she wouldn't. She never did.

I trudged up the sidewalk, the wind whipping around me from all directions. It was no wonder he didn't want to come out in this weather, and I hated that he'd sent me instead. By the time I entered the corner market, my whole body shivered, the cold seeping into my body through my thin jacket. It was too small, but it was all I had, so I dealt with it.

The teen at the counter barely looked up from their phone when I entered. I slapped the money on the counter, used to this song and dance. The store wasn't legally allowed to sell to me, but my stepfather had set something up with the owner to allow me to get his cigarettes so he wouldn't have to leave the house.

"Red ones," I said, my teeth chattering.

The teen rolled his eyes but reached down and

handed over the carton, putting the money into the till. Shoving the box into my coat, I hurried back out, wanting to make it home before the storm worsened. My foot caught on a bike as I turned the corner, my body falling forward as I braced my hands out in front of me.

In my fall, I kicked a box, revealing what was hidden beneath it. A small girl with dark hair stared back at me, her blue eyes wide. Her tiny body shook in the few layers of clothes she had on.

"What are you doing here?" I asked, something about her called to me.

"Just leave," she said, putting her head on her knees. She wrapped her arms around them, probably attempting to keep her body heat in. Her sadness overwhelmed me, and the need to do something to make her smile felt important.

Without a thought, I removed my jacket and placed it around her shoulders. She gasped, looking up, her blue eyes watering as she stared at me.

"I live at the third house down. If you come to the back window at dark, I'll sneak you in. It's going to be too cold out here tonight."

I didn't wait for an answer, placing the box back so she was covered, and ran the rest of the way home with the cigarettes.

For the next week, she snuck into my house at night, eating whatever I could scavenge throughout the day,

and slept next to me on the mound of covers that acted
as my bed.

"What's your name?" I asked one night.

She shook her head. "I don't have one anymore."
Her eyes closed, and I knew something terrible had
happened.

"Then I'll give you one," I whispered. "How about...
Petunia?"

She giggled, covering her mouth, but shook her
head.

"Hmm, what about..." I trailed off, looking her over.
Her small features were so delicate, her voice as pretty
as the songbirds. She'd run away from home, escaping
her cage, something I wish I could do. "Your name
should be Birdie, but I'll call you Little Bird."

"Okay," she said, smiling. "And I'll call you Otto."

"Deal." I grinned, feeling happier than I'd ever
been.

Of course, that hadn't lasted long. The next night,
we'd held one another while my stepfather went on a
rampage, breaking things and hitting my mother. I
knew then I couldn't stay there any longer. It wasn't
safe for her.

Throwing some stuff into a bag, I pulled out the bag
of coins I'd collected over the past year, hiding it away
from my stepdad. Throwing on clothes, I shoved some
into her bag as well, placing a few more layers on her so
she'd be warmer.

"You sure?" she asked, her lip quivering.

"Yeah."

I opened the window, the old panes squeaking as it rose. We both froze, the sound in the rest of the house ceasing. Fear ran through me, and I pushed her out, climbing on the chair and shoving one leg over as my door crashed open, and my stepdad stood in the doorway.

I didn't hesitate; I jumped and sprinted with her hand in mine. He shouted at us through the window, but we didn't stop, running as far as we could. A week later, we discovered the secret entrance to the attic of the old theater, making it our home until the night I got sick and we were torn apart.

I'd later learn that if Little Bird hadn't gotten me help when she did, I would've died in that theater attic. There were some days when I suffered with the remnants of that night that I almost wished she had. But then a new day would appear, and I'd remember my promise to find her, giving me my own happy ending to create.

"We'll find her," Rueben said, shaking me out of my memories.

"Yeah. We will." I smiled, believing it just as much. "And when we do, we'll be complete."

Rueben grunted, his allotment of words used up for the day. He sat the bags on the floor before rolling out his yoga mat, falling into his nightly yoga routine before bed.

Taking that as my cue, I headed back to the main room, wanting to review the plans again. That tug that it mattered hadn't left, and I knew I couldn't sleep until I was confident I had every single contingency planned for.

Raven

AFTER SPENDING MY EVENING AND EARLY MORNING surveying the first location, I'd slept in, waking as most of the town was closing for the day. The hotel didn't have an onsite kitchen, so I'd been forced to venture into town for something to eat. My stomach growled, reminding me it had been a while since I'd last eaten. Being on a job was the one time I didn't constantly snack; too focused on the task at hand.

So, with my Ghostbusters tee, black skirt, black tights with ghosts, and red Converse on, I meandered down the main street of the small town my mark had decided to hole up in. It wasn't the cutest town, but it had a little of that quaint small-town feel to it. A hardware store, bookstore, and a cafe were along one side, with a bank, theater, and what looked to be a candle store along the other.

A medium brick building stood in the center, and I assumed it was the town hall with the flags raised. Potted plants hung from every pole, giving the town an ethereal quality, hiding some of the lingering dirt and grime. Not seeing any other food places on this block, I headed to the cafe, hoping it would still be serving food.

"I'm so hungry, I'll eat about anything," I said out loud, forgetting I was in public. A woman looked at me curiously, so I hurried to the door.

The bell jingled as I walked in, smells of fried foods and meat hitting me. My taste buds exploded as I inhaled, my stomach rumbling louder in protest. Most of the tables were filled with families with a few empty stools at the counter. Walking to the front, I took one of the stools and smiled as the waitress brought me a menu.

"I'll be back in a minute, darlin'," she said, her accent thick. That had been the one thing I'd consistently failed at in training, mimicking the perfect accent.

My eyes scanned the menu, and I couldn't decide what I wanted. So when the waitress stopped by, I ordered it all.

"I'll take the cheeseburger with a side of fries for here and the fried chicken with mashed potatoes, an order of chicken and dumplings, and three slices of pie to go. You can pick the flavors."

The waitress wrote it all down, thankfully not commenting on how much I'd ordered. I'd learned early on that if I got most of it to go, people believed it was for my imaginary family back home. I didn't care what people thought, but they tended to ask questions and remembered the short chubby girl who ordered enough food for a week. And since my goal was not to be caught for my recreational pursuits, I played along, giving them a narrative that was easier to swallow and faded from their mind.

A colossal piece of chocolate cake was placed down in front of the space next to me, drawing my attention. I hadn't noticed the person sitting there, too zoned in on my mission to get food. My eyes widened, and I licked my lips as I looked at it. I wanted to roll around in that cake.

"And I'd like a piece of the chocolate cake first," I said before the waitress could escape.

"Sure thang, darlin'. I'll have that right out for you," she said, smiling at me before she moved away.

Now that my food situation had been handled, I glanced closer at the rest of the patrons. No one stood out, just the typical middle to lower-class families living in a small town like this. The families looked happy, so I watched them, wondering what it would be like to have a mom and dad who cared. It was an odd game I played, putting myself in the kid's position, trying to imagine what it would've felt like to have a mom fix your hair and pull you into her chest as she spoke.

"I'm sorry, hun. We sold out of the chocolate cake.

Can I offer you anything else?" the waitress asked when she returned. I glanced, meeting her eyes, trying to decipher what she was saying.

"No cake?" I asked. I hadn't meant to sound so sad about it, but it felt like the world's biggest disappointment right then.

She shook her head, her eyes landing on the piece next to me. I guess they'd gotten the last one.

"Would you want to try the cherry cake?"

"No, thank you," I said, my voice small.

She nodded and walked away, my eyes falling to the counter as I debated getting up and leaving. This was a flaw I didn't fully accept about myself, more like I tried to ignore.

Often, when something went wrong, I didn't have the emotional capacity to handle the disappointment. It wasn't all the time, but with the case on the line, and the need to punish these marks, I guess I'd overwhelmed my system.

Tears pricked at the corners of my eyes, and I was two seconds away from bolting out the door so I could cry alone in the alley.

A large arm covered in tattoos nudged me holding a bite of the chocolate cake I'd just been crying over on a fork. I whipped my head around, peering up and up and up until I met the eyes of the man the tattooed arm offering cake was attached to.

Everything about him was dark—dark hair, eyes,

skin, and beard. Most people probably gave this man a wide berth, crossing to the other side of the street when he neared. But I'd always preferred the dark, seeing the truth of a person better when the light wasn't there to shield them.

And while this man appeared to be menacing, I could tell deep down he had a good soul. Life had scarred him, but he wasn't a threat to me. In fact, his quiet presence was comforting, and I felt safer with him than I did with most people.

His eyes watched me, letting me take my time to assess him fully. It made me sad to think people were afraid of him. I smiled at him, wanting him to know I saw who he was and wasn't scared.

The corner of his beard moved, and he nudged the fork again, reminding me what had started my perusal.

"Oh, that's kind of you, but I don't want to take it from you. You got it first, so you should enjoy it." I shook my head, smiling at him so he knew I wasn't mad he had it.

He didn't drop it, lifting the fork with the cake closer to my lips. His eyes fell to my mouth, and I licked them under his gaze. The little bit of space between us allowed him to press the chocolate cake closer, my mouth automatically opening and wrapping around the utensil.

Chocolatey goodness exploded in my mouth, and I

barely contained the moan that wanted to escape in response. He pulled the fork from my lips, allowing the cake to slide the rest of the way into my mouth, melting as it hit my tongue.

My eyes glanced up, not surprised that he was watching me. I smiled in thanks, my insides vibrating with happiness. The opposite corner of his mouth ticked up, making him almost have a full smile. He cut off another bite, taking it to his mouth. With his eyes still glued to mine, he placed it on his tongue, wrapping his lips around the silver utensil as chocolate icing spread across his lips.

Never in my life had I been so jealous of a fork.

I sucked in a breath, my heart racing as heat spread through my body. Shit, this was turning me on. I never thought chocolate cake and a hot guy... okay, I should stop right there and acknowledge I'd been lying to myself this whole time if I didn't think this was a fantasy come to life.

Crossing my legs, I waited with bated breath for what he would do next. This had suddenly become the most intense conversation I'd ever had, and he hadn't spoken a word. It should've probably been weird that I was eating cake off a random guy's fork, but it wasn't. There was a connection I couldn't describe between us that went past the strangeness.

He cut off another bite, bringing it to my lips again. I didn't resist opening my mouth for the cake. Back and forth, we took bites until nothing was left but a few crumbs. He sat the fork down on the plate, and I weirdly wanted to snatch it back and keep it forever.

That fork had seen some things.

It felt wrong to let it back out into the general public now that it had been part of my mouthgasm.

We continued to stare at one another, comfortable with the silence. The waitress interrupted it when she sat my food down, the to-go bags placed next to me.

"Here you go, darlin'. Let me know if you need anything else."

She hurried away on a mission to serve her next customer. I picked up my cheeseburger, taking a huge bite of it. Then moaned around the greasy goodness as cheese melted in my mouth, some dripping down my fingers. I lifted the burger to the man beside me, offering him a taste. It only seemed fair.

A full-blown smile sat on his lips, stopping my breath for a second. He shook his head, motioning for me to continue.

I shrugged, going back to my meal. When I was mostly done, I wiped my face, not wanting a ketchup chin when I looked at him again. I picked up a fry and turned, the thoughts in my head ready to escape.

"Thanks for the cake. I want to feel bad for stealing half of it, but it was so good that I can't lie about that. So, thanks." He nodded, his body turned more toward me. He leaned one of his elbows against the counter, resting his head on his hand as he watched me. "I don't know if you noticed, but I was at a real low point. Sometimes I get that way and am unaware until the simplest thing pushes me over that edge."

He continued to stare at me, his eyes speaking to me as he listened.

"Most of the time, I'm this happy-go-lucky girl, ready to take on the world. I'm okay with how my life is and where it's going. But then, sometimes, I wonder if I will repeat the same day over and over and if that's all there ever will be. It's hard because I do like my life. It's safe and comfortable because I know what to expect. I live with people who understand me and accept me. I have everything I could possibly want. But..." trailing off, I realized how deep I was getting with this stranger. I cleared my throat, shoving a few more fries into my mouth.

The quiet man nudged me, his eyes soft, and I knew he understood. The emotions tumbled inside me; he'd felt them too. Even without him voicing any words, I instinctively felt them. He placed his big palm on my forearm; the warmth seeping into me, hugging me from inside. Taking a deep breath, I let it out slowly, nodding that I understood what he was saying.

That it was okay to feel alone even when you were surrounded by people. That it was okay to want something just for yourself. And that it was okay to be sad when, for all intents and purposes, you shouldn't be. It. Was. Okay.

"So, yeah, that," I said, using my fry to emphasize my point. "You're an excellent listener. I'm glad I sat beside you and stole half your cake." I giggled, the action making his eyes widen, and I could practically feel them smiling at me.

I finished off my food, wishing I didn't have to leave. But I still needed to do a few things before today's activities.

"Well, I guess I better head back. Gotta love a secrets and chocolate cake dinner." I smiled as I paused, not sure what else to say. "If I never see you again, thank you for touching my heart with your beautiful soul."

The quiet man took my hand, squeezing it between his giant paws. We held eye contact for a second longer, only interrupted by the waitress placing my bill down. She eyed me, looking between the man who held my hands and me. She only saw his outside; her face worried for me as she peered back.

"You good, hun?"

"Yep." I nodded, giving her a reassuring smile. "Thank you."

I hated dropping his hands to reach into my purse to grab some cash. Placing some bills down, I scooted off the stool and grabbed my food bag. The man stood, and I realized just how tall he was. He had to be double my size, my head barely reaching his abs. He watched me, his eyes shielded, his face guarded as he waited to see how I would respond to him. Carefully, he pulled out his wallet, placing some cash for his cake.

Giving him a big smile, I tilted my head as I debated. He lifted an eyebrow in question.

"I was just debating if I could climb you like a tree. Pretty sure I could do it. I have strong leg muscles, and I'm very limber."

His jaw dropped open, and I giggled, my face blushing as I realized how that sounded.

"I didn't necessarily mean it like that, but..." I shrugged, my smile turning coy as I fluttered my eyelashes as I attempted to flirt. Something shifted in his gaze, a new part of him waking up.

I turned on my heels, spinning with the bags of food, wanting to get out of the cafe before I spontaneously orgasmed from my quiet giant's eyes alone.

I didn't have to look to see if he was following me; I somehow knew he would. Not in a predatory way, but wanting to make sure I was safe. The thought was comical, but I appreciated the sentiment. I hadn't had anyone to look out for me since Otto.

The sun was setting as I exited, the air cooler as the temperature dropped. My silent stranger fell into step next to me, placing himself on the edge closest to the road. It was a simple gesture, but my lady parts about exploded from it all the same.

That same feeling of not wanting to leave this man filled me, and despite knowing I had somewhere to be, I stopped, turning to him. My mouth opened a few times, words escaping me for once. The door to the bookstore opened, jolting me as I realized we'd paused right in front of it.

"There you are," a guy said, then stopped.

I didn't understand his words, so I broke eye contact with my stranger and glanced at the voice. The blond guy from yesterday stared at me with a curious expression, glancing between my cake provider and me.

"Oh, um," I mumbled, realizing how it might look. We'd had a spark, and then here I was with someone else. "Looks like we did find one another again. Small town perk," I said. I gave him a soft smile, hoping it said, "*Hi, this is, but it isn't, what it looks like.*"

He lifted a brow, frowning. "Do I know you?" he asked, looking back at the tall man.

Shame and embarrassment filled me, my words toppling over one another as I rushed to get out of this awkward situation. The thoughts from earlier that had been stalled with the cake flared to the forefront of my mind.

"Right. Yeah. A momentary lapse of judgment." I dropped my eyes, not able to meet my silent friend's gaze, knowing I'd be able to feel the pity emanating from his expressive orbs. "Thanks again," I said, darting off and running with my bags of food down the sidewalk before he could stop me.

For the first time in my life, I wanted to look back, to see if he chased me, but the fear that he hadn't was far worse than that of being captured. So I focused ahead, tears streaming down my cheeks as I ran toward the hotel.

This was why I didn't venture out of my room and lived vicariously through *Phoenix Hospital* and smutty books for all my romance needs. Real life never measured up.

I shoved away the thought that it was a lie. That not only had the past twenty-four hours shown me differently, I knew in my soul that true love existed. Because I had found it when I was six years old.

Raven

After a shower, I parted my hair into two French braids to keep it out of the way. I shut off my emotions like I'd been taught and focused on the mission. Later when I returned to my room with a new tally to add to my death tracker, I could eat my feelings as I binged on the food I'd shoved into the tiny refrigerator. Yeah, that was a good plan.

Taking my clothes out of my bag, I laid the black leather pants next to the tight-fitting black top and leather jacket. They were so outside my regular clothes that they helped me fall into the Silent Blade. Yeah, that was so much better than the Peppermint Killer.

Wiggling my way into the pants, I zipped them up and fell back to the bed, my body heaving for breath. "And this is why I avoid pants," I grumbled, rolling over. I slipped on the tank top and placed my leather jacket into the bag designed as a medical kit. It also held my weapon of choice, my hypodermic needle. The bag of peppermints was nestled next to my collection of chemicals disguised as perfume bottles and a few feet of dynamic rope in case I needed to make a quick exit.

Once everything was secure, I pulled on a pair of scrubs over my leather outfit and a curly red wig to leave the hotel. Hitting play on my laptop, the room filled with noises of me entertaining a guest in case anyone stopped by. I'd made the clip from various scenes in Phoenix Hospital, splicing them together for a long night of fun.

"At least invisible me gets laid." I giggled at my joke, locking the deadbolt after putting the 'Do not disturb' sign on the front. Slipping through the connecting door, I exited the adjoining room we'd reserved with a different name. I took the stairwell and exited out the back door, avoiding a single soul. I quickly removed the scrubs and wig, swapping them for the long leather coat with a hood.

Now that I was as black as the night, I could sneak through the shadows to my destination. Most of the town was asleep; only a lone bar appeared open this late, giving me ample time and cover to reach my mark's house unnoticed.

The three-story brick house sat on a corner, with houses on both sides. Across the street was an apartment building and a shoe repair shop. The shop roof was my lookout as I used my night-vision and infrared binoculars to check out the surrounding area.

The house on the left was vacant, with only a few rodents populating it. The one on the right showed two figures sleeping in their upstairs bedroom. The apartment building had seen better days and, therefore, wasn't full. A few people still lingered in their apartments, but none were directly across from the house, so it was unlikely they would notice anything.

A van five houses down caught my attention. It hadn't been there the previous night. The binoculars picked up a few heat signatures, and I wrestled with the decision of waiting or going in.

"You'll be in and out. You're the Silent Blade. No one will see you. You've done this a hundred times," I muttered, trying to convince myself.

Taking in a deep breath, I nodded, reassured. My muscles bunched under the leather, ready to get into action. I focused on the crimes Millicent had committed; the innocent lives she'd destroyed. She might not have created the drug, but she'd still signed off on it, making her just as responsible in my book. Perhaps more.

Checking my surroundings one last time, I secured my bag to my back and slipped off the roof. My feet landed quietly in the grass, and I crept toward the back of the house, knowing it was the weakest entry point. My heart raced, the adrenaline pumping in me with each step.

A sound further down the street rang out, stopping

me in my tracks. I waited a few seconds, dismissing it as an animal. No one inside the house stirred, pushing me to continue. Lifting myself up on the roof overhang that covered a back porch, I adjusted my weight to avoid the rotted spots I'd found last night. It made me weirdly happy that Millicent had ended up in such a crappy place.

She'd gotten rich from the deaths of others, and now she'd die in a rundown house in the middle of nowhere, Kentucky.

Taking a deep breath, I jumped from the roof to a balcony, my fingers gripping the bars as I pulled myself up and over the railing. Sitting against the brick, I took a few seconds to catch my breath and ensure no one had heard my movement.

Despite the house being a piece of crap, Millicent had installed a state-of-the-art alarm system. But they hadn't considered someone climbing all the way to the attic. Every other window had an alarm on them, but not that one. Granted, it was about 20ft off the ground, which would dissuade most people. But I wasn't like most people.

"One more story," I whispered, standing up and balancing on the balcony railing. This was the trickiest part since I only had a small ledge to pull myself up on.

"Next invention, some of those sticky feet things you see in spy movies," I grumbled, my fingers digging into the brick. With one last deep breath, I reached up and gripped the ledge, heaving myself onto it.

I leaned against the window, my heart racing as I caught my breath. Cursing myself for eating that cake now. "Actually, that's a damn lie, and you know it. You loved every second of that cake. You're just mad now that you didn't spend more time on arm definition. Don't blame the cake!" I hissed, narrowing my eyes at myself. "And this is why you don't have friends," I mocked.

Ignoring my own debate, I got to work, lifting the window I'd been able to unlatch last night with a magnet. It had taken a few squirts of WD40 to quiet the hinges, but it now slid up with ease; not a squeak could be heard.

Once it was up, I squared my shoulders, dreading this next part. Part of why they didn't put an alarm on this window, outside the fact it was up so high, was that it was... well, it was tiny. Small. Miniscule. Close to a dog door opening and not human size.

I had a small frame, but it was well padded with muscle and my love of cake.

Knowing I needed to get on with it, I sucked in a breath and dove through arms first, hoping the quicker I did it, the faster it would be over with.

My hands touched down on the floorboards, my body moving with gravity as it propelled itself through the opening. My torso cleared, and I let out the breath

I'd been holding, only to curse with that same breath as my hips snagged.

"Beetlejuice!" I cursed, my feet dangling out the window as my front half hung. Pushing against the floor, I wiggled my hips, my stomach scraping across the metal latch. I ignored the pain and shoved up with my foot on the ledge, hoping to add enough force. Sucking in a breath, I squeezed and pulled myself with all my might.

My hips screamed in pain, the sides of the window digging into my flesh, but as I debated giving up, they cleared, and I tumbled to the floor as I rolled into a ball. I lay there briefly, praying no one had heard me. The house remained still, my hips throbbing in response. Shutting the window, I was glad I had a different exit planned for later.

"Ow. That's going to leave a bruise."

I sat up, my eyes quickly adjusted to my surroundings, and I moved around the clutter overtaking the dusty space to a small door on the right wall. It was about four feet high, meaning I only had to duck slightly to fit in this one. I'd found this passageway in the oldest blueprints, used for the servants when they'd lived upstairs. The door went directly to the main bedroom where my mark was.

Plucking my small pin light off my belt, I ducked into the space and descended the stairs. The wood creaked with each step, so I took them slowly, allowing my weight to settle with each one before I moved to the next. When I reached the second floor, I turned and counted the doors, stopping when I got to the third one.

Turning the knob, I unlatched the door slowly, unsure if it would make a sound. The door opened into a walk-in closet, an addition to the house in the past fifty years. Boxes of shoes had been placed in front of the door, so I moved a few over until I could climb over the rest. It was funny how people could make their minds forget something by covering it up.

But I was here to make sure she remembered what her actions did.

Stepping into the bedroom, I watched the couple on the bed, their chests rising and falling with sleep. Pulling out my needle, I filled it with air as I neared and calculated my next move. While between the toes was my favorite spot to inject the bubble, it wasn't always the easiest when they were sleeping, especially with a spouse next to them. It looked like her husband would be my first test subject for my newest spray.

Nearing the man, I pulled off the bottle of sleeping spray and wafted it under his nose. His nose crinkled for a second; then, his whole body went lax. Lifting his arm, I let it drop back to the bed, catching it before it hit the mattress. I poked his cheek and lifted his eyelid. None of my ministrations roused him, so I took it to mean my combination worked.

Fist pumping the air, I moved over to my mark, lifting the covers at the end carefully. Millicent took several sleeping aids at night, so I didn't worry about her waking just yet. Pushing her toes apart, I pressed the needle into the fleshy part, pushing down the plunger until it emptied. Standing, I lowered the covers and moved toward her head.

Pulling the bottle of peppermint oil off, I wafted it under her nose. I didn't need to do this part, but for the really horrible ones, I wanted them to know who it was that had killed them.

Her eyes flared open, her body temporarily paralyzed with the fast-acting agent I'd added to the oil. I had to act fast, only having a few minutes before the air bubble did its job.

"Hello, Millicent. Your crimes have finally caught up to you." I smiled, nothing innocent or joyous about it, as I stared down at her through the hood. "I just wanted you to know it was me who killed you."

She licked her lips, her eyes wide as she stared at me. "He told me you would come. The Peppermint Killer," she whispered, her breathing growing ragged.

"What? No! I'm the Silent Blade!"

Her mouth opened, but no words came out, and I knew my time was over. Placing a peppermint on the nightstand, I put my needle away and headed back to the closet.

"Stupid people and their stupid nicknames. I

should be able to veto the moniker since I'm the deadly killer. But no, they spread that name around without my consent and take all the joy out of a kill," I groused, opening the secret door and putting the shoe boxes back.

Closing it a few seconds later, I turned on my flashlight again, pouting as I headed toward my exit. I hadn't wanted to come in through this way, too worried someone would spot me since it was on the first floor. Plus, the secret passage only opened from the inside, the rest of the doors blending with the wallpaper, so I had to enter it from the attic. Taking a right, I counted until I was in front of the door I needed and pressed my ear to listen. Feeling confident it was clear, I pushed it open and stepped into the room.

Movement in the corner caught my attention, and I spun, not noticing the shelf that protruded from the wall. The side of my head caught the corner, sending a jolt of pain through me. My hood fell down, and I cursed, then froze, remembering something had caught my attention.

A tall, dark figure stood still, a bag on their shoulder and an instrument pressed to a safe in the wall. I relaxed when I realized it wasn't anyone who lived in the house. I held up my hands, stepping back.

"Sorry, I didn't mean to interrupt. Just finishing up my job; not here to encroach on your territory. Just avoid the master unless you want to contaminate it with your DNA. Your choice. Carry on your thieving, and I'll get out of your hair," I said, taking another step back toward the crawl space I wanted.

The figure chuckled, stepping closer as I put the pieces together.

"Wait... Oh my God, you-you're—" I gestured with my hands, unable to get the words out. It was the Loxley Crew! I'd finally done it. I ran into one of them. The person stepped into the light, pulling his balaclava off, shocking me even more.

"Well, if it isn't the cutie-pie. I knew we were destined to meet again." He smiled at me, his hair all skewed from the balaclava. My mouth dropped open as I searched every inch of him, not believing what I saw.

"You!" I spat, planting my hands on my hips.

"Yes, me. Who knew we had even more in common, Robyn Banks? That's even funnier now that I found you here."

I rolled my eyes, trying to stave off the adorableness of him and his flirting. Do. Not. Be. Swayed.

"Funny. You ignored me completely earlier, but now that no one else is around, you're all friendly again. I've dealt with guys like you before, only wanting to date the chubby girl in private. Well, newsflash, I can kill you six ways to Sunday, so do me a favor and leave me alone. I've had enough self-doubt today to last me a lifetime."

His eyes dropped, a frown deepening as I spoke, confusion etched over his face. But I wouldn't fall for his cute little puppy dog act. Not this time.

"Wait, what are you talking about? I haven't seen you since I dropped you off," he said, stepping closer. His eyes shifted to my face, concern now shining in them.

"Yeah, okay, whatever, dude. I gotta go. Thanks for ruining my favorite thieves' organization, jerk." I stepped back, not liking how close he was. I needed to get out of here. My head throbbed where I'd hit it, and I was too scared to touch it.

"Are you okay?" he asked.

I rolled my eyes. "Yeah, of course, you're playing that card. I'd have to be 'mental' to deny you, right? Fuckety-bye." I rarely used the f-word, but this time felt appropriate.

"No." He shook his head. "I think you're bleeding."

Everything in me seized up at his words, my heart picking up a quicker pace as it galloped off, blood pumping in my ears. Shit. Shit. Shit. I needed to leave here before I passed out in my mark's home. That would not go over well with Man if I were found at the crime scene.

Yes. Must. Leave. Now.

Spinning, I took one step toward my exit, only to

run smack into a hard surface. Strong arms reached out to grab me, lifting me up. My legs were too weak to fight, the blood trailing down my face and into my eyes and over my nose. The copper and rust smell filled my nostrils, my vision going red.

It was too much, and I couldn't stop the flashback, my brain catching up and spiraling back to the past as my body gave into the panic and went offline.

Porter

IN A MATTER OF MINUTES, MY HEART HAD SOARED AT discovering my blue-haired beauty was the assassin we'd been tracking for years, then confused as she ripped me a new one, and finally, it plummeted as blood trailed down her face as she swayed.

Rueben stepped out of the shadows, and she turned, smacking into him. I sighed in relief as he caught her, hoisting her into his arms. He stared down at the blue-haired pixie, something passing over his face.

"You done?" he asked, reminding me what I'd been doing before she'd walked into the room out of thin air.

"Just about." I rushed back to the safe, finishing the combination and opening it. My usual adrenaline when I cracked a safe was nowhere to be found. My eyes kept jerking to the right to check on Robyn. Pulling the rest of the items into my bag, I shut the safe and turned the dial, putting the painting it had been behind back.

"The other rooms secured?" I asked.

Rueben nodded, stepping out of the room and going to the backdoor. I tapped the comm to get Phoenix's attention.

"Heading out, let me know when the alarm is off."

"On it," he said, tapping his keys. "Any problems?"

"Um, not a problem, per se. You'll see in a minute."

"And go, you have fifteen seconds."

I opened the door, gesturing for Rueben to go first, and closed it a few seconds later. Typically, we could manage the alarm longer, but the system here was top of the line despite the state of the house. The longest we could disrupt it without setting off the monitoring company was fifteen seconds, giving us just enough time to open and close the door.

Rueben stayed in the shadows, moving silently and quickly for a man his size. I never knew how he did it, but it made working jobs easier for him. The van parked a few houses down came into view, and I quickened my steps, curious about how Robyn was doing.

I stepped in front of Rueben and knocked on the door with our signal; the lock disengaged a second later. Opening it, I hopped in and cleared a spot for him to lay her down.

"What the hell?" Phoenix muttered, jumping up. I

shoved the bag of goods in his arms and reached up to grab the first aid kit. Rueben laid her down gently, brushing the side of her face softly. It surprised me, freezing me to my spot for a second.

"Holy shit, it's the girl from the bookstore," Phoenix whispered.

"No, it's my ride-share girl," I said, wiping the blood off her face. It had stopped bleeding, so I didn't think she needed stitches. Once it was cleaned, I applied a butterfly bandage just in case.

She whimpered, and Rueben pulled her back into his lap. I couldn't even argue about it; the look on his face and how he held her stopped me. Phoenix's words penetrated my mind, some dots connecting.

"She's who you met at the diner and then later bumped into Phoenix with?" I asked Rueben. His dark eyes lifted to mine, nodding in response. "That explains why she yelled at me then. She thought you were me." I slapped my twin, and he rolled his eyes, not bothered.

"I didn't say anything mean to her!" he exclaimed. He glanced at me for a second before returning to her. I internally smiled; he was smitten, even if he wouldn't admit it. Now I just had to convince Otto to give her a chance.

Phoenix liked to point out how often and quickly I fell in love with girls, only to discover something about them later and break it off. He was only half right in his assessment.

The reason I fell out of love with them was because they were never the right girl for *all* of us. Since the other knuckleheads barely ventured out of our rooms, it had been up to me to meet the one for us. So, I'd meet someone I liked and talk her up to the others, bringing her around so they could meet and fall in love with her too. But for one reason or another, one of them wouldn't like her. So, I'd make a random excuse for why she wasn't the one and move on.

But it finally looked like I'd found her. And she was our little assassin, to boot.

Phoenix and Otto had thought I was crazy the first time I'd seen her. She'd been jumping out of a window as we entered a room. I didn't think she'd even noticed us. She'd intrigued me, and I hoped we'd run into one another properly.

Over the years, I'd find evidence of her being there, sometimes before us, sometimes after when it broke on the news. But we never crossed paths again until tonight.

Picking her up at the airport, Phoenix and Rueben running into her in town and stumbling into her now on this job... I knew it all meant something. This was fate bringing us together.

What better way for a girl to accept our lifestyle than to have a secret one of her own?

She stirred in the big man's arms, her eyes opening as she came to. Her blue eyes landed on me, and I smiled, not wanting her to be scared.

"Blue cheese! How hard did I hit my head? I'm seeing double." She blinked again, turning her head from side to side. "Yep, definitely Diplopia. Okay, possible conditions include concussion, brain aneurysm, stroke, infection, brain tumor..." she said, listing off medical conditions as if she had them memorized.

"What's Diplopia?" I asked, confused.

"Double vision," Phoenix and Robyn said at the same time. Robyn gasped, looking back and forth between us again.

My twin smiled, reaching out to take her hand. "You don't have double vision. There are two of us. And I think I owe you an apology, though I'm unsure what I did wrong earlier."

"Two of you," she mumbled in disbelief.

I waved, my tattooed hand on display. She glanced down at the one in her grasp, spotting Phoenix's tattooed hand.

"Right. Twins?" she asked like she was still confused.

"Yes. Porter, Phoenix," I said, pointing us out. She followed my finger, taking it all in. "Does your head feel okay? You clipped it on the corner. I cleaned it and bandaged you, but we can take you to the hospital if you prefer."

Her eyes shuttered as she winced. "Yes, of course. I was leaving and ran into the shelf. You mentioned... You mentioned that word, and everything went dark. Is there any on me?" she asked, keeping her eyes closed.

"None on your face." I lifted her hand and spotted a little smear, so I wiped it off and checked her clothes. There was a little smudge on her hood, so I wiped it clean next. When I didn't spot anymore, I tossed the wipes away. "All clear."

Her whole body relaxed, and she let out a breath as her eyes opened; her blue eyes softened as she looked between Phoenix and me.

"Thank you. I can't..." She shook her head. "Yeah, I just can't. It makes it difficult to watch my favorite show too. No matter how many times I write to *Phoenix Hospital,* they refuse to do away with the red stuff. I mean, I get it, but also... eww."

"You watch *Phoenix Hospital*?" my brother asked, his eyes wide as he smiled down at her.

"It's only the best medical drama ever," she said, some of the spark I'd seen the first time I'd met her returning. "If you're going to make fun of me, just know I can kill you a hundred different ways."

"He's obsessed," I said when Phoenix's mouth dropped open. I couldn't tell if he was scared or turned on. Knowing him, probably a little of both. He swallowed, nodding.

"It's my favorite show, too. The guys get tired of me talking about it all the time."

"Same! The other Belladonnas don't understand my commitment to it, especially after—"

"Dr. Romano left," they said together.

Robyn giggled and went to sit up but was blocked by Rueben's arms holding her. She glanced down, finding the large tattooed arm across her middle. Tilting her head back, I nervously waited for her to freak out at the silent giant's arms she was in.

She smiled, her hand reaching up to touch his cheek. "My chocolate cake hero," she said sweetly. Rueben's eyes fluttered closed as he leaned into her touch. He'd never been this at ease with a woman before. I didn't know all of his history, but based on what I'd gathered over the years, I believed his abuser had been his mother, making his trust in women difficult.

I'd only seen him with a handful throughout the years, but they never lasted long. Even when he liked one, he never treated them like this. He was stand-offish and kept them at arm's length, keeping their relationship physical.

"The three of you are with PROP, aren't you? You're the Loxley Crew?" she asked, looking back at the three of us. "I've wanted to meet you for so long. I follow all your heists as best as I can." Her cheeks tinted red, pride filling my chest at her admiration.

"We are. Along with one other. Boss man is back at the house we rented. He had... to rest," I said, not wanting to disclose Otto's secret. He worked hard to not let it be a hindrance to his life, so I wouldn't be the one spilling the beans.

"There's four of you? I could only ever count three. That's very clever." She brightened as she looked between the three of us.

"And you're the Peppermint Killer," Phoenix said, earning him a scowl.

"No, I absolutely am not! I'm the Silent Blade. Or at least I am tonight. I haven't decided if I'm committed to it yet. No one ever asked me if I wanted to be the Peppermint Killer; they just started calling me that, and now it's stuck! So, I'm on a mission to change it."

Her outburst was so cute it made us all smile as we watched her huff and puff. Our laughter had her crossing her arms over her chest, her lower lip dropping into a pout that I knew would be the end of us all. I needed to do something quick!

"Do you need to get in touch with anyone, Robyn? Are the Belladonna's your organization?" I asked, hoping to learn more about her and distract her from the pout.

"Oh." Her mouth formed an 'o' as she sat up, Rueben letting her this time. He didn't release her entirely, though, settling her back against his chest. She shook her head, cringing.

"My name's not Robyn. That's just my cover. I'm Raven. Sorry for lying. And pretend like I didn't mention the Belladonnas."

"Raven," I said, rolling her name over my tongue. It fit her so much better. "I like it. And you don't have to apologize to us. We know the importance of keeping identities hidden. You can trust us. I know that sounds cliche, but you can."

She deflated, her eyes shining as she nodded. Her trusting us felt significant, and I wanted to shout from the rooftops. She took a breath, swallowing.

"I don't have anyone I need to get in touch with yet. The Belladonnas are my adopted sisters, my fellow assassins. But should we move? I don't normally stay around the crime scene this long." She looked around at the van, something clicking in her mind. "You're the van parked down the street. I thought it was out of place," she mumbled.

"Yeah, I guess we better. Um..." I paused, looking between the others. I didn't want to let her go just yet. The two others seemed to agree, giving me a subtle nod. "Would you want to hang out some more? We have food, and we could trade war stories or something?" I asked, my cheeks flushing.

"Oh, are you sure? I don't want to interfere."

"You wouldn't," Phoenix and I said together as Rueben's arms tightened around her.

"What's your name, big guy?" she asked, looking up at him again.

"Rueben," he said, his voice deep and hoarse.

"I had a Care Bear named Rueben once!" she exclaimed, her eyes big as she smiled, successfully making my insides turn into a million butterflies.

"It's settled. Do you want to stop by the hotel first?" I asked, standing up in a hunch.

She bit her lip, grabbing all three of our attention. "How long will we be?" she asked, looking down at her clothes.

"However long you're comfortable with, baby assassin," Phoenix said, earning himself a nose crinkle and head shake.

"Um, no. That makes me sound like I kill babies, and I would never!" she gasped.

Phoenix's cheeks heated as he nodded, rubbing his hands through his hair and making the ends stick everywhere. "Right, um, Raven?"

She nodded, pleased with the correction, then remembered the question. "I guess I would like to change. This isn't my normal attire."

"Then it's settled. We'll swing by the hotel and let you grab whatever you need. Phoenix, alert the boss man so he doesn't freak out when we're not back."

"On it," he said, sliding into his chair at the

computer and sending a secure message. I climbed into the driver's seat, trusting Rueben would keep her safe in the back without a seatbelt. For the first time since we started PROP and became the Loxley Crew, I wasn't buzzing to see what we'd stolen; instead, my mind and heart were completely enraptured by a girl. One I hoped would change our lives as we knew it.

Raven

I directed the van around to the back and pulled my disguise back on. The guys watched with amused expressions, curious about my process. It had taken some convincing for Rueben to let me go once we arrived, and I didn't want to admit how nice it had felt to be held like that.

"I'll be right back," I said, touching the back door handle.

"Wait a second," Phoenix started, reaching over to stop me. "Shouldn't we go with you?" he asked, his green eyes big as he peered at me and the outside world.

Now that I knew there were two of them, I could tell the difference, even if outwardly they looked exactly the same, except their tattooed sleeves. Phoenix seemed less trusting of things, whereas Porter jumped in without looking. It would be interesting to be around them more and find other ways they differed, something I looked forward to.

"Assassin," I said, pointing at my chest and smiling.

Phoenix blushed, dropping his arm that had paused mid-air. "Right. I'm going to take a bit to get used to that." He cringed, dropping his eyes sheepishly.

"I'll be lickety-split!" I cheered, climbing out of the door and ducking into the shadows. The sun would rise soon, so I needed to handle this before I blew my cover.

The tape I'd placed on the back door latch was still intact, and the door opened with no problems. I climbed the stairs, my breath huffing out as I neared the third floor.

"Always with the cardio," I mumbled, hating having to admit I needed more. Slipping through the door, I paced myself as I approached the extra room, using the key card to open the door.

Stepping in, I leaned against the wall and counted to ten as I let my eyes adjust to the darkness. The shapes of the room came into focus, nothing appearing to be out of place. I could hear the TV in my room still on; the recording had finished an hour ago when I'd expected to return.

Something felt off, but I couldn't place it just yet.

Convinced it wasn't anything in this room, I smiled before opening the room door. Porter and Phoenix fell through and immediately righted themselves, attempting to look around like they didn't know how they'd gotten there.

"How did you know we were here?" Porter asked, his cheeks pink.

"Assassin," I repeated, giggling. The twins stopped their shuffling, looking at me with awe. "Plus, one of you, I'm guessing Phoenix, since you don't go into the houses as often, isn't as quiet as he thinks he is."

Porter laughed, clapping his brother on the back as the grumpier twin pouted, crossing his arms and frowning.

"You can come out, Ruebear," I said, keeping the door open for a few more seconds. The most silent of the trio popped from around the corner and walked through the door, shrugging.

"How did you know he was there?" Phoenix asked. "He's the quietest of all of us."

"I didn't actually hear him, but I knew he wouldn't stay put. It was his cologne that gave him away. I've been inhaling it for the past hour, so when I smelled it again when the door opened, I knew he was just better at hiding."

Rueben gave me a broad smile, lighting up his entire face, his beard moving with the action. It felt like I'd just won the lottery with how beautiful it was.

"Holy shit!" Porter exclaimed, looking at the big man in question. "That's it. We're keeping you now,

Raven. I hope you don't mind four smelly dudes because you won't be able to shake us."

I giggled again, my face flushing with his words. It had been a long time since someone had shocked me with their proclamations, making me feel wanted in an entirely new way.

"Hmm, I bet I could shake you if I wanted," I teased, tapping my finger against my lips.

Phoenix slapped his brother against the stomach. "Shut up, bro. She'll take that as a challenge. I'll never underestimate your skills ever again, Silent Blade." He motioned like he was bowing with his hands, making everything in me tingle with delight.

"Just for that, you get a reward." I moved over, pulling his arm until he crouched down. I kissed his smooth cheek, giggling as his eyes widened in surprise, his hand touching where my lips had just been. "Now, you three stay here so I can change."

"No fair! I want a reward," Porter mumbled, making me laugh even more.

I slipped through the adjoining door, leaving it open a smidge so I could still hear them. I wasn't convinced someone hadn't been in my room yet, which left me on high alert until I could confirm it was clear. So, I took a few seconds to orient myself to the room, the TV casting shadows around it as it flashed.

Everything looked in place, but my sixth sense told me something was off. Pulling out a spray from my belt, I tiptoed across the floor toward the bathroom, the only room I couldn't see from here. The door was open, the long mirror reflecting the images from the TV as they bounced around. A shift in the mirror's background caught my attention, and I ducked just in time to avoid the knife now lodged into the wood.

The next few seconds happened quickly as they readjusted, jumping over the bed to strike me. I picked up the nearest thing, throwing it into their path as I leaped on the bed out of their way. They stumbled into the dresser, so I quickly grabbed the hotel binder and tossed it at the adjoining door, shutting it completely. I didn't want this person to know they were there, or worse, for them to charge in here and get killed.

Hopping off the bed, my attacker and I watched one another as we circled the area and waited for one of us to strike.

"Who sent you?" I asked, despite already having a good guess. When they didn't answer, I took a different approach. "It's nice to see you again, Steel Strike. What's it been, three years since the last Assassin get-together? Who's on that committee? We should message them and see what the holdup is."

"You always did talk too much, Peppermint—"

"It's the Silent Blade, thank you very much!"

Steel Strike laughed, not taking their eyes off me. "Funny, since you never shut up."

Rolling my eyes, I dove, tired of the standoff. The

longer I took, the higher the likelihood one of the guys would come to investigate, and I would not let them get hurt.

I swiped Steel Strike off her feet, rolling back to my position a second later. Steel Strike growled, charging me now that I'd pissed her off. I jumped over the chair, tossing napkins at her face to distort her view. I spotted the bottle I'd dropped by the bed and jumped up to grab it.

Steel Strike grabbed my ankle, turning me around as they pounced on me, holding my arms down. "If you wanted to make out, all you had to do was ask," I said, my fingers wrapping around my bottle.

Steel Strike sneered, her head moving to slam into mine, but I got my bottle between us, squirting it in her face. She screamed instead of passing out, so I looked down in confusion, realizing I'd grabbed the wrong one. Instead of the knockout spray, I'd grabbed the dirty bombing spray—part instant laxative, part chlorine. It was not a pleasant combination.

Wincing, I watched as she scrambled back, kicking me in the side as she tried to find her way to the door, her stomach already cramping as she held it. I rolled off the bed, standing and tripping over something we'd thrown, cursing as my ankle twisted in my boots. Giving up trying to help her, I watched as she fumbled for the handle. Her face was bright red, the chemical burns already taking effect.

"Honest mistake!" I hollered, waving at her back.

"This isn't over!" she screeched, slamming the door as she ran, probably to find a toilet.

Choking on a laugh, I fell back to the floor, the high of a good fight filling me as I lay there. Banging on the inner door reminded me of what I'd been up to before the showdown. Sitting up, I pulled myself to my feet and gingerly pressed down on my ankle, wincing when it pulsed with pain. Hopping over to the door, I opened it, giving my best innocent look.

The twins stared at me, their eyes wide as they assessed me and tried to peer into the room. "What's up?" I asked. "Miss me already?"

"Rueben said he saw someone leaving your room, their face all red and holding their stomach. We were just concerned?" Phoenix said, the last part coming out as more of a question as his eyes scanned me.

My heart warmed at their concern for my safety. It wasn't that my fellow Belladonnas didn't care, but we all knew each other could handle shit, so you didn't worry in the same way.

"I'm fine. Just a tussle with my nemesis. I'll only be a second." I stopped, realizing what Steel Strike being in my hotel room meant. "Crash Bandicoot! My cover's blown." I rubbed my temple, the night catching up to me with each new event.

"It's settled then. You'll come and stay with us

until you figure out your next move," Porter said, not even hesitating.

"What?" I asked, being the one not to understand this time. Porter gave me that smile that said I was being cute, pushing the door open and walking into my room like he owned it.

"We'll help pack. Put us to work, Cutie-pie!"

I spun on the balls of my feet, my right leg still bent at the knee, my foot lifted. I blinked as I tried to process his request.

"A bunch of guys I just met want me to come and stay with them?" I asked. His face fell, and I struggled to understand why.

"No, we didn't mean it like that!" Porter blurted, confusing me more.

"Huh? You don't want me to stay with you? Or, you do? Sorry, you're going to have to spell it out. I spend most of my time talking to myself, watching *Phoenix Hospital*, and eating snacks while playing with my chemistry set. Sometimes altogether, sometimes separately." I waved my hands in the air. "What I mean is, it doesn't leave much time for boys."

His smile returned as he stepped forward. "First off, we're men, not boys." He winked, sending flutters through my belly. "And I thought you were scared about being in a house with a bunch of guys you don't know," he admitted, taking my hands in his.

I crooked my head to the side, replaying his words. "Um, no, I didn't think about that. Assassin, remember?" I giggled. "I, um, was making sure it wasn't a prank."

Phoenix placed his hands on my shoulders, his body pressing into my back. In between the twins, their intoxicating scent of rain and citrus swirled around me. They touched me together, sending my nerves off-kilter as I peered at Porter. One of his hands moved to my cheek, cupping it as he stared into my eyes.

"I think we were meant to find one another, Raven. You deserve all the best things in life. To be pampered and adored. Cherished. We'll give that to you if you let us."

Whoa. My eyes felt so big I worried they would fall out of my head. My heart galloped in my chest, my skin heating under his stare. What he was offering might sound crazy or ridiculous to other girls, but I'd never been one to fit into the status quo. His words felt like a promise, a declaration built on a lifetime of searching for that missing piece. I wanted to be that piece.

"Okay."

Porter grinned, his eyes practically sparkling. Phoenix bent down, kissing a spot behind my ear.

"You're ours now, pipsqueak. I'll never let you go. Please don't break our hearts." His words were a whispered plea, emotion thick in their meaning.

I leaned back, staring into his deep green eyes. While they were the same color as his brothers, Phoenix's were more haunted, mirroring some of the pain I held in mine. Porter's were the color of grass after a good rain, but Phoenix's were the dark green of an evergreen tree, bordering on black.

"I promise," I said, not scared to make the declaration.

Perhaps it was a flaw, but it was one I definitely accepted about myself. I'd never been afraid to go all in. When I decided on something, I stuck with it, no matter what. Some of my tutors found my stubbornness endearing, while others said it would get me killed in the end. But right now, I didn't care whether it was a flaw or not because the smile Phoenix gave me was worth everything.

For so long, I'd been given everything I wanted—food, clothes, sisters, knowledge, skills, and toys (both kid and adult versions). But in the past few hours, I'd earned smiles from a group of men I didn't think gave them often, and I knew it was exactly what I'd been missing.

Companionship. Laughter. Love.

I wasn't deluded enough to think I was in love with these guys, but I could see myself falling for them quickly. Being an assassin, I understood tomorrow wasn't guaranteed, making me not waste moments on societal standards of do's and don'ts.

"Alright, Porter, you grab my things from the bath-room, and Phoenix, you can grab my electronics. I'll change and pack all my clothes."

The three of us got to work, and I laid out an outfit to change into. A soft pair of leggings and an oversized sweatshirt called to me.

"Don't look," I ordered, keeping my back to them as I pulled off the scrubs and leather jacket, placing the sweatshirt over my tank top. Sitting on the bed, I removed the wretched boots and wiggled out of the pants. I panted for a second, sitting in my underwear before I could pull the leggings on. Once I had them up, I laced up my Converse and shoved all the dirty clothes into a separate compartment.

"Okay, I'm done," I said, letting them know they could look again. Porter handed me my bathroom bag, and I set it in the suitcase, glancing around at every-thing else. Phoenix had all of my electronics in my bookbag, the strap over his shoulder.

"I guess that's it," I said, zipping my suitcase up and sitting it on the floor. Porter took the handle from me, and I motioned for them to exit back through the adjoining room. I took a few seconds to wipe any areas I might've touched in my fight, hobbling out of the room a few seconds later.

"You're hurt!" Rueben exclaimed, rushing toward me. His brows furrowed, his lips frowning as he bent to me, checking me over.

"I just twisted it. It will be back to normal tomorrow," I said, waving him off.

His eyes shot to mine, a storm brewing in them. I placed my hand on his cheek, and his eyes closed, his nostrils flaring as he took a few deep breaths. I felt the sudden urge to do something to make it okay for him.

"How about you give me a piggyback ride, Ruebear? That way, I stay off it?"

His eyes flew open, and he nodded, turning around so I could hop onto his back. The twins now watched me with worry on their faces at missing it. I felt terrible that I'd hidden my injury from them. It hadn't been on purpose. I was just so used to taking care of myself.

Rueben stood up, my eyes wide as I realized how tall he was. "So, this is what it looks like from up here?" I teased, hoping to settle some of the tension.

The guys relaxed a little but still seemed worried I'd fall apart in the next second. Acting like Rueben was a horse, I made an imaginary whip sound as I twirled my hand in the air.

"Giddy up, horsey!"

Rueben's chest vibrated, and I hoped it meant he was laughing. The twins chuckled, finally heading out the door, and the three of us escaped the hotel, no one else the wiser. As we drove to their rental, I prayed that the fourth member of PROP was as cool as these three guys had been.

Raven

PORTER PULLED UP TO A SMALL COTTAGE THAT FIT THE quaint town. I couldn't make out many details at this hour, but it looked like it would belong to a sweet old grandmother who made you chocolate chip cookies.

"Mmm, chocolate chip cookies," I moaned, my tongue salivating at the thought. Damn. I'd left my food in the fridge.

"Farwell, pie. You will be missed," I whispered.

"I have the sudden urge to run to the store," Porter said, reminding me I wasn't alone in the van.

"Why?" I asked, turning to look at him, my brows furrowing.

"He wants you to make that sound again," Phoenix supplied, his brother hitting him in the arm.

"Oh." My eyes grew big as I stared at the twins. I didn't know what to do with that. Were they flirting? Did they like me like that? They were hot, and my mind was short-circuiting.

"I think you broke her," Porter whispered, hitting Phoenix again.

I'd been serious when I said I didn't spend much time with boys. I had a few awkward times with a random guy I met in one city early on and a tech guy I'd hooked up with at one of the conferences. Neither had left much to be desired, in my opinion. I hadn't sought out male companionship after that.

When they'd asked me to stay, I assumed it meant as friends. I couldn't deny the heat between me and the guys, but I'd never assume it was mutual. I was prepared to fall for them and live an unrequited life as their cute friend. But this...

Rueben tapped my leg, drawing my attention to him. He'd already opened the van door and turned, lowering himself so I could climb on again.

Smiling, I wrapped my arms around his shoulders, inhaling his coffee and sweat smell. His large hands grasped my legs, holding me to him. Heat radiated off him, warming me instantly.

"And we're off!" I chuckled when he stood. "I might have to switch to RuebenAir for all my transportation needs from here on out," I teased. His chest vibrated, and my skin tingled from the sound.

The twins hurried out, the doors shutting after they grabbed my bags and theirs. Rueben waited at the door for them, his hands busy with me. Porter unlocked it, pushing it for us to step through. Rueben had to duck down to get in the door, the top of my head brushing the frame.

"Raven, what did you mean earlier about a nemesis? Did you know who broke into your room?" Porter asked, concern on his face.

I waved him off as Rueben bent down, lowering me to the couch. "Oh yeah. It's nothing. It's not the first time someone's tried to kill me," I said nonchalantly.

"Um, what?" Phoenix asked, his face falling. "They were there to kill you?"

"I'm beginning to wonder if you guys understand the definition of assassin. I. Kill. People." I pointed at myself, then gestured like I was cutting my throat, my head lolling to the side at the end.

"Yes, Cutie-pie, we got that part." Porter held his fist to his mouth like he was holding in a laugh. I shrugged, not embarrassed about my macabre charades.

"Okay, well, I'm sure Jerome Fulton isn't too happy with me or my cause and has therefore hired my nemesis to kill me."

"Why do they want you dead? You didn't steal from them. We did. Speaking of, we need to inventory what we gathered tonight, so Otto has it all in the morning when it's recovered."

"Otto? I had a friend named Otto once," I hummed, my mind bringing my first friend to the forefront of my mind. I'd need to check my search once I was settled.

"Why do they want you dead, Raven?" Phoenix asked, squeezing my thigh to get my attention. I hadn't noticed him sit beside me, too focused on the memories playing in my head.

"Oh." I blinked, re-buffering my mind. "He's the board president of Good Meds Pharma, and I made it my mission to take out the board, saving him for last. So, self-preservation is probably his motive."

Phoenix's mouth dropped open, turning his head to look at the others, then back to me. "I have the sudden urge to lock you in a room and not let you leave," he said, narrowing his eyes.

I rolled my eyes, pulling his arm closer to me so I could snuggle into him. "Oh, please. Steel Strike is not half as good as I am. You seriously underestimate the Belladonnas. Not a smart move, dude."

He chuckled, pulling me closer to his warmth. My stomach growled, reminding me I hadn't eaten.

"Food!" I sat up, my eyes wide. "I do believe I was promised some food."

Porter smiled, padding into the kitchen. Rueben had disappeared but returned wearing a black shirt and athletic shorts. He walked over and sat on the floor in front of me, pulling my leg over his shoulder, his hand wrapping around my ankle. He peeled my sock off, looking it over as he gently handled it.

"Ice," he said, glancing toward the kitchen. Porter lifted a finger, spinning in a circle as he looked for something.

"How's boss man?" Phoenix asked.

"Asleep," Rueben said, his eyes shifting to look at Phoenix, a message passing between them. My curiosity about their fourth team member grew even more. Porter handed Rueben an ice pack and towel, returning to the kitchen to gather food.

Rueben motioned for me to turn, my back resting against Phoenix's side, my foot propped on a pillow with the ice pack. A strange flutter took off in my belly. I'd never been taken care of like this. I'd always been the one to treat the girls when they were sick or injured.

"Thank you," I whispered, suddenly feeling shy. Rueben's eyes met mine, nodding as he stood and walked over to the table, taking things out from a bag. Phoenix turned on the television, finding a channel with an older episode of *Phoenix Hospital*. I sighed, settling back into him, happy to have someone to share it with.

"Oh, I love this episode," I said, smiling, tilting my head. Phoenix's eyes were on me and not the TV. "It's the first time Mary performs her solo surgery, and all the other residents get jealous. Plus, there's not that much blood in this one."

Phoenix's green eyes twinkled, and some of the

haunted shadows I'd noticed earlier disappeared. "Yeah, you're right. I'll help you cover your eyes," he offered, those tingles inside multiplying. No one had ever gone out of their way to help me before with my blood issue. The girls knew, but I didn't think they understood what happened to me in those moments and just saw it as another Raven quirk.

"Thank you," I whispered, lifting his hand to my lips and kissing it.

"Ah, man. Phoenix got another kiss. How come I met you first, and I've gotten the least amount of kisses?" Porter asked, pouting. He stood at the end of the couch with a platter of food, my eyes going wide as I took in all the delicious things.

"If that's for me, I'll give you three!" I said, sitting up a little. Porter perked up, his green eyes shimmering with a playfulness I liked. He placed the tray on my lap, bending down with his face turned.

Reaching up, I pulled his face close, kissing one cheek and then the next, debating where to place the third.

"Can I save it?" he asked.

"Why?" I turned my head, trying to figure out his reasoning. Did he not want me to kiss him?

"So I have something to look forward to," he said, the words soft and sincere. My cheeks heated, my stomach tumbling over itself.

"Yes, of course," I stammered, dropping my hands. "Thank you for the food, Porter."

"Anytime, Cutie-pie."

"I have a feeling a bizarre game of earning kisses just started," Phoenix mumbled, sighing at his brother. Porter stood, his face smug as he walked back to the kitchen, grabbing more plates for the others.

Rueben stayed at the table to eat, but Porter joined us on the couch, shifting my foot into his lap. I tried to focus on the show as I ate, but I had so many new things to process.

What did this all mean? What did I do from here? Could I like all of them? It felt like I did. I didn't want to leave, enjoying their company more than I wanted to admit. They felt safe.

True to his word, Phoenix covered my eyes when blood appeared on the screen, allowing me to watch the episode in relative freedom for once.

"Is this how you usually wind down after a caper?" I asked.

"A caper?" Porter repeated, chuckling.

"Thievery? High-jinks? Monkey business?" I asked, giggling. "What do you call your jobs? Heists?"

Porter tilted his head in thought, strands of honey-blond hair falling into his eyes. "I hate to break it to ya, but we mostly just call them jobs. Though, I'm kind of digging high-jinks. What do you think, Rueb? Want to get into some high-jinks?" he asked, laughing.

Rueben turned his head from the floor where he'd settled once he'd finished his food; his brows raised as he shook his head at Porter.

"Ruebear prefers caper," I said matter-of-factly, my hand dropping to his shoulder.

He looked up at me, shrugging, his dark chocolate eyes dancing. I moved my arm, but he kept it in his grip, so I shifted it over, running my fingers through his hair, causing his head to fall back against the couch at my ministrations.

The twins watched me as I ran my fingernails over his scalp, their eyes focused on my hand. I didn't think it was all that interesting, but I wasn't one to judge another's curiosities.

"I'm glad I met you all," I whispered, scared to say it too loud. "Do you think Otto will like me? Is that a common name? I've only heard it once before," I rambled; images of a brown-haired boy with gray eyes and a big smile filled my mind.

"He'll love you, pipsqueak. You don't have to worry about that," Phoenix said, his hand skating over my arm up and down, leaving goosebumps in his trail.

"How did you guys meet to form the Loxley Crew?" I asked; my mind needed something else to focus on. The guys looked at one another like they were deciding who would speak. In the end, it was Porter.

"We all met at a group home. Phoenix and I had survived a while on our own as pickpockets. It was a hard habit to break even when we weren't on the streets. Rueben caught us one night sneaking out and told Otto. The next day, we were moved into their room. I never knew why he did it, but that's Otto. He's a collector of lost souls." He sighed at the memory, a small smile lifting the corner of his mouth. Porter leaned back against the couch cushion, his thumb caressing my shin as he recalled his youth.

"Otto has this way about him, you'll see. He can get just about anyone to do what he wants. He's always planning and strategizing, looking for the best angles for any problem. At night, well, he gave us a reason to stay—"

I yawned loudly, interrupting him. All three males looked at me, calculating everything about me in that one look. I yawned again, unable to stop it now that it had started, the tiredness of the night catching up with me.

"Go to sleep, Raven. We can finish in the morning." Phoenix curled his arm around me, his shirt soft against my cheek, his rain smell invading my nostrils.

"You smell yummy," I mumbled, my eyes drifting shut. I could feel his chest vibrating under me, his shoulder shifting as he laughed.

"Sleep, my little harbinger of death. We'll keep you safe until you can resume regular duties."

"Thanks, you're a peach." I patted his cheek, his lips curving up against my palm.

His lips moved to my forehead, pressing against me before he drew back. "I had no clue how much we needed you, dearest. Please don't leave us," he whispered, again reiterating his plea.

Sleep took me under before I could respond, my body relaxing into the twins' embrace.

Phoenix

THE THREE OF US SAT IMMOBILIZED FOR A LONG WHILE, OUR focus on the magnetic girl between us. I'd never met someone that had captured my heart so quickly. Raven captivated all our attention and did it effortlessly. I loved her carefree spirit, wanting to know what brilliant and hilarious thing she'd say next.

She soothed something in all of us, bringing us even closer. I had no doubt that Otto would feel the same. We needed to figure out a way to keep her with us. I couldn't imagine losing her now that we'd found her.

"She's perfect for us," I whispered, tracing my finger over her cheek.

"I knew she would be," Porter sighed happily, rubbing his thumb over her leg.

"How?" Rueben asked, peering at us. I didn't know if he meant her or how we'd keep her.

"We'll figure it out. Otto will have a plan," Porter

said confidently, apparently understanding what Rueben had meant.

"Speaking of, someone should check on him and bring him some food. He's going to need it after that crash," I said.

"And we need to contact the client and get everything ready to be transferred," Porter added, yawning.

"We need to sleep as well." I looked down at the pixie of death, not wanting to move but knowing I needed to.

"I'll stay," Rueben said.

Nodding, I placed one more kiss on her forehead and gently laid her head on the pillow Rueben put in my spot. Porter lifted her legs, keeping her sprained one on the pad as much as he could. She twisted, turning her face toward the cushions as she rolled. We both stepped back, our arms extended as we cleared the couch.

Rueben stayed where he was on the floor, resting his head back on the cushion. I didn't know how he did that. I'd be stiff as a board in the morning. With one last glance, I grabbed a bottle of water and some crackers from the kitchen and headed to the other room. Otto slept on his side; his covers twisted around him.

I checked the time before shaking some pills out of the bottle next to the lamp, and wrote down the dosage and time on the pad of paper. Sitting down on the edge of the bed, I gently shook him.

"Hey, man. It's time for some more meds."

Otto groaned, his eyes sluggish as he tried to open them. He blinked a few times, wiping some sleep from the corner, focusing on me when he could see. I showed him my hand and the water. He nodded, sitting up so he could take them.

"I brought some crackers. Do you think you could eat some?" I asked. Otto scrunched up his nose.

"I know, man. But if you don't eat anything, you'll have a more miserable time later. And while that wouldn't usually matter as much, I think you'll want to be present tomorrow."

He lifted his eyebrows, sipping the water, and hesitantly reached out for the cracker, nibbling a little. When he'd finished one, he took another sip of water, wiping his mouth when he was done.

"Why?" he asked, his voice hoarse. "Everything go okay with the job?"

"The job went well. But the guys encountered a surprise inside," I said, chuckling.

"What? How? We planned for everything."

"Everything but our secret assassin."

Otto's mouth dropped open, color returning to his cheeks. "You guys made contact?"

I nodded, moving next to him against the headboard. "Yeah. She came stumbling through a secret door into the room Porter was in. She hit her head on a shelf and passed out when she saw the blood. Rueben carried her out once everything was clear."

"A she, huh? That makes sense, actually. Is she okay?" he asked, nibbling on another cracker.

Otto and I didn't often go in on the jobs, our skills were better used on the outside, but there had been an occasion or two when we were all needed or if Porter was out of commission, like when he had mono. So, we didn't have as much crossover with the assassin, but we'd heard stories of their kills the same as Porter and Rueben.

"Yeah, it was only a minor scrape. Raven can't handle the sight of blood."

"Raven." He smiled, rolling the name around. "I like it. Suits them. Harbinger of death."

"Well, it gets better." I nudged his shoulder, eyeing the crackers. He lifted another, eating it as he waited for me to continue. "Raven is Robyn, the girl Porter picked up on the ride-share."

Otto's eyes went wide. "No shit. Wait, it wasn't a con, was it?" he asked, his face falling.

"No. I don't think so—more like fate. Because, earlier, Rueben met her at the diner and was completely smitten with her. They were walking out, and I bumped into them, and she mistook me for Porter. Apparently, she gave him an ear full before she passed out." I chuckled, making Otto laugh as well.

"Fate, huh? Okay, I can get on board. Rueben never likes anyone."

"Exactly, and he's so far gone, I think he's microchipped her already. Dude straight up has hearts in his eyes."

Otto's jaw dropped again, more of his color returning to his face. He cleared his throat, adjusting his position as he took a drink of water. "Well, damn."

"We'd invited her to hang out here. None of us were ready to leave her company."

"Good call," Otto said, nodding.

"We took her back to her hotel so she could change out of her 'assassin wear,' as she put it. We tried to follow her, but she wouldn't allow it. So she went in—"

"You let her go alone?" Otto blurted, interrupting me. I held my hand up, laughing.

"We gave her a few seconds head start and followed her in. She's good, though. She caught Porter and me, then called Rueben out, even though he was hiding." I smiled big, remembering how we'd fallen into that room. "After she reminded us once again she was an assassin, she went into her room to change. There were some tussling sounds, and then a person dressed in black ran from her room."

"What?" Otto asked, his breathing halting. I patted his leg, reassuring him.

"This will take longer if you keep interrupting me,

man." He closed his eyes, nodding for me to continue as he took a deep breath. "Long story short, the head of Good Meds Pharma has it out for her because she's gone after the board, saving him for last. When she realized her cover was blown, it gave us the perfect opportunity to invite her to stay with us. So, we packed her up and then came here. She'd sprained her ankle in the fight, so we iced it, fed her, and watched some *Phoenix Hospital*."

Otto narrowed his eyes at me. "You put her through that? I'm surprised she didn't leave."

"For your information, she's a Phoenix junkie." I smiled, liking how that sounded.

"You like that too much," Otto said, echoing my thoughts. I shrugged, not complaining.

"So, she's here?" I nodded in confirmation. "And it sounds like... you three like her? What's that going to mean? How will that work?"

I shrugged. "I think you'll like her just as much, bro. There's something about her. I'm not sure what it means; other than that, we all want to keep Raven here with us; however that works. It might sound weird, but I dunno. I think we all need her in different ways."

"How does she seem to take that? Does she know who we are?"

"She does, and before you get your panties in a knot, she won't use that information to hurt us. I promise, she's..." I trailed off, realizing I was about to start speaking in sonnets and riddles. She was the sun, moon, and the whole damn sky. "She belongs with us."

Otto seemed intrigued and perplexed at the same time. His shoulders drooped, and I knew he needed to rest more. Taking the water and crackers, I sat them on the nightstand. "Get some rest. We need your crazy brain to figure out a plan to keep her with us when you wake up."

Otto blinked, his eyes heavy as he moved down the bed and laid his head on his pillow. I started to stand, but his tattooed forearm reached out and grabbed mine.

"Will you stay for a little bit and tell me a story?"

Sitting back down, I crossed one ankle over the other as I rested against the pillows. Otto scooted closer, his body pressing up against my legs for contact. There had never been anything sexual between the four of us, just a bond that had been formed and fortified in the trenches. We were one another's family, both Otto and Rueben as close to me as my twin. With that closeness came security and understanding, a trust that we could be vulnerable with one another.

Otto needed physical contact, a reassurance that he wasn't alone, especially after one of his episodes when he felt the weakest. Wrapping my arm around his back, I hugged him to my side, giving him pressure and comfort. It was a shame men couldn't physically console one another without judgment. If everyone hugged more, there would probably be less anger and violence in the world. There was no room for that toxic masculinity shit in our bond.

I recited Otto a story from our past, one we all knew by heart, as Otto's breathing evened out and his body relaxed into a deep sleep. Kicking off my shoes, I scooted down next to him as tiredness settled through my bones. I'd just sleep here for a bit. It was already warm.

THE SOUND of giggles and my brother's voice woke me, the crick in my neck telling me I hadn't moved once I'd fallen asleep. I rubbed my eyes, spotting Otto still sleeping next to me. His complexion looked better, and I relaxed, knowing the worst was past us.

Stretching my arms, I twisted side to side and stood, my back cracking as I leaned over. I sniffed my armpits, not something I typically cared about in a house of guys, but now, I wanted to smell as good as Raven had said I did.

Grabbing my stuff from my room, I quickly showered and changed my clothes. Porter had always been the more fashionable one, paying attention to styles and trends. I'd never cared, happy to wear a T-shirt and joggers if I could get away with it. I didn't think Raven was one to judge a person by what they wore, but I wanted to present myself in a good light. Earning her smiles felt like a reward. Using some of Porter's gel, I tousled my hair, hoping it looked nice, then brushed my teeth.

When I felt presentable, I hurried back to Otto's room despite my urge to go to Raven. I needed to help my brother first. He hadn't budged, so I checked the time and saw it was time for his next dose. Nudging him again, I held out the giant pill and vitamin with some water. He sat up, not fighting me as much this time, taking the medication I offered.

"Feel up to a shower?" I asked.

"With you?" he joked, swallowing down the rest of the water.

"You're about twenty minutes late on that offer, dude. I'm willing to help your stinky butt, though, so you don't smell like a dead rat when you meet Raven."

He grumbled but nodded, moving to get out of bed. Otto wobbled a little on his legs, his muscles protesting, but he gained momentum as we approached the shower. Once he ate, he'd be good as new. Turning on the water, I hopped on the counter while he got in. He grumbled more about having a babysitter, but I knew, deep down, he appreciated the company.

"How long do we have the rental?" I asked, my head leaning back against the mirror and my eyes closed.

"Maybe one more day. I'm off on my days after sleeping for ten hours," Otto replied as the water shifted.

"Were we heading after the other board members? Or was it only for this one?"

The water shut off, and Otto reached out to grab his towel. "I wanted to discuss it with everyone. The other two weren't on the job list, so we'd need to figure out where they are if we wanted to continue. This one was supposed to have some information in her safe that might lead us to them. I need to look through it."

He stepped around the curtain, a towel around his waist. I didn't budge as I thought through the information.

"I bet Raven knows. That's where she's going next. Maybe we can join forces or something. It's at least a way to keep her with us for a little longer before we need to consider a long-term plan."

Otto snorted. "I honestly can't wait to meet her. You sound more like Porter than ever before when you talk about her. I'm not sure what to think, hearing it from you. From him, I expect it and know he'll burn out as fast as he flamed... but you and Rueben." He shook his head, pulling his jeans up. "That complicates it for me. I do hope she isn't a con artist. I don't want to be the one to break all of your hearts in order to protect us."

"I understand where you're coming from, Otto. I do. And I know it sounds so bogus and fake. But... it's not like that. She's pure and light, despite killing people for a living. Promise me you'll take the day to get to know her before you decide she's lying to us all."

Otto searched my face, scrubbing his hand over his stubble. "Yeah. Okay. I promise."

Grinning, I hopped off the counter so he could finish and opened the door to let out some of the steam. The smell of pancakes and bacon greeted me, my stomach growling in response. Otto joined in, stopping next to me as he inhaled deeply.

"God, I'm hungry."

I clapped him on the shoulder, excited for him to meet our harbinger pixie. "Then let's get some grub and introduce you to Raven. You're going to love her."

Otto lifted one side of his mouth but nodded, walking with me as we entered the small kitchen area. Raven faced away from us, her braids down, leaving her black and blue hair in waves around her. If it was possible, her hair seemed to be bigger than she was. Rueben was to her left, and Porter to her right, both grinning as they watched her eat. I couldn't blame them. Watching Raven eat was a treat all on its own.

"Raven, this is our brother and friend, Otto. The last member of the Loxley Crew," I said, grinning wide.

Otto tensed beside me, his trademark smirk in place, and I prayed he wouldn't eviscerate her too badly. Mostly because I didn't know if Rueben would allow it; he'd punch Otto if he made her cry.

Raven turned, the fork with a bite of pancake still in her hand and a beautiful smile on her face as she met my eyes before moving to the man next to me. I felt Otto's body grow rigid as he gasped, and Raven's eyes bulged, her face growing slack as she dropped the fork, and it clattered to the floor.

A sudden jolt of panic rose in me, afraid Otto had been right, and she was conning us, breaking all of our hearts. That was until Otto said the one thing I never thought he'd utter again; freezing us all to our spots.

"Little Bird?"

Raven

GRAY EYES I'D KNOW ANYWHERE—THE SAME ONES I HOPED but never thought I'd see again—stared back at me. The faded image of the brown-haired boy with a cute smile I'd known came into high-definition focus, shattering every vision I'd created in my mind. The cute kid no longer existed. Instead, he'd been replaced with a man—slightly shorter than the other three—built with muscles and tattoos. His hair was the same chocolate brown, now longer on the top and short on the sides. Stubble covered his jaw where none had been before, and his nose appeared to have a slight bump like it had been broken and never healed properly.

Time froze as I stared at him, wondering if I'd somehow conjured an adult Otto from my mind after thinking about him over the past twenty-four hours.

"Little Bird?" he whispered, breaking the paralysis I'd been in, his words jump-starting my heart.

The other guys disappeared as I bolted from my

chair, leaping into Otto's arms. He caught me easily, wrapping his muscled forearms tightly around me, his head falling into the crook of my neck. I could smell his body wash and shampoo as my face pressed against him.

"Peppermint," I whispered; the smell was so intertwined with Otto in my mind.

We stood holding each other for a few seconds, absorbing one another, neither of us saying a word. When his body trembled, the comments the guys had made last night about him filtered through, and I pulled back, not knowing if it was serious. I scanned him for any sign of sickness, not finding anything standing out.

"It's really you," he said, his voice full of awe. The corners of his eyes were shiny, the smile I'd committed to memory now fully on display.

I nodded and lifted my hand, my fingers shaking as I placed them against his cheek. His eyes closed at my touch, and he sucked in a breath. His stubble tickled my palm, and I smoothed my thumb over his face. Otto leaned into me, pressing into my hand more.

"Holy shit!" someone behind us said as the chair scraped against the floor, reminding me other people were in the room. Otto's eyes opened, flicking behind me like he'd just realized it too. He glanced back down at me, something clicking in his head.

"Raven?" he asked, and I nodded, smiling. "The Peppermint—"

"No!" three other voices shouted, cutting Otto off. I giggled, my brain and body coming back online.

"Cutie-pie's the Silent Blade. Check your sources," Porter said, tsking.

Otto's eyes went wide as he looked down at me in response. I tapped his arms to set me down, but he refused, tightening his grip. Leaning into a backbend and placing my hands on the ground, I shocked Otto— and the others if their shouts of surprise were anything to go by—as I flipped out of his arms and stood.

Phoenix smiled wide at me, happiness radiating from him. I spun on my heels, not putting too much pressure on my ankle, and spotted Porter behind me. I motioned for him to bend down, his cheeks turning red as he did. Leaning close, I kissed his smooth cheek and spun back around.

"So, after we got separated, you met these three?" I asked, glancing at Otto again, still shocked he was standing in this kitchen. I was worried if I blinked, he'd disappear.

"Yeah. Well, sorta. I bounced around a few foster homes first. I kept running away to look for you," he admitted sheepishly. "Eventually, they were tired of reporting me, and I ended up in the group home and met Rueben. The twins showed up a year later. We've been together ever since."

"You looked for me?" I asked, hope shining in my voice.

Otto moved closer, placing his hands on my hips as he looked down into my eyes. "I made a promise, Little Bird. Together—"

"Forever," I finished. My lips curved up in the biggest smile, my heart beating a mile a minute. He hadn't forgotten me.

"I never gave up, even though everyone told me you'd died. I knew you were still out there somewhere." His forehead rested on mine, and we breathed in the air between us. "What happened to you? Where did you go?" he asked, stepping back.

"Not to break up this beautiful moment," Porter started, appearing next to Otto, his eyes searching both of us. "But Raven needs to rest her ankle some more, and you should eat something."

Otto swallowed at his friend's words, digesting them. When it clicked I was hurt he bolted into action. "Your ankle. Yes, Phoenix told me. Sit back down, and we can all talk."

Rueben took my hand, lifting me into his arms for the few feet to the table. "Not that I'm complaining, Ruebear, but I'm starting to believe you just like picking me up."

His dark chocolate eyes dropped to mine, his beard moving on one side as the corner of his mouth ticked up. Mirth danced with protectiveness in his dark orbs, an alluring combination. It felt like there was a story there, one he wasn't ready to share yet. If I had to sacrifice walking to help him, then it was a price I could pay.

"Fine, don't blame me when my hips get bigger because I'm not burning any calories walking," I teased.

"There are other ways to burn calories, Raven," Phoenix purred beside me, sending shivers down my body. I didn't know how to handle my desire, so I focused on something else.

"That was a flirt, right?" I asked.

"A flirt? Oh, sweet harbinger of death, we have so much to teach you." He chuckled and leaned in, kissing my cheek, making my face burn. It felt nice, though, better than any of the kisses I'd had before.

Rueben sat down in a chair, keeping me in his lap. I started to protest but realized there were only four chairs, so I'd have to deal with my human-sized high chair. Not that I hated it. His arms were warm around me, his touch soft and soothing. Plus, he smelled like chocolate and coffee, and I couldn't decide whether to eat my pancakes or lick him. Probably both.

I glanced at Otto, wondering what he thought about his friends being so touchy with me. It felt natural to me, and it would be hard to stop, but they were his friends first, and I wouldn't want to upset him. Thankfully, he smiled at me as I caught his eyes. Porter placed a plate of pancakes in front of him, taking his seat as Phoenix sat down with his plate.

Their love for one another was so sweet. I adored how they cared for each other in big and small ways. It was something I wish I had more of in my life. I never realized how much it was missing until I witnessed it before my own eyes.

A fork with a piece of pancake appeared in front of my face, the syrup dripping down the utensil. I peered back at Rueben, and he nudged me to open my mouth. Accepting it, I did as commanded and wrapped my lips around the fork, the fluffy piece of pancake falling apart on my tongue. My eyes closed as I enjoyed the bite, doing a little happy dance in Rueben's lap.

"Holy cow. Is that how she always eats?" Otto whispered. I opened my eyes, finding three pairs staring back. The twins nodded, gazes locked on me as they ate their meal. Shrugging, I accepted another bite, letting the buttery goodness take my mind off the fact they were watching.

"You were going to share what happened after you and Otto lost one another," Porter said once my plate was clean. I nodded, grabbing a piece of bacon and leaning back into Rueben's arms. Despite all of his hard muscles, he was incredibly comfortable. My free hand trailed up his tattooed forearm, my fingertips brushing against his skin as I thought.

"After I escaped the badge lady, I ran and ran until I couldn't. I didn't know where I was or how to return to the theater. So I stopped and sat on a curb to figure out a plan. I hadn't meant to run so far, and I didn't want to lose you, so I mentally tried to retrace my steps when a car pulled up. At first, I worried someone wanted to take advantage of me since I was alone, but it wasn't. It was Man."

"Who's Man?" Porter asked.

"The man who rescued me and made me into who I am. He said I could get revenge on all the people who'd hurt me, that he would teach me how. I didn't have to do anything other than try. I'd get my own room, access to unlimited food, clothes, and toys. Everything I desired would be available to me, and I could learn anything I wanted. Even though I was young, I knew he was being honest, and I'd already concluded my chances of surviving on the streets alone were risky. Before I met Otto, I hadn't done well, so without him, I didn't have high hopes of surviving. Man offered me a chance to learn and have the resources to do something, to be someone. He even promised to help me find you."

I bit my lip, worried now about what he said. If he'd been looking for me, I should've tried harder too. I could've been reunited with Otto sooner if I'd stayed.

The fear that I shouldn't tell them my history didn't even register. I'd felt safe with them from the start and knew I could trust them with it.

"I'm glad you went with him, Little Bird," Otto said, erasing all my doubts.

"You are? Why? I thought you'd be mad I didn't try harder."

He shook his head, his eyes growing wide as he looked at me. "I'd never be mad at you for trying to survive, Little Bird. I'm ecstatic that you didn't have to suffer on the streets and found a home where you were cared for."

We held each other's gaze, filling our minds with this new version of one another. Hearing his voice, seeing him in the flesh, was doing wonders for my heart.

"What was it like there?" Phoenix asked.

"It was everything I dreamed it would be. Other girls were training with me, giving me instant friends. We all lived together, just like I wanted in my stories. I spent a lot of time learning how to be a doctor, wanting to know how to care for people so I wouldn't have to lose anyone again."

"I told you that you were the best doctor I ever had," Otto said, smiling warmly, my cheeks heating again. I shrugged one shoulder, hiding my face as I traced Rueben's tattoos.

"Well, I took all the courses but couldn't go to

medical school or perform any surgeries. So, I only have theoretical knowledge. Passing out at the sight of blood is a big hindrance in the medical field."

"I'm still proud of you, Little Bird. You've done amazing things with your life."

"Even if I kill people?" I asked, looking up from under my eyelashes. The other guys had accepted it about me, but for some reason, I worried that Otto wouldn't be able to, seeing me as that little girl from our past.

"Have any of them been innocent?" he asked, lifting his eyebrow like he already knew the answer.

I scoffed, shaking my head. "Man is very thorough. If he gets the job, they're bad news bears. Every kill I've made has deserved it." My voice was cold, the killer in me showing through. I'd accepted long ago that the darkness in me had a purpose, and I could use it to make the world better for other little girls. The world was too corrupt with laws and rules designed to help the rich. There wasn't justice for girls like me unless I took it.

"Do you care that we steal from the rich, taking what we want?" he countered.

"No, I love that. It's just like my story..." I trailed off, looking at the guys with different eyes, remembering what they'd told me last night now that I knew their Otto was indeed *my* Otto. "You told them our stories." I didn't make it a question. It was written all over their faces. Even without meeting me, they'd gotten to know me through the stories Otto and I told.

Porter nodded, giving me a soft smile. "The stories I mentioned last night are yours, Raven. I guess it makes sense now why we already feel connected. We've known you most of our lives."

I sucked in a breath, considering what he was saying. *They'd known me.* Even if I hadn't known about them, they'd been out in the world, thinking about me as they went about their days. That realization blew me away, pushing aside any residual doubts and fears.

I'd been trying to reconcile how these guys could feel so comfortable and safe and figured I'd gone crazy. But it turned out they'd been carrying a piece of me with them. When we'd all met, it slotted into place, connecting us on a deeper level than any of us had been prepared for.

"Wow. I don't know what to say. Which, for a person who routinely talks to herself out loud, is rather shocking."

The guys chuckled, their focus still on me, making those butterflies turn into a full-blown frenzy.

"I've finally found my lost boys, my home."

Their smiles could've powered an entire town as they beamed at me, warming me from the inside out. Rueben bent down, his beard tickling my skin as his lips moved against my ear.

"And you're ours."

My eyelids fluttered closed, the promise and depth of those three words sending my body into overdrive as my skin heated, my body shuddering, and my breath hitching. A throbbing built in my core, a needy feeling pounding in time with my heart. I opened my eyes, seeing how the guys focused on me, watching my body respond to their attention. Rueben's leg shifted, hitting me right where I wanted, his large hands flexing against my body.

A tingle raced down my spine, and quicker than I knew what was happening, my body convulsed as fireworks spread through me, lighting every nerve ending on fire. I gasped, a moan slipping out as I shuddered in Rueben's arms, liquid heat pouring from me.

"Fucking hell, did she..."

"Yeah, I think so. It was magnificent."

"The most amazing thing I've ever witnessed."

When my breathing calmed, I braved the silence, opening my eyes. Hungry eyes full of heat watched me, and for once, I wasn't scared of what it meant.

Raven

THEIR GAZES TRACKED MY EVERY MOVE; MY SKIN WARMED under their attention. I licked my lips, not used to this many people focusing on me at once.

"So, um," Otto cleared his throat, shaking his head like he had to clear the cobwebs. "Want to see what happens the day after a heist?" he asked, his smile reaching his eyes.

"Heist!" I pointed my finger at the twins in triumph. Otto watched me curiously, his eyes bouncing between us.

Porter rolled his eyes, groaning as he lowered his head to the table, barely missing his plate covered in syrup. Phoenix chuckled, grabbing my finger and taking a playful bite.

"Fine, you win. Apparently, we do call it a heist, though; I've never heard it before," Porter said, pouting playfully.

"I still think it should be hi-jinks," Phoenix muttered, shrugging his shoulders. He hadn't let go of my finger, swinging it around as he spoke. I giggled, enjoying being around them all so much. It was easy, and I didn't have to worry if I was boring them.

"I take that as a yes?" Otto asked, reminding me he'd asked a question.

"Yes, that would be amazing! I love to learn new things, and I've been a healthy stalker of Loxley Crew online. Watching you work sounds exciting."

"Healthy stalker." Porter chuckled before he got up and collected the plates. "Just when I think you can't get any cuter, you go and show me up."

He dropped a kiss on my forehead as he took my plate, singing as he started to wash the dishes. Phoenix hopped up, joining his brother at the sink, and grabbed a towel.

"I'll be there in a minute," he hollered over his shoulder.

Rueben stood, taking me with him as he walked to the living room and sat me on a table I hadn't noticed until then. It was pressed against the wall and covered in blueprints, notes, and schematics. I picked one up and looked over it.

"You don't have the original blueprints. The ones that had the secret passageways," I muttered before dropping it back.

"Passageways! Phoenix had mentioned you came through a door we hadn't known about, but I hadn't considered passageways," Otto mused, taking a seat and pulling on a pair of glasses to look closer to where I'd pointed. He looked adorable, and I wanted to pinch his cheeks. To stop myself, I picked up another sheet, my eyes absorbing the information about the safe and its presumed contents.

"Wow, I never thought about the details of thieving. It's as complex as killing someone."

Otto chuckled, the sound as familiar to me as my own. I reached out, brushing my fingers through his hair, unable to stop myself this time. He froze, and I withdrew, remembering I couldn't just go around touching people. Otto reached out, grabbing my hand before I could tuck it away.

"Don't," he whispered, his voice rough. He cleared his throat, lifting his eyes to mine. "You don't have to stop. *Please*, don't stop."

He tugged my hand back, and I continued to brush my fingers through the long dark strands on top, feeling the sharp edges of the sides as they tingled my hand. After a few seconds, he focused back on the papers.

"Phoenix mentioned you were going after the other two board members." It wasn't a question, but I nodded in response, out of habit. His eyes had focused back on me, abandoning the papers. He swallowed, closing his eyes for a second when I pressed my nails into his scalp. "We hadn't planned on it, but I'd like to.

Maybe we could coordinate plans of attacks and see how the other works?"

His question hung in the air, the answer feeling more important than a simple yes or no. I stopped my ministrations and assessed him. His gray eyes were clear, unwavering as he watched me. I sank into his eyes, the comfort and feeling of home I'd missed for twenty years returning.

"I usually work alone," I whispered, my heart racing. Otto didn't respond, giving me time to process. I couldn't figure out if I was scared they wouldn't like the killer I became in those moments or if I was excited about not having to do it alone.

Though, if I was honest, it was the after that terrified me.

After I got used to them and they left.

After I showed them my darkness and they left.

After the novelty of me wore off and they left.

Because I was always left.

Left in a closet. Left on a street corner. Left out of the cliques. Left on the sidelines. Just plain left.

Tears I hadn't expected welled in my eyes, threatening to fall.

Otto stood suddenly, the chair scraping back against the floor in the process. Stepping between my legs, he placed his hands on the table next to my hips, his body crowding my space. Our faces were at eye level. One of his hands lifted, softly stroking my hair back as he gripped my chin in his fingers.

"Together forever, Little Bird. Now that I've found you, I'm never letting you go again. Do you understand me?" Otto asked, somehow knowing what I'd been thinking. He didn't give me time to answer before he continued. "No matter what. You don't have to leave your life if that's what you're afraid of. We can still be part of it, even if we're not together every day. I'll hate it. All the guys will hate it, but we'll deal if that's what you need."

His thumb stroked away the tears, his eyes imploring me to say something.

"What if you don't like that version of me? What if it changes how you feel?"

"Impossible, Little Bird."

His words were spoken with utter conviction, branding my heart with their truth. Otto loved me. I could feel it. I didn't know what that love meant to him yet, but it was enough to soothe my fears and allow him time to figure it out. Because there was no doubt in my heart that I loved him, too.

Nodding, I took a shaky breath, letting it out slowly. "I never want to go another moment without you in my life, Otto. And I know I've only known the others for a day, but I feel the same way about them."

He smiled, the tension leaving my body. "We all feel the same, Little Bird."

Returning his smile, I threw my arms around his neck, squeezing him tightly. "Then I would love to merge our two worlds together. The Loxley Crew and the Silent Blade. It's going to be the best thing since peanut butter and jelly."

"I can't wait to watch you work. But first, let me show you ours."

OTTO HAD SPENT a few hours demonstrating his process of going through the items collected, their value, and setting up drops to his fence. The whole thing fascinated me, and he'd been patient in answering my questions just like he had when we were younger.

The guys moved in the background, packing up their belongings and cleaning up areas. They'd taken showers and changed clothes, their intoxicating smells of chocolate and coffee, rain and citrus mixed together and tickled my nose every time one of them came out of the bathroom. The twins would come and sit with me for a while but eventually would get bored and get up to do something else.

"And that's it until we hear back from my contact. Now, we usually begin planning for the next one," Otto said, closing his laptop and arranging the papers into a stack. I bit my lip, going over my usual to-do list.

"I was headed to South Carolina next. I'm saving Jerome for last," I admitted, sitting on my hands.

Otto looked over my shoulder, so I peeked, finding all three guys watching us. "We only had Millicent and were hoping information on the others was in her possession. You've saved us a day of work. So, what do you guys think? Should Loxley Crew head to South Carolina with Little Bird?"

"Duh," Porter said, giving me a golden smile.

Phoenix screwed up his face, sticking out his tongue. "What did I tell you, pipsqueak? You're not getting rid of us. I'll stalk your ass if I have to."

"Yes," Rueben said, his eyes searing into me. They said so much more than that simple word.

I turned back around, my cheeks on fire. Otto lifted his brow, proving his point from earlier. They were all in.

"Okay then. I'd planned to leave in the middle of the night, but I could change my plans. I'm already checked out of the hotel, so I can move whenever."

"We have the rental until tomorrow morning. How were you traveling? We haven't purchased tickets yet," Otto said, opening his computer and pulling up a travel website.

"Oh, well, you won't need tickets. We can use my plane. They'll leave whenever I tell them."

Otto froze, turning slowly to me with wide eyes. I tilted my head, not understanding. I peered back at the others, who all wore similar expressions. Porter was the first to break, jumping off the couch and picking me up to spin us around as he chanted.

"Private plane! Private plane! Private plane!"

I laughed at his enthusiasm, loving how excited he got at things. "So, I take that as a yes?" I asked, peeking over his shoulder at Otto. While they were a group, it was clear Otto was the leader.

"If you're offering, we'll accept, Little Bird."

"I'll message them to expect five of us. Could I use your shower before we leave?"

"Need a hand?" Porter asked, wiggling his eyebrows. My face heated. That had definitely been a flirt.

"Tempting, but I have a feeling if we want to leave at some point today, I should go solo."

His head moved closer, his lips brushing against my earlobe as he whispered, "The offer will never expire, babe. So, just let me know when you're ready." He kissed my cheek, sending shivers through me.

"Okay," I said, my voice huskier than I'd ever heard it.

He smirked, looking more like Phoenix in that second, that I had to check his tattoo sleeve to make sure it had been Porter.

"Right arm," I mumbled, making him tilt his head in question.

"Hm?"

"Nothing," I squeaked, patting his arms to let me down.

The second my feet touched the ground, I grabbed my suitcase and hightailed it into the bathroom, too nervous to look at the others. Sprained ankle, who?

Things had definitely progressed since last night, and my body was fully on board with the invitations to explore things. It was just my heart and brain that kept getting in the way.

"Just go with the flow," I said, taking a deep breath. "You'll never learn if you don't try. They won't laugh at you like Mike." A wicked smile spread as I remembered how Darcy helped me get back at him. "Who was laughing in the end, Mike? That's right. You don't mess with a Belladonna!"

I did a few air punches and kicks in the air, imitating taking down a foe. A knock on the door had me jumping; a tiny squeak that was nowhere near badass sounding escaped out of me.

"We're ordering some food. Anything you don't like?" Phoenix asked.

"Nope! I'll eat anything," I shouted back, hoping to sound more assertive than the squeak had portrayed.

Once I heard feet moving away from the door, I turned on the shower, remembering I was in here for a reason. Opening my suitcase, I pulled out my phone and checked in with Man, letting him know the first mark had been taken care of. Then I messaged Phillip, confirming my takeoff time and that there would be additional passengers traveling with us.

With both tasks done, I hit play on my "shake booty" playlist, stripped my clothes off, and hurried into the shower. The warm water rushed over me, soothing the aches from the night before. My ankle had mostly healed, only a little tender if I placed too much weight on it. I'd also gained a massive bruise on my sides from the window and the takedown with my nemesis. I'd put my body through the wringer yesterday.

Humming along to the music, I dried off and picked out some clothes. I selected my "I aim to misbehave" shirt and constellation skirt, pairing it with some lunar tights and black Converse. Spraying detangler in my hair, I opened the door and headed out with my comb. My hair took forever to comb out, and my arms always got tired halfway through, so I often did it while I watched some *Phoenix Hospital,* so I didn't notice it.

No one was in the living room, so I sat down and turned on the TV, finding the channel we'd watched last night as I ran the comb through sections of my hair. I jolted when someone touched my knee, having gotten sucked into the show.

"Geez, sorry. You'd think for an assassin, I'd be more aware of my surroundings," I mumbled sheepishly, meeting Rueben's eyes.

He smiled, finding humor in my response. He held his hand out and motioned for me to sit between his legs on the floor. Hopping down, I crawled into his lap and gave him the comb.

"You sure?" I asked, biting my lip.

He nodded, his dark eyes warmed as he watched me. His tattooed fingers turned my head around to the TV before they softly trailed through my hair. His touch was gentle, just like him, as he took his time combing out my knotted strands.

Soon, I was so relaxed that I forgot he was detangling my hair; my scalp and neck adored the soft massages he gave them in between sections.

"Blow dryer?" he asked, leaning down to ask me. Nodding, I moved to get up when a blur raced across the room, sliding into the bathroom.

"I got it!" Porter shouted, running back out with it, a triumphant smile on his face. That was when I looked around, noticing that Otto and Porter had joined us.

"Where's Phoenix?" I asked. It felt strange watching the show without him. I'd enjoyed looking at him for reactions last night or talking about our theories. It added a whole new layer to watching something.

"He went to pick up the food."

"Down," Rueben said before I could ask more questions. The blow dryer came on, his fingers picking up my long locks and drying them with as much care as he had combed.

Now, this was the treatment. If I didn't have to comb or dry my hair, I'd spend more time on styling it. As it was, I only fixed it when I knew I'd see people. Which, for someone who spent days and weeks on end in the mansion, wasn't a lot.

"Whoa," Phoenix said a while later, the door shutting behind him. I glanced up from my curtain of hair, wondering what had caught his attention. Both Otto and Porter still watched me, so it wasn't them.

"Right?" Porter said, apparently understanding what his twin meant.

"What?" I asked, looking back and forth, trying to figure it out.

"I volunteer to do Raven's hair next time," Phoenix blurted, surprising me.

"It's definitely a job suited for both of us, Brother," Porter added, his hand on his chin as he watched.

Rolling my eyes, I focused back on what Rueben was doing. Honestly, I didn't know if I wanted anyone else to do this. It felt nice having this moment with my silent giant. It seemed like he needed this, too, rewriting something from his past. Yeah, I needed to say something.

"Too bad. Rueben's got first dibs. You'll have to find your own thing," I said. Rueben paused, placing his large palm against my back. I took that as a thanks, and I smiled, liking that I'd made him happy.

"Oh! I vote for cuddles. The twins get dibs on cuddles!"

"Yes, perfect, Brother."

"Wait! What's all on the table? I feel like I'm behind," Otto interjected, his voice almost a panic-whine.

Okay, maybe I'd misinterpreted their gawking. Perhaps this was Rueben's job, and he did it for everyone? I didn't want to be a burden and make their group dynamics off-kilter.

"Um, whatever you want. I'm not used to doing things in a group. How does that work with you guys?"

Rueben's hand stopped; Otto and the twins as well, the three of their gazes locked to me, their mouths partly open. I couldn't be sure, but there almost seemed to be heat in their eyes as well. Just what had I said now? I ran the words through my mind, trying to figure out what I was missing. My brow furrowed.

"Like, do you take turns doing the dishes? Cooking? We had maids and cooks, so I have to admit I'm not the greatest at household duties. I can learn if you tell me which one you want me to do. Hm, I am great at facials," I said, pausing as I tapped my lip, trying to think of more.

Otto practically choked, and the twins weren't

fairing much better. Phoenix had to grab Porter before he fell over. I didn't think it was that shocking that we had people to do things for us, but maybe I'd become spoiled.

"Oh!" Pointing my finger in the air when a thought struck. Aha! I so was not spoiled! "I can make all kinds of chemical gadgets. I'm also great at first aid, as long as no blood is present. I'm an excellent taste tester and napper. Do you need help in any of those areas?"

There. I could add to their group, too. Otto's face softened, his eyes no longer bulging out of his head.

"Little Bird, we'll appreciate any help you want to offer us. But you don't have to do anything to earn your place with us. In fact, we were fighting over spending time with you, not jobs."

"Oh." My cheeks heated, and I turned, checking in with Rueben. He smiled, smoothing my hair down. I hadn't realized the blow dryer had shut off. "Well, I'd like that too. I want to do things with each of you separately and all together."

I could've sworn I heard another gasp/choke sound from one of the twins, followed by a slap on the back, but I kept my eyes on Otto.

"Sounds good, Little Bird. Besides, we already have our thing—stories. I think we could all use a few new ones. What do you think, guys?"

"Yes. Absolutely," the twins said, and Rueben

nodded against my back. My stomach rumbled, and the guys jumped into motion again.

"Let's eat! I get to be Raven's seat this time," Otto proclaimed, lifting me from Rueben. He took in my outfit, licking his lips.

"You're too cute for words, Cutie-pie," Porter said, taking my hand and spinning me in front of them.

Otto waited until he was done, taking my other hand to walk to the table where Phoenix unloaded Chinese food containers. Sitting in Otto's lap, I ate and laughed, knowing I never wanted my life to be separate from them again. It didn't matter if they only wanted to be my friends, or if we could all be something more like the heat in their gazes suggested, I just knew I'd be here for it all.

WE CLIMBED THE ROLLAWAY STAIRS TO THE JET, MY EYES checking every direction someone could possibly attack from. I trusted in Raven's abilities, but I didn't know these people, and my past dictated my constant vigilance. I wouldn't let anyone endanger my family— and that included Raven now.

"Holy cow, babe. This is incredible," Porter gushed, taking in the leather couches and chairs. "Otto, I'm afraid I can no longer be happy with flying first class. It's private or nothing for this bum from here on out."

Raven giggled as Otto rolled his eyes, sitting beside her. I watched my closest friends, enjoying how much they'd softened since she'd entered our lives. We'd needed her more than I realized, having become too jaded and untrusting of others. Though, each of us for good reason.

"Miss Raven, we'll be taking off in a few minutes. The flight is only a few hours, and we should land around 3 am. There are some light refreshments and snacks in the galley. Otherwise, let me know if you need something, and I'll see you when we land," the pilot said. He was an older man with white hair, a tall frame, and a kind smile for Raven. His eyes had taken us in with a calculating gleam as he observed us. His protectiveness settled my nerves, and I had a feeling there was more than met the eye with him. He gave off a retired Air Force vibe.

"Thank you, Phillip. These are my friends," Raven said, motioning toward all of us, her smile so sweet, it was a wonder there weren't people dropping at her feet just to see it.

He nodded his head, smiling. "Welcome. I'm glad Ms. Raven has made some friends. She's a special one. We'll be on our way momentarily."

"That she is," Otto said, wrapping his arm around Raven. She snuggled into him, her cheeks reddening at his praise.

I took my seat after ensuring everyone was buckled, my eyes roaming over the airstrip. It was hard to turn off my protector mode, wanting to stop anything from harming my family. I hadn't always been this way—a partial mute with possessive tendencies. But that was the thing about trauma; it had a way of making you into something you'd never intended to be.

The plane's lights dimmed a moment before it moved, taxiing down the airstrip. With the time of night and private field, we were taking off in a matter of seconds, with no other planes to worry about.

Raven's fingers entwined with mine, pulling my attention away from the window. She smiled at me when my eyes landed on her, my heart galloping at the sight. As cliche as it sounded, everything was different with her.

Most women didn't look twice at me once they realized I wouldn't talk to them. And the ones that did weren't anyone I'd want to spend time with. They saw me as a project, someone to fix.

My voice wasn't the problem—words were. There weren't ones in the English language that could convey the damage I felt inside, the pain I'd experienced. After screaming for hours and months on end, I finally realized it didn't matter what I said or how loud I cried.

No one was coming for me.

No one was stopping her.

No one was listening.

At some point, when your words no longer mattered, you quit trying to use them; the rejection stinging a little less each time when no one cared. If you said nothing, there was nothing to hope for, no savior coming to rescue you. My words had become the only control I had, holding all my broken edges together. The abuse hurt a little less if you refused to give it a voice.

Now, I only used my voice in the rare moments I wanted to be heard. It was funny how by not speaking, it made people listen more.

Raven didn't look at me as someone to fix or pity. She found a way to speak to my soul, communicating with me beyond words. She softened the edges, the sharp blades of my past not piercing my skin quite as deeply. I could breathe around her, just like I could the guys.

Maybe it was because we'd known about her for years; her stories had become a part of our hearts, pulling our damaged pieces together. But I didn't believe that was all of it. I'd felt the connection before I even knew who she was. Fate had brought us together, our connection beyond comprehension.

"Did you find a rental to stay in?" Raven asked, turning her head slightly to look at the others.

"Yeah. Thankfully, this town had a little more to offer, being on the coast and more of a tourist destination," Phoenix supplied, pulling out his phone. He turned it, showing her the pictures.

"Ooh! It has a jacuzzi tub!" she cheered, making our next spot on the heist/assassin tour sound like a vacation. I didn't understand how she could exude such light and optimism, finding joy in the small things with her job. But maybe that was it. She saw the darker parts of life and could tiptoe in them when she needed, but she didn't linger or let them stick to her.

"Is it safe to talk here?" Phoenix asked, peering around like someone might jump out. Not on my watch, buddy.

"As safe as any. What's on your mind?" she asked, leaning her head back on my shoulder.

"What's your process? Anything we can help with?"

"Oh, um," she screwed up her nose, her brows furrowed as she thought. "I did a lot of research back at the mansion. The file I have is pretty extensive as well. For John, I'll be posing as a traveling nurse. He's on dialysis among other medical problems and has a nurse who stays at the house. The night nurse conveniently won a vacation and will be gone for a week."

"Whoa, so you have covers and things?" Porter asked, leaning forward.

"Sometimes. Most of my kills I can do in the dead of night, slipping in and out with no one the wiser. But some have such tight security that having a way in is easier. I tend to go undercover as a nurse or doctor because I know the lingo and pass without detection. I'm not the best at other personas, so I stick with what I know."

Otto's brows pinched as he turned. "What's the security like? It seemed standard to me. What did I miss this time?"

Raven patted his arm, naturally soothing his nerves over missing something.

"John understood the assignment when he went on the run and secured himself a fortress, unlike Millicent's run-down house in the middle of nowhere. There's a monitored gate, security that walks the grounds and house, and cameras. I have an app that will distort the cameras, but I didn't want to deal with the other complications. Sometimes the easiest way in is the simplest."

"Shit," Porter cursed, flopping back in his seat. "How are we going to get in?" he asked, looking from me to Otto.

Otto didn't notice, his gaze distant as he ran the risks and odds through his head for various plans. The guy had a knack for solving puzzles.

"I could potentially get one of you in as my intern or something," Raven offered.

"That could work. How many days were you planning to be there?" Porter asked.

"At least a few days, so it's not suspicious that he dies the moment I get there. I have some things I'll give him to show his decline leading up."

"Hmm, it would give me time to do a walkthrough, locate all the hiding spots, and figure out the guard's rotations. What do you think, Otto?" Porter asked.

"We'd just need to find Rueben a way in. I don't want you two going in alone."

"Please. I could take all the guards out without breaking a sweat," Raven huffed. "I just don't want to. It's a lot of bodies to cover up. I'm fine on my own. Always have been."

A growl rumbled in my chest, my hand tightening at her words. "No more," I said gruffly, causing her head to spin toward me. Her eyes were wide, and I worried for a second I'd gone too far, scaring her. She licked her lips, and her pupils dilated as her cheeks turned a delightful shade of pink.

Oh. *Oh.* She was turned on.

A smug smile spread across my lips before I could stop it, my beard stretching with the action. Her eyes glazed over a little, making my heart hammer harder as my cock stiffened. I was sunk for this girl. There would be no turning back for me. Raven was it. I could see similar looks in the others, so we'd need to discuss what that meant the second we had a chance. I wasn't opposed to sharing; we'd shared everything for years, and with how we worked, it would be easier to have one woman.

Hopefully, the others felt the same because I didn't want to fight my brothers.

The conversation turned to Raven sharing some of her favorite kills and spotting marks we'd overlapped. It was interesting to find how many times we'd almost met.

Eventually, her eyes drifted closed as she snuggled

deeper into my arms with her feet in Otto's lap. We'd raised the arms on the chairs so she could stretch out an hour ago. The cabin was quiet, her soft snores the only thing I focused on. Looking up, I met the twin's eyes, both locked on the girl in my arms. Otto's were also, and I knew this was the moment I'd been waiting for. Taking a deep breath, I wetted my lips and swallowed.

"We need to talk." My voice came out hoarse from disuse, the last few words more of a croak. It was nearly the longest thing I'd said to them all in years.

Everyone's eyes lifted to me, nodding.

"I think I know what you want to talk about," Otto said, motioning toward the girl in our arms.

I nodded, happy to sit back and let them hash it out now that I had the ball rolling.

"We all like her," Porter said, putting it out there plain as day. I appreciated that about him. I nodded, as well as the others. He smiled, his shoulders relaxing. "I've been waiting for the right girl to come along and win all of our hearts. I never imagined it would be Little Bird."

Phoenix's skeptical gaze swung to his brother, his jaw dropping in protest. "What do you mean, you've been waiting for the right girl? Every girl you meet has been the right one." He crossed his arms, daring his brother to deny it.

Porter just rolled his eyes, not taking the bait.

"Each time I liked a girl, it was because I saw something in her I thought we'd all like. But every time, at least one of you wouldn't like her, so I'd find something to send her on her way. This has been my plan all along. Can you honestly say it's not ideal?" Now it was Porter's turn to raise his eyebrow, waiting for his brother to argue.

"What? Huh?" Phoenix stuttered, his eyes bulging at the revelation.

Porter sat back with a look of triumph, his grin wide as he crossed his ankles out in front of him. Otto chuckled at them, shaking his head in mirth.

"It never would've been anyone but her for me," he admitted. "I've been looking for her," he said, his eyes sweeping to mine, a secret we carried. "I hoped she'd be the one to complete us. It wasn't my intention, but by sharing her stories and telling you all about her, she became a part of you, too. I think we've all been in love with a version of her for a long time."

Phoenix sat back; his eyes narrowed as he thought. "So both of you figured we'd need to share a girl? I understand your reasoning, Otto, because it was Little Bird, but I don't get yours, Brother." He turned to his twin, sadness etched on his face as he looked at him, something from his past triggering him at this moment.

"Bro, how often has someone tried to break us apart?" Porter whispered, clasping Phoenix by the neck, their foreheads touching. "At first, I wanted someone for us both to love so we'd never have to worry about being separated." Phoenix took in a deep breath, nodding that he understood. Porter turned his head, addressing us, "Then, when we all became a family, I knew it had to be the four of us. I couldn't stand the thought of losing anyone else I cared about. Plus, with how our lives are, traveling from one place to another and the secrecy, it seemed logical to limit the number of people involved."

He stopped, closed his eyes for a second before a smile spread, and sighed.

"You can't deny how hot it is having someone between us, Bro. We work well together, and bringing a woman to orgasm with our combined forces is sexy as hell. Cutie-pie deserves all the pleasure."

Phoenix gaped at him before shutting his mouth, a look of understanding and acceptance coming over him. He cleared his throat, shifting in his seat.

"Yeah, okay. You make a lot of good points. And I wouldn't walk away from Raven even if you hadn't. I hope she's on board with this. I don't want to lose her."

We could all hear the unspoken words in his statement. *He couldn't lose her.* He wouldn't survive it. I had a feeling we all felt the same.

When their eyes landed on me, I realized they were waiting for my answer. Swallowing, I nodded but pushed the words out, knowing it was important to say it.

"I'm in."

The three of them relaxed, their eyes falling back on the girl in my arms. I'd felt her stir a little bit ago and knew she'd been listening. I smoothed her hair back, caressing a thumb across her cheek. Her blue eyes opened, meeting mine as she peered into my soul again. I raised an eyebrow, hoping she knew what I was asking. The others froze, realizing she was awake now, silently panicking over what they'd said and how much she'd heard.

She licked her lips, turning her head to peer at all the others. Porter braved the silence, asking her outright.

"What do you think, Cutie-Pie? Do you want to be our girl?" His smile was crooked as hope brimmed in his eyes, his lungs barely moving as he waited for her to respond.

"I've never been anyone's anything before," she admitted. "It's kind of hard to date when you live with a bunch of girls in a secret house, and your job is to kill people. I've met others through things, but it was just a way to pass the time. There wasn't romance or anything. What if I'm not good at it?"

"Little Bird, you don't have to be good at it. You just have to be ours. That's all we want. But just so you know, you're already great at it," Otto assured, squeezing her hand.

"Oh." Her cheeks turned that beautiful pink again. "And I don't have to choose? I can be with you all? As in dating and sexy things?" she asked, gulping.

"Yes, you'd be with all of us. However that looks for you. We won't pressure you into anything. You'd never have to choose between us. I know this has been fast and out of the blue, so if you need time to think about it—"

"I don't need time," Raven said, cutting off Otto. "I want to have you all—no one else. And you won't date anyone else?" she asked.

"No," the four of us said at once. Her body relaxed as she smiled.

"Then yes. I want to be yours."

Never had words sounded so beautiful to me before.

She was ours, and I was hers.

Raven

My heart overflowed with happiness at the guys claiming me. I pinched myself just to make sure I hadn't been dreaming. The small bruise now joined my others, evidence that it had all happened.

The plane landed shortly after, and we gathered our belongings, waving goodbye to Phillip as we descended the stairs. I headed toward the black SUV that waited, in a bit of a daze from the past few hours. I wasn't used to being around people this much. There were a million thoughts trying to escape my head that I'd kept contained, not wanting them to think I was weird. Or... At least weirder.

"You can only hide it for so long," I mumbled, rolling my eyes at myself.

"Huh?" Porter said behind me. My cheeks heated as I peered over my shoulder.

"Our ride is here. You won't have to drive this one," I said instead. He looked skeptical, but I opened the door before he could question me more. A packet lay on the seat with my name on it, so I picked it up and opened it.

"Who am I this time?" I pulled out the nurse's badge, blinking as I giggled. "There's no way Man picked that name. Gah, I love you, Darcy, you silly girl."

"What is it?" Phoenix asked, sliding in next to me.

"My name for this mission." I turned it toward him, wondering if he'd get it.

"Molly Cule." His eyes lifted, a grin spreading across his face. "As in from the *Magic School Bus*?"

I nodded. "Yep, and because I'm a science nerd."

"What are you two laughing at?" Otto asked, getting in the other door and sandwiching me in. Rueben and Porter got into the seat in front of us, turning to look back at his question.

"My alias for this mission is Molly Cule." I giggled again, finding it too hilarious.

"I love hearing you laugh," Otto whispered, his breath warm against my face. He nuzzled his nose along my neck, the soft touch sending goosebumps all over me. I shuddered, my eyes closing as I took in a deep breath.

"Shit, she's so responsive," someone said. I was too focused on how Otto made my body feel with the barest touch. He placed a small kiss on my cheek before he pulled back, giving me time to calm down.

"This is going to be fun," Porter said, my eyes

opening and meeting his. The green shimmered, and his pupils grew as he stared at me. I sucked in a breath at the desire clearly written all over his face.

The SUV started forward, so he turned, breaking the connection and letting my heart return to my chest. I didn't know everything he meant, but I had a feeling I would agree with him. Discovering all these new sensations would be a lot of fun. For the first time in my life, I felt excited about that. Before, it had been perfunctory. A way for me to understand and check off that I'd done it and never needed to again.

With these guys, there weren't enough checkboxes in the world to ever be done with them. My mind devoured every new sensation, absorbing it so I could chase more of that feeling. The need to research and learn as much as I could itched under my skin, my brain's way of handling new information.

"You okay?" Phoenix asked, his hand squeezing my thigh.

"Mmhmm," I hummed, my lips pressed together. Taking a deep breath, I focused on the stitching of the seat before me and not my body's reaction to their very presence. After ten big gulps, I felt more centered, my heart no longer galloping.

The car slowed, and I leaned over Phoenix's chest to see out the window. His arm dropped around my back, his thumb landing on the small space of skin between my shirt and skirt. All the work I'd done earlier went out the window, my body practically purring at his touch.

The house had a curved driveway that wrapped around the front, and the driver stopped at the front door. The gray wood shimmered under the moon, the black shutters standing out against the soft color. It had a classic Craftsman style to it, with angled roofs over the windows and doors. Flowers grew in beds and pots all along the front. It was welcoming and precisely like the type of house I'd want if I lived in this town.

"It's perfect," I said, turning to Phoenix, forgetting how close I was to him. His nose bumped mine, his eyes drifting down to my lips.

For a second, everything else disappeared as I waited for him to decide if he would kiss me. The slamming of the door jolted me, and I pulled back. Phoenix grabbed my arms and held me in place. His eyes closed as he moved closer, his lips touching mine softly. He pulled back before I could investigate them more.

"Stay with Porter and me tonight?" he whispered.

My hand drew up to my lips as I nodded, the ghost of his kiss lingering. His eyes sparkled at my response, letting me go so I could unbuckle and climb out of the car. Rueben already had my bag, so I took Porter's hand and walked into the house, waving bye to the driver as the SUV pulled away.

Rueben opened the door, but the guys kept me back. I huffed, realizing they didn't think it was safe. I was mildly insulted that they kept forgetting I was a badass killer. But the overprotectiveness and caring for me felt nice, so I'd let it go for now.

My quiet giant returned, nodding that we could enter. Yawning, I blinked my eyes in an attempt to keep them open. It had been a long night, and I was ready for bed despite the fact the sun would rise soon. Oh well, I didn't have to be anywhere until tomorrow evening.

I walked through the house but didn't take in any of the information, my mind shutting down with each step closer to a bed.

"We'll take this one," Porter said to the others. I dropped Phoenix's hand and walked over to Otto, startling him when I pulled his shirt so he'd lower. He was the shortest of the guys but was still a few heads taller than me. Deciding to be brave, I kissed him on the lips, just like Phoenix had earlier. It felt right and important to make the same effort.

I dropped his shirt and moved to Rueben. I motioned for him to bend down; he smirked, squatting to my height. I'd be offended, but he was easily six-foot-four, and I barely topped five feet. I grabbed his beard, my fingers scratching through it before kissing him.

"Goodnight," I yawned, waving over my shoulder

as I stumbled toward the door Porter stood frozen at. I didn't know why and was too exhausted to figure it out.

Grabbing my bag, I undressed in the attached bathroom, tossing my clothes into the dirty side. I'd need to do laundry soon. Brushing my teeth, I leaned against the counter, barely able to stay standing. Spitting when I was finished, I grabbed an old t-shirt and pulled it on, remembering I couldn't sleep naked if I was sharing a bed.

Shuffling my feet, I climbed into the middle of the bed and pulled the covers over my head. Relaxed and warm, I drifted to sleep, hoping neither of the twins snored. I'd been known to stab someone for that nonsense.

WARMTH ENCASED me from both sides, and I tried to remember if I'd fallen asleep in my grilled cheese Oodie last night. My fingers found the hem of my shirt, so I pulled it over my head and tossed it. Gah. I hated wearing clothes to bed. They felt too constricting, and I always overheated. Air hit my bare skin, cooling me off. *Aww, that was better.* Soon I fell back into slumber.

WHISPERING WOKE me the next time, my mind fighting to hear what was being said or return to my dream.

"Holy shit. She's naked. Did you do that?"

"I'm good at sleight of hand, but I'm not good enough to remove someone's shirt, Bro. But thanks for the vote of confidence."

"Should we be looking? I feel bad, but also like I can't look away," the voice in front of me said.

"What do they look like?" the voice behind me asked.

"Perfect. They're plump and round. My fingers ache to touch them, to cup them in my hand, to feel their weight. Her nipples are plump and puckered, the areolas are a dark pink. They would fit into my mouth so easily," the voice purred.

My heart rate increased as I listened to them describe my body. I'd never heard anyone say such erotic things about me before. A pulsing in my core beat the same speed as my heart, and the urge to move my legs overwhelmed me. I kept my eyes closed and my breathing as even as possible, wanting to hear more from them.

"Fucking hell, that sounds divine. My dick is so hard right now it's practically straining my boxers. I'm having to hold myself back from grinding into her pert ass."

The voice in front of me groaned, the sheets rustling as he moved. "You're stronger than me, Brother. I don't know how you've managed to keep your hand still without running it over her."

His voice sounded different this time, a little breathier and huskier. It made me want to open my eyes to discover what made him sound that way. The throbbing intensified, a slickness developing between my legs.

"Her skin is so soft, and she smells divine."

A nose behind me trailed over my shoulder, goosebumps spreading everywhere he touched. I bit the inside of my cheek to stop myself from gasping. A sound of faster movement in front of me pulled my focus back as I tried to distinguish what it was.

"Are you spanking your monkey, Port?" the voice behind asked, their voice shocked. I tried to understand what Phoenix meant now that I could identify them. In the dark room, half asleep, their voices were too similar to distinguish.

"Uh-huh. I can't help it. If you had this view, you would too. Fuck. My dick is so hard and leaking just from her tits. I'm going to explode all over them the first time I taste her," Porter said unapologetically.

"You're going to scare her," Phoenix hissed.

I didn't know why Phoenix thought I'd be scared.

If anything, it turned me on more. Giving up the battle to keep myself still, I moved my legs, my butt moving backward and bumping into a hard length. Phoenix moaned at the action, the hand on my hip tightening. I did it again, liking how he sounded. Fluttering my eyes open, they landed on the honey-blond man in front of me, his green eyes bright and focused on me.

I licked my lips, his attention ramping my desire up tenfold. He smiled and winked. His shoulders dropped back down, and I wondered if he'd been nervous I would freak out like his brother had suggested. I still didn't understand why he thought that.

The hand behind me flexed again, his fingers moving ever so slightly up and down my thigh, bringing goosebumps to the surface. My eyes trailed down Porter, taking in his bare chest. The tattoos that covered his right arm continued over his right peck. It was an intricate design; I wished I could see better. Going lower, my legs shifted again as I took in his abs, the muscles defined. I'd never understood the appeal before, but staring at Porter's naked body, I wanted to lick and touch every single one.

The sheet covered his hips, his hand moving beneath it. He stopped as I spotted it, his face grimacing as if it pained him to do so. Reaching out, I gripped the sheet and met his eyes as I asked if it was okay. He nodded, licking his lips, and my legs moved again, garnering another groan from Phoenix as I rubbed up against his hardness.

Slowly, I lowered the sheet, blinking at what I discovered. Porter's hand was wrapped around his cock, squeezing it and making the dark purple tip leak. I kept watching, entranced as his hand stroked it slowly at first. The longer I looked, the faster his movement began.

The body behind me moved closer, his dick nudging my butt on its own. Phoenix's head nestled into my neck, his cheek pressing against mine.

"Do you like to watch, Raven?"

I nodded, licking my lips. "I've never seen someone do that before," I admitted, my voice soft and husky.

"Is this okay?" he asked, moving his hand over my belly, his thumb brushing against the underside of my boob. I rocked back into him, liking how he felt against me.

"Yes," I breathed, struggling to keep my eyes open to watch Porter.

"Hot damn, Rave. You're the hottest thing I've ever seen."

His words felt like hot pokers, searing into me and making me feel sexy. Confidence I never had in the bedroom before emerged. Pushing my hand down my stomach, I took Phoenix's hand and placed it between my legs. He froze behind me, so I moved his fingers for him, opening my legs as wide as I could in this position.

"Is she?" Porter asked.

"Uh huh," Phoenix groaned, rocking into me more. I took a second to show him how I wanted to be touched, then reached out to place my hand on Porter's. He moved the sheet down, watching his brother's fingers rub my clit, bringing the wetness up from my folds. I squeezed his hand, and he moved. I focused on how fast he went and where he pressed, and after a few turns, he dropped his hand, his head falling back on his pillow.

Porter panted as I stroked him, enjoying how he felt in my hand. His cock was hard as steel and as smooth as velvet, my hand gliding over him with ease. The bead of pre-cum caught my attention again, so I rubbed my thumb over it, and Porter moaned loudly, the sound vibrating the bed.

"Shit. I'm so close, babe. Your hand feels so good. Don't stop. Squeeze me just like that." I did as he said, feeling accomplished in my task at his verbal accolades and praise. He let out another groan a second before hot liquid squirted out, covering my hand as I continued to pump him. When he was done, he fell back to the bed, his body heaving as he came.

"My turn," Phoenix growled, plunging his finger into me as he bit down on my shoulder. The intrusion sent shivers down me, pleasure, unlike anything I'd experienced before, coursing through me.

Porter moved closer, taking my mouth with his as he kissed me. This one was deep and dirty, his tongue swirling into my mouth and making my head dizzy. Phoenix continued to pump his fingers in deeply, his cock rubbing between my butt cheeks as he rocked into me.

Feeling brazen, I reached back and pulled him free. I couldn't grip him from this angle, but I shifted so he rubbed between my legs. Phoenix had halted his movements while I situated him, his breathing stuttering at each stroke.

"Fucking shit, that's hot," Porter said, watching Phoenix rock into me, his cock slipping between my folds. "It's the sexiest hotdog I've ever seen."

Moaning at the thought, I pulled his face back to mine, kissing him like he'd just done to me. My hands dug into his hair, our lips pressing hard against one another.

Phoenix matched his strokes with his cock, picking up speed as he grew closer. He curled his fingers just right in my pussy, setting off an explosion of sensations. My belly grew tight before vibrations pulsed through me. My muscles tightened as my core convulsed around his fingers, gripping them tight. I pulled back from the kiss, panting for air as Phoenix groaned into my neck, his fingers slowing as he came on my butt.

"That was the sexiest thing I've ever been part of, and we didn't even have sex yet," Porter gushed, brushing my hair back. The three of our faces were close to one another, breathing the same air. I smiled, liking how nice it felt to be held by them.

"I might die when I feel your pussy around me, babe. I thought you were going to squeeze my fingers to death."

"Is that bad?" I asked, worried I'd done something wrong.

"No. It's fantastic. I'd gladly die inside of you."

Giggling, I realized he was being dramatic, but I appreciated the sentiment.

"What do I do with my hand?" I asked, realizing it was still covered in cum along with my butt.

"Shit. One second, Cutie-pie." Porter jumped off the bed, walking to the bathroom. His butt flexed with each step, and I couldn't wait to explore his body more. He returned with a washcloth, using it to clean me up between my legs first, and then wiped my hand before tossing it to his brother.

"Aw, you're not going to clean off my dick, Bro?"

"Nah. Mine's prettier," Porter teased, climbing back into bed.

Phoenix snorted, moving back so he could wipe me

off before getting up and cleaning himself. When he returned, he pulled me back to his body.

"I like sleeping between you two," I whispered, my eyes closing again.

"You can be the cream to our twin sandwich anytime, babe."

Kisses were placed on my cheeks, a smile flitting across my face. "I think twin sandwiches are my new favorite."

Raven

For a split second when I awoke, I worried the twins would regret what happened and think I was a slut for doing that with them. But then I remembered how hot it had been and that they'd been the ones to initiate it, letting me direct what I was comfortable with. It had been the first time I ever felt free in my sexual expression, making me crave it more.

Activating my hyper-focus to learn everything I could about sexual pleasure wasn't a great idea in the middle of a job, but I'd always been a quick study. I was sure this wouldn't be any different. Plus, I had four gorgeous boyfriends to practice on.

"What are you smiling about, Rave?" Phoenix asked. I'd rolled over at some point, facing him.

"Just that I have four boyfriends." I grinned again, the word making me happy.

"Yeah, you do. I like hearing you say that. I'm your boyfriend." Phoenix leaned forward, kissing me deeper as he pulled our bodies closer. We were both naked under the sheet, my nipples pebbling as they brushed against his chest.

"I'm half tempted not to interrupt you for breakfast and join you," a voice from the door said.

I turned my head, spotting Otto staring at me with hungry eyes. I licked my lips, desire filling my belly as I watched him. Only my stomach growling broke our stare off, Phoenix laughing as he pulled back.

"Food first. Our girlfriend's hungry."

"Girlfriend. The word has never sounded better," Otto said.

I sat up, forgetting I was still topless, the sheet falling to my lap. Otto's eyes widened as he stared. I'd never been embarrassed about my body; it was other people who had problems with it. With the way Otto stared, I didn't think he was one of them. So I stayed sitting, letting him take his turn.

He placed his fist in his mouth, biting his knuckles. "Who needs breakfast?" he muttered.

I raised my hand, my boob moving with the action. "Um, I do. Very much."

Otto laughed, nodding. He pulled his shirt over his head and walked toward me. "Here then. If we want to get through it without an orgy, you better cover up."

"Orgy," I said, the word sounding funny to my ears.

Phoenix groaned as he stood, my eyes moving to the cock I'd felt rubbing against me last night. He pulled on his pants, hiding it from view. Otto pulled my arms through, dropping the rest of it down. It was a little snug, stretching across my chest.

"Damn. That's not any better. You're too fucking gorgeous, Little Bird."

My cheeks heated, liking his compliment. "I have my own clothes, you know. They fit better."

"No!" Otto and Phoenix said at the same time. "Keep the shirt on. Maybe just add some shorts or something?" Otto added, grimacing.

"I can do that." I nodded, and they groaned as I walked to the bathroom, my lower half still bare.

"How did you sleep next to that all night and not bust a nut?" Otto asked.

"I didn't." Even from here, I could hear the smugness in Phoenix's voice.

"You...?" Otto trailed off, his voice soft, and I worried he wouldn't be happy despite his assurance last night. I looked over my shoulder to gauge his expression. There wasn't a hint of jealousy present, more like envy and desire. Okay, I could deal with that.

Quickly, I slid on a pair of leggings and pulled my hair into a messy bun. I turned in the mirror, liking how Otto's shirt looked on me. I lifted it up to my nose, smelling him.

"I could get used to this."

Walking back out, I found Otto waiting for me, his chest still bare. He had tattoos covering his chest, so I walked closer to take a look. My fingers reached out to trace the smallest one on his heart.

"A bird?" I asked, glancing up.

"Funnily enough, it's a raven. A little bird on my heart for my Little Bird." He covered my fingers with his hand, holding it there. A tear ran down my face at his sentiment.

"I'm so glad I found you, Otto."

"Me too, baby." He wiped my tear with his thumb, trailing it down my cheek, pulling my lip down with it. My tongue peeked out, tasting the salty tear on the tip. Otto groaned, his eyes rolling back.

"I get you tonight, Little Bird."

Nodding, I smiled at his request, wanting to spend more time with him as well. Otto dropped my hand, bending down to pick me up bridal style as he carried me from the room.

"I can walk. My ankle doesn't hurt anymore," I said, reminding him.

"I know." He lifted his eyebrow in a challenge. Rolling my eyes, I let him carry me, secretly liking it.

When we neared the kitchen, I glanced around at the open space, observing it more this time. The kitchen was white with navy blue accents, spilling into a navy and orange living room with a huge couch and fireplace. A massive TV hung from the wall over the fireplace. The entire space was warm and cozy.

"Good morning, Reubear," I said when we neared.

He turned from the stove, looking me over from head to toe. His eyes lingered over my chest, noticing how the shirt stretched tight. His nostrils flared slightly, and I hoped he didn't hate that I wore Otto's shirt. He cleared his throat, his eyes returning to mine, speaking directly to my heart.

Good morning, precious. You look beautiful.

My heart settled once I knew he wasn't angry with me. Otto sat in the chair, keeping me in his lap.

"This table has enough chairs," I pointed out, but the guys ignored me.

"It's more fun this way, Little Bird."

Shrugging, I didn't have an argument for that, so I let it go. I much preferred their laps to chairs, too. Rueben placed a plate of food in front of me with scrambled eggs, bacon, toast, and fruit. Smiling, I kissed his cheek before he could move away.

"Thank you, Ruebear. It looks delicious."

He smiled softly before returning to the stove to make the other's plates. I loved how they all took turns waiting on each other. They were a solid unit in every way, and I felt privileged to be part of it now.

Reaching for the fork, I glanced down to find it missing. Otto tapped my thigh, and I glanced up, finding a bite of egg in front of me.

"You're going to feed me?" I asked, smiling.

"Yep. I want to pamper you, Little Bird. Please let me."

Opening my mouth, I let him feed me as the others gathered around and dug into their food. When my belly was full, I took the fork, wanting to return the favor. Otto laughed but opened his mouth, letting me feed him this time. Giggling when I dropped something on his chest, I moved down to lick it up with my tongue. His hands tightened on my thighs, a hardness growing beneath my butt. Oh. *OH*.

"Sorry," I said, licking my lips.

"Don't. That was hot. I just hadn't expected it," Otto admitted, kissing me.

I looked at the guys, their eyes all on us as they shifted in their seats. I tried to hide my smile, liking too much how I affected them.

"You enjoy that, don't you?" Porter asked, not letting me get away with it.

"Kinda. I've never had men respond the way you guys do. It's addictive and powerful." I shrugged one shoulder, my eyes focused on the empty plate. Would they think I was weird for feeling that way?

"It's the same for us, Little Bird," Otto whispered into my ear. "You drive us wild with the simplest things."

"Really?" I asked, not believing them.

"Yup," Phoenix said, popping the p. "I'm hard as steel just from watching you eat."

"Huh." I sat back, no longer hiding the smile I had. I definitely needed to do some research. If I got this reaction from simple things, what kind would I get from something more seductive? The nerd in me wanted to find the scale and test my theories.

"Were you able to get one of us to accompany you?" Porter asked, breaking me away from how to integrate seduction and the scientific method.

"I haven't checked my phone yet. I'm going for two hours tonight to learn the routine with the regular nurse. She leaves tomorrow, and that's when I'll be there longer. So, it might be better to wait. My stetho-scope has a pin camera in it, so I can get a layout of the house and all the potential escape routes. I can get you a copy as well."

"That would be amazing. The blueprints weren't very forthcoming, and with the added security, getting in and out won't be easy. Any inside knowledge would be beneficial," Otto said, his arms wrapping around my waist and pulling me back further.

"Could I give you something to take that lets me hack into their system?" Phoenix asked, tapping his fingers on the table.

"For sure. Tonight is recon, so let me know how I can help." The guys all nodded, lost in their thoughts about their upcoming heist. "Do you know what they have worth stealing?"

"Some valuable pieces of art and jewelry. The usual rich person stuff. But there's a rumor he has a top-secret document with the knowledge of the side effects that would prove they'd known the risks and sold it anyway. The court could never prove without a shadow of a doubt, so the families settled when their lawyers advised it, worried they'd get nothing," Otto explained.

"*Settlement*. It was peanuts compared to what they should've gotten," Phoenix said, scowling.

"I'm glad you guys hate them as much as me. Not everyone understood my need for vengeance. I know Artevac wasn't responsible for killing my parents. But it feels too similar, and I know how those families must feel. Not everyone can do what I do, so I'm doing this for them. For the little kids who lost their parents first to drugs and then to the hope they'd found a solution, only for them to take their own lives. All because a few people were greedy."

My fists clenched, my words angry by the end.

"Now I can totally see the deadly killer. Is it wrong I find her just as hot, knowing she can kill me as I do when she looks innocent and pure?" Phoenix asked. Porter shoved him, shaking his head, but I didn't miss how no one corrected him. My cheeks flushed.

"That's where you're wrong," I said, leaning forward. "I can kill you any time—especially when I look pure and innocent."

Four groans sounded around the table, making me grin. This was so much fun. I'd just found my new favorite game.

"I see what you're doing, Little Bird. Don't forget there are more of us. Want to wager something?"

"Like what?" I asked, tipping my head to the side.

"First one to break and give in to the other is the last to come in our future orgy."

I sucked in a breath, both at what he was promising and the action to lose. I suddenly doubted my ability to win. Porter caught my eye, winking, and I remembered how he'd pleasured himself while I slept from my naked body. I just needed to embrace that confidence.

"Game on. Though, it doesn't count while we're working. I can't be distracted like that," I said, knowing I needed to have my head clear when I was there.

"Agreed. Only while in the house, so everything here is fair game. Deal?"

I looked at the three guys before me, the hunger clear on their faces. "Deal." They smiled at my words, and I hoped I hadn't walked into a trap.

Though, I think it would be a trap I'd happily enter with these four.

"Okay, well, I have some research to do. I'll see you boys later." I scooted off Otto's lap, rushing from the room, giggling at the look on their faces. Oh yeah, this was going to be fun.

Pulling out my laptop, I shut the door and sat on the bed as I typed into the secure database. I quickly reviewed tonight's information, ensuring nothing had changed since I'd left. Everything was as I remembered, so I closed it and moved to a new tab. My fingers tapped against the keys as I tried to think of the right words to search for.

"Four boyfriends? Four dicks? Hmm... how to satisfy four men? Maybe I should start with blow jobs and sex, then add the numbers." Nodding, I typed it in, settling back as the screen filled with educational videos.

After watching a few on how to give a good blow job, I moved on to different sex positions, amazed there were so many.

"Cowgirl? That sounds fun."

Watching the video, my skin heated as I studied the woman and man, watching their faces and movements, committing them to memory. Moving a pillow between my legs, I put myself in the same position, rocking forward as I watched.

"That's not too bad. Feels pretty good too."

With each video I watched, I felt more confident, finding the moves easier to do when I craved the four men they were for.

"Maybe I wasn't bad at sex after all. I just needed to be attracted to the guys in order to enjoy it," I mused, something lifting off my chest at the realization.

I'd always felt defective, not enjoying sex or

wanting it. But this.... The slipperiness between my legs told me a completely different story. The urge to touch myself and relieve the pressure overwhelmed me, but I didn't know if that would count in our bet. They hadn't turned me on; I'd done that myself.

But I'd imagined them, so maybe it would. Knowing the twins, they'd find a loophole and say it did. Huffing, I laid back on the bed and pulled out my kindle, focusing on a light and fluffy book to help quell some of the lust.

Yeah. I was so losing at this game.

Raven

It took a lot of convincing, but I eventually got the guys to let me go to the mansion on my own. I still wasn't certain Rueben wouldn't follow of his own accord—he'd agreed far too easily—but he'd at least be discreet if he did.

"Don't forget to text us when you get there and when you leave, Little Bird," Otto demanded for the tenth time in thirty minutes.

"I'd like to remind you I'm a trained assassin, but at this point, it just feels like a waste of time," I muttered, double-checking my bag. I'd need to stop and get some supplies before tomorrow. I was a little low on a few things. Adjusting the wig, I secured it with pins, giving myself a long blonde ponytail. Adding on some big wire-frame glasses, a fake mole, and a nose prosthetic, I was unrecognizable in the mirror.

I checked my camera on the app, placing the

stethoscope around my neck and an extra pen camera in my pocket. If the video didn't work due to blockers or interference, the camera could take pictures.

"Whoa, you look so different," Porter said as I exited the bathroom. They'd gathered in the twin's room while I'd gotten ready.

"That's the point." I laughed, spinning in a circle. "Be good. I'll be back in a few hours. Try not to miss me too much."

I kissed them all on the cheek, not wanting to smudge any of my makeup or get lost in their kisses. My phone vibrated, alerting me my ride-share was here, so I waved and hurried out the door before they changed their minds about accompanying me.

The driver asked a few questions on the trip but mostly left me alone as I peered out the window. The houses became further apart as we neared the mansion that John Mathis, or John *Duke* as he was known here, resided in. Trees lined the road, disappearing when an iron fence came into view. It spanned a few blocks before we arrived at the gate where a security guard stepped out, walking toward the car.

"State your business," the man said. The driver motioned toward me, so I rolled down my window and handed him my badge.

"Hello, I'm here to shadow Rebecca today." He looked over my badge with the agency name on it, then back at me. The guard stepped back to pick up a

phone in the booth and pressed a button. He spoke
with someone before hanging up and handing me my
badge.

"You'll have to get out here. Only cars that have
been inspected are allowed to pass."

Sighing, I nodded and grabbed my bag. "Thanks
for the lift." The driver nodded, their knuckles tight on
the steering wheel, their eyes not meeting mine in the
rearview.

Whelp, it looked like they wouldn't be accepting
any more jobs from me.

Closing the door, I stepped out, and not a second
later, the car reversed out of the driveway and sped off.
Rolling my eyes, I walked toward the gate, noticing
how long the drive was. Yay. More cardio.

"I'll need to inspect your bag, Miss."

"Of course... I'm sorry; what's your name?" I asked
with a smile. Seduction had never been my skill, but
being friendly and kind were. People relaxed around
me, my unassuming appearance and height making
me seem like a non-threat. And since people naturally
tended to ignore anyone who didn't meet the beauty
standards of size and weight, I became invisible,
fading into the background.

Which was funny when you thought about it. The
chubby girl being invisible. But I was most often. I
didn't let it bother me, using it as a strength instead.

"It's Mark," the guard answered as he peeked

through my bag. I held in my laugh at the fact a guard named Mark was guarding my mark. He handed me back my bag, stepping toward me with a wand. "Lift your arms."

I did as he asked, spinning in a circle when he needed me to. And this was why I handled these jobs. My murder weapons were inconspicuous and easily explained with my role.

"You're really good at your job. I can tell you take it seriously, Mark." His chest puffed out at the compliment, some of his earlier hardness melting away.

"You're clear, Molly. Sorry about the hike. I'll try to remember to bring the golf cart down here tomorrow. If you call the guard box at the end of your shift, I'll have someone bring you back."

I touched his arm, smiling brightly. "That's really kind of you, Mark. Thank you. I appreciate that so much." His cheeks tinged a little red, and I dialed it back a little. I didn't want to accidentally send him a flirt.

"Have a good day, Miss Molly." He cleared his throat and dipped his head like he was from a country-western. Mark opened the gate from his stand, and I waved, hoping my camera had gotten the controls.

I'd have to try to get a clearer view later in case we couldn't get a car through and needed to open it ourselves. Strolling, I took in my surroundings, making sure to get the gate and fence to show how expansive it was. The walk to the house wasn't bad, despite the forced cardio. I had on comfortable shoes, and the weather was pleasant for this time of night, lacking the earlier humidity the south was known for. As I strolled, I spotted a few men patrolling the grounds ensuring to capture them. It might suck to walk, but it gave me a great view of the perimeter.

"This place is bonkers," I muttered as I approached the front of the house. The dark brick appeared obsidian in the night, expanding as far as I could see with a driveway that wrapped around to a garage. Windows covered the front, only a few lights visible from the outside. It stood three stories high with no trees close by.

This would be difficult for Loxley Crew to breach. They'd need to get past Mark and all the guards on the grounds. Not to mention the fact if they checked vehicles, stealing anything would be impossible. My mind plotted out differing scenarios and escape routes over the last few steps, listing the risks. When I made it to the door, a guard nodded at me. I smiled, hoping to make another friend.

"Hello, sir. Are you having a good evening?" He grunted, opening the door without a word.

Okay, so he wasn't much of a talker. But unlike my Ruebear, who spoke mostly with his heart and eyes, this man's were dark and hollow. He'd take out another person without hesitation. I labeled him as a threat in my head. We'd all need to be wary of him.

A frazzled nurse met me a few feet inside, her red hair frizzy and out of its clip, a grimace on her face. Despite her messy appearance, she had a kind face and didn't give off any predator vibes.

"I'm sorry about the walk. I told the agency about the car thing," she said, motioning for me to follow her. "I'm Rebecca, by the way."

"Molly. It's nice to meet you. And the walk was fine. It's a nice evening." I ignored the sweat that had developed under my boobs, knees, and arms. Gross.

She gave me a tight smile, and I hoped Rebecca would lighten up a bit on her vacation, especially since she wouldn't have to return to this home. I felt slightly bad about that, but the agency would find her a new place. Maybe she would be happy to be rid of this evil bastard.

I tried to swivel as much as I could as I followed her, trying to capture the room layouts. We climbed the stairs, my legs groaning by the time I reached the top floor. I really did need to think about increasing my cardio because there was no way I was cutting out donuts. An image of a donut hanging in front of a treadmill had me snorting out loud. Rebecca turned, lifting her eyebrow at my odd behavior. I coughed. Hoping she'd think the first one had been one too.

"So, how long have you worked here?" I asked, trying to soften her a bit.

"About a year at this house, but I've been with the agency for about five years. This is actually the first vacation I've taken since then." She relaxed a little with that news, making me happy we'd thought to do that. Everyone needed a vacation—especially in the medical field.

"Very exciting. Are you traveling with anyone?" I asked as we walked into a room. She paused, a slight smile gracing her lips.

"I kind of have a thing going with one of the guards. He's hoping he can get off work. He's put his request in and is waiting to hear if it's approved."

That was good intel to have. Maybe Reuben could pose as an extra guard. I'd have to get the name of the guard so we could hack into the security company's system. It would make things much easier for Loxely Crew if they had an in with the security.

"Ooh, that sounds delightfully clandestine." I giggled, making her smile more. "Good for you, girl. I hope he's able to get off. Though, I must admit the security was slightly more extreme than I expected."

She nodded, walking over to a table with a chart. She motioned for me to take a seat.

"Yeah. It's a lot at first, but eventually, you get used to it."

I leaned forward, hoping I wasn't pushing too

soon, but with us already on the topic, I didn't want to bring it up later, and it appear out of place.

"Do you know why they have so many? Is he famous or something?" I asked, opening my eyes wide to give myself a look of innocence. It made me feel like they would pop out of my head.

"Not in the way you're thinking. He's not a rock-star or professional athlete."

"Darn. Don't tell anyone, but I once got to work for one of the doctors from a top-rated TV show." I sat back, pretending to be disinterested and hoping she'd rise to the bait.

"It wasn't *Phoenix Hospital*, was it?" she gasped. "Dr. Romano?" Rebecca wiggled her eyebrows, her cheeks flushing.

I gave her a wink as I leaned forward. "Let's just say it was bigger in person, if you know what I mean." I giggled, moving my hands to indicate size. Her eyes grew wide, a hand covering her mouth as she laughed.

"What are you ladies giggling about in here? Shouldn't you be working?" An older man who looked like he had a stick up his butt while sucking lemons appeared from the hallway. Rebecca stiffened, a grimace appearing at his interruption. Okay, so this wasn't a friend. Nosy buttstick might be difficult to handle.

"Hi, I'm Molly. I'll be here while Rebecca's away. We're just going over the details. She's been a great tutor so far," I gushed, hoping to earn some brownie points with the redhead. Her shoulders relaxed marginally, giving me a win.

The man glanced between the two of us before stepping closer. He placed his hands behind his back, puffing out his chest. I hated him already.

"You may address me as Mr. Silver. I'm the head of staff for the house. You'll be under my authority while you're here."

I stood, pretending not to notice how dismissive he was, not wanting to make an enemy of the small man just yet. I held out my hand, his eyes dropping to it with a frown before shaking it carefully with two fingers. His hand was cold and wet. Gross. I'd need to wash it before I touched anything I wanted to keep.

"It's a pleasure to be working with you, Mr. Silver."

Rebecca stood, carrying the binder with her. "I'll show you the room and the medication schedule and run through the machines with you."

She left out a side door, ignoring the man. I nodded, spinning on my heels to follow. I leaned in to whisper when I was out of range of the creepy butler.

"He seems fun."

She smiled, but it was tense. "Watch out for him. He likes to think he's more important than he is. He'll turn anyone in for the smallest thing. Bethany Duke uses him to know what's going on. She mainly stays in her wing of the house, but he has her ear and will make your life hell. Word of advice... stay out of both of their paths."

"Got it. Nose down. Do you really have to call him Mr. Silver?" I asked, hoping to catch his first name so we could do a background check. The staff's names hadn't been public knowledge since they'd been hired privately.

She snorted, a smile appearing. "Yes. Because he hates his real name." She paused, bending down to whisper. "It's Fern. Fern Silver." She giggled, and I joined in as we approached an ornate door. Her eyes lit up as she spotted the guard near the door. Her eyelashes fluttered as we neared. The man was good, keeping his focus straight ahead, but I caught how he watched her, one side of his mouth ticking up at her arrival.

"Hey, Nate. This is Molly. I'm training her for when I'm gone. Any changes with Mr. Duke?"

His eyes assessed me, but there was no heat like I felt from my guys. It was purely clinical as he cataloged my level of threat. He nodded in greeting before his eyes landed on the older nurse, the corners softening toward her.

"No changes to report. He's sleeping, and Mrs. Duke has already been by to say her goodnight. It's nice to meet you, Molly."

"You too." He too gave me a nod, making me

wonder if the men here were born with that imaginary hat they all seemed to dip.

Rebecca brushed past him, her hand touching his arm as she did—smooth, girl. The room we entered was massive, spanning at least six windows in the front. Heavy drapes hung off to the sides, the night sky filtering through. A medical bed sat in the middle, with IVs and machines hooked up to the man resting there. Time had not been kind to John Mathis. His skin was thin and sagged on his bones, and he had a slight yellow pallor. His hair drooped off his forehead, the strands limp and oily.

My eyes trailed over the room, taking in the paintings, grand piano, and ornate couches. The room resembled more of a sitting room than a medical one, but I guess the man could choose where he wanted to die. A few cameras were visible in the corners of the ceiling, the red light flashing a steady rhythm. I wondered if the safe was in here or if that was a different room.

Rebecca walked over to the patient and wrote down the readings she found. "We have to input how he's doing every two hours, then scan into the computer so that Mrs. Duke and his doctors can tell if there's a problem right away."

Shit. That might create an issue. I would need to make his numbers decrease, but not enough that they would intervene. It would be a delicate balance to figure out. My hand itched to grab a pencil and write down the equations so I could solve them out. Math soothed me when things got too complicated in my head.

Rebecca went through everything, and I could tell she cared about her job and ensured her patient was well taken care of. She made a good nurse, someone who could put the person aside and focus on their health. Assuming she even knew who he was and what he'd done since he'd used an alias.

Separating the person from their crimes hadn't been anything I'd ever been able to do. Bad people deserved to be punished—end of story.

After another flirty encounter with Nate, Rebecca showed me a few other rooms I would be allowed to be in, which staff to avoid, and which ones would be helpful. The two hours went by fast, so by the time she walked me to the door, my brain was overloaded, and my feet hurt.

"Thanks for everything, Rebecca. Have a wonderful time on your trip!"

I waved goodbye, climbing down the stairs as I pulled out my phone to order another ride-share, but there weren't any cars close by at this time of night. "Just great," I muttered.

"You okay, miss?" a voice asked me from the shadows. I jumped, clutching my hand to my chest.

"Sorry. I didn't see you there. I'm fine. Thank you."

"Would you like a ride down to the guard station to wait?" he asked, motioning to the golf cart.

"Yes, that would be amazing. Thank you." I practically ran to the golf cart, sinking on the leather cushion. "I'm Molly," I said once I was seated.

"Nice to meet you, Molly. I'm Sean. You covering for the lovely Rebecca?"

"Yep. Seems like an interesting household. I've never worked anywhere with security before."

"The Dukes take their privacy seriously. You won't find a safer place here."

"That's good." I smiled like that was what I was worried about. I pointed my camera around some more, capturing anything I might've missed the first time. The ride was much quicker than my trek, and I waved goodbye as the gate opened.

"Have a good night, Sean."

"Everything go okay, Miss Molly?" Mark asked as I stepped through. A car sat off to the side, but I didn't know who it was.

"Yep. I'm looking forward to my first solo day." I smiled, wondering when he got off and if I could convince him to give me a lift into town.

"Good, good. I've already confirmed your ride, so I'll see you tomorrow." He nodded toward the car parked off to the side.

My ride? I glanced at the car closer, the driver's window lowering with a familiar head popping out.

Smiling, I waved bye to Mark as I walked slowly to the car and leaned in like I was checking. Porter beamed at me, making me laugh.

"Your ride's here, Cutie-pie!"

I climbed into the back, grateful he'd come to get me. I guess there was a benefit to not doing this alone. But I wouldn't tell Otto that just yet.

Raven

ONCE PORTER HAD DRIVEN PAST THE FENCE, I REMOVED THE wig and disassembled my disguise. The wig cap had been hot and itchy, making me wish this job was easier so I could wear my usual garb of black leather.

"Ahhh, that feels so much better," I said, sighing in relief as I scratched my hair. Porter chuckled, his eyes moving to the rearview to watch me.

"How did it go?" he asked, his fingers tapping along to the song on the radio.

"Cover-wise, it went fine. I made contact with a few of the staff and learned the routine. As for security and window of opportunity, that will be tricky. It's tighter than expected. They have a lot of protocols in place that will inhibit both of our missions."

"I do like a challenge," Porter chirped from the front.

Laughing, I finger-combed my hair and rubbed at my scalp as I let my hair down. The scrubs were itching, so I grabbed my change of clothes and took off the top. Porter gasped, and I jumped, looking up. I searched behind us and in front for what caused him to gasp. When I couldn't find anything, my forehead creased.

"Are we being followed?" I asked, scooting forward so I was in between the front seats.

"Nope. You're just trying to kill me." Porter's voice was strained, his hands tight on the wheel.

"Huh?" I asked, my nose scrunching as I tried to figure him out. I glanced down at my hands, finding them empty. "I'm not holding a syringe or a wire. I know I'm good, Port, but I wouldn't endanger myself to prove a point."

Porter groaned, biting his fist now. "Cutie-pie, you're gonna have to add being topless to your list of ways to kill a man."

At his words, I peered down at my boobs pressed between the seats with my black lacy bra on display. "Oh. Sorry, I didn't think it would be a big deal." I shrugged, moving back now that I knew we weren't in danger. An idea came to my head from my earlier seduction education, and I decided to put my new skills to the test.

"Just give me a warning next time," Porter grunted in response, his eyes flicking back to me every few seconds. Smirking, I kicked off my tennis shoes and shimmied my pants down. Then I deliberately turned, my butt now in the space between the seats, as I pulled out my leggings.

The car swerved as Porter cursed, spurring me on. Returning to my seat, I pulled off my panties and dragged the soft cotton up my legs. Moaning in relief as the soft fabric met my skin, I sighed happily. I toed my shoes back on, folding the scrubs and underwear into my bag.

"I feel like this is a real-life *Dirty Dancing* moment," I said, moving my hands to the band of my bra.

"Oh? How so? You going to dance in the water with me, Raven?"

I smiled, loving that he'd seen the movie. "You going to teach me? I'm not great at dancing, but I could balance on the log without any problems. But no, more like the time she changes in the backseat after their first performance. So, keep your eyes up front. There's your warning."

Slowly, I mimicked the lady I'd watched earlier and pushed the straps off my shoulders, shimmying the cups down my arms as I pressed my boobs together. I didn't glance up to see if Porter was watching, but his inhale and swerve told me he was. Putting my arms into the shirt, I raised them to drop it down over my head, my tits perky and alert from this angle. I pretended to be oblivious as I wrestled the shirt down, tugging it down in the front last.

"Fucking toadstools," Porter cursed, making me laugh. "You knew what you were doing, didn't you?"

I climbed over the console, trying not to bump him with my hips as I took the front seat and put on my seatbelt. In shock, I turned to him. "Who me? I have no idea what you're talking about!"

Porter shook his head good-naturedly, grinning as he focused ahead. He shifted a few times, drawing my attention to his crotch—a long length pressed against his thigh, visible through his tight jeans. I gulped, the one taken by surprise now. It had felt big last night, but seeing it there, it seemed twice the size.

"If you keep staring at it like that, I'm going to pull this car over and do something about it."

"You'd lose the game," I whispered, licking my lips and wondering what he'd taste like.

"That's where you're wrong, Rave." He chuckled darkly, the sound deep in his throat. "There's no losing in this game."

Building up my courage, I was about to reach out my hand and touch his leg when he pulled into the rental, turning the car off. I quickly pretended to be observing my nails.

"Oh, look, we're here!"

Porter laughed but let me off the hook. "Come on. Rueben grabbed some food on his way back from checking out the layout." His eyes twinkled at the confirmation that one of them had followed me.

"I knew it," I grumbled, opening the door. Though inside, warmth spread through me, knowing I hadn't been there alone. All my talk of doing this solo was proving to be just that... talk.

If these guys made me depend on them, they had another thing coming if they ever tried to leave me. I'd cling to them like a koala. Rueben was as tall as a tree, so I was confident we could work out a living arrangement that would work.

Deep down, I knew in my heart they weren't playing me. Otto had been in my heart since I was a child. He'd shared me with his brothers, and I'd become part of them in exchange. They were as likely to let me go as I was them. So, what was I afraid of?

"I hope he got some cake or pie. I have a sweet tooth that has to be fed after a mission. It's mandatory!"

Porter grabbed my bag from the back, throwing his arm around my shoulders. I spotted an SUV parked next to the car and figured it had to be the one Rueben used. They'd been busy in the time I'd been gone.

"If I know Rueben, he bought one of everything. He'd want to make sure he got you what you liked. Plus, he loves his sweets just as much. Probably what drew him to you. You're as sweet as they come."

He nuzzled my neck, kissing me under my ear. My

face flamed at his words as my insides heated from his kiss. All my progress at seducing him went out the window as he turned me on with such simple things. I'd never felt this aroused before, and it was becoming glaringly obvious that I wasn't asexual like I believed, but perhaps demisexual.

Accepting myself, I lifted my head and wrapped my arm around Porter's waist. He grinned at me, and I felt like I'd won the lottery.

The door flew open, and Phoenix flew out, scooping me into his arms as he picked me up. My legs wrapped around him as he hugged me tight to his chest.

"Um, hello. Did you miss me?" I laughed.

He nodded, his eyes big as he stared at me. "How was your day, sweetie?" he asked as he turned and walked into the house, leaving his brother behind.

"I'm here too, Bro!"

"You're not as pretty."

"I look the same as you, dweeb."

"Nah, I'm cuter. Right, Raven?"

"I'm not getting in the middle of that. Wait!" The twins laughed as I tried to fix my blunder. "You know what I mean."

"Aw, our girlfriend's cute when she gets flustered," Phoenix said, giving me a megawatt smile.

We entered the house, the smell of food hitting my

nose, and I turned, almost causing Phoenix to drop me. "Food!"

"Bro, I think she's happier to see food than you," Porter teased, elbowing his brother.

"My turn to be chair!" Phoenix claimed, acting goofier than I'd ever seen him. Rueben and Otto came into the kitchen at the noise, trying to pull me away from Phoenix to hug me, but he denied them.

"Mine for now." He locked his arms around me, squishing me to his chest to the point it was hard to breathe. I tapped his shoulder.

"Phoenix. Can't. Breathe."

Rueben heard and smacked him upside the head. Narrowing his eyes as he pointed a finger. Phoenix grimaced, releasing me so I could breathe easier.

"Much better," I sighed. I reached out a hand to Rueben, and he clasped it, squeezing. I tried to ask him with my eyes how he was, wanting to learn how to eye speak as well. He gave me a bearded smile and nod, kissing my hand. I took that to mean he understood and was good now that I was here.

Otto plastered his front to my back, turning my chin to peer back at him. His hands landed on my ribs, his fingers flexing against me. I sucked in a breath. Being held by one man and touched by two others proved difficult.

"Do not rub yourself against Phoenix. Do not rub yourself," I chanted in my head.

When Otto smirked, I wondered if it had actually been in my head. I'd gotten so used to talking aloud that I couldn't tell the difference. Shrugging my shoulders, I decided it didn't matter.

"Missed you, Little Bird." Otto kissed my cheek before stepping back and walking off like he hadn't just set me on fire.

"Stupid handsome boy," I grumbled, making Phoenix laugh. I crossed my arms over my chest as Phoenix shifted me in his arms, his hands gripping my butt, and I tried to pout.

His smile turned devilish, and he nipped me, pulling my protruded lip free with his teeth. The sting sent a jolt straight to my clit, and I gasped, opening my mouth. Phoenix took the opportunity to kiss me, plunging his tongue into my mouth and stealing my breath.

When he drew back, I felt dazed, my eyes blinking as I tried to acclimate myself. "You're a freaking wizard," I whispered. The guys laughed, reminding me we were in the kitchen where there was food. Yes. Food. I needed to focus on something other than taking a ride on Phoenix's disco stick.

"Disco stick?" he asked, and I spun around, my eyes attempting to fall out of my head. Okay, maybe I needed to remember not to say things out loud.

"Hairy sloths!" I grumbled, reaching for the first

thing I could see. A large hand with tattoos intercepted me, placing a cheeseburger in my grip. "You're my favorite."

I immediately began eating, my stomach growling at me in protest for waiting so long.

"Did she mean Rueben or the cheeseburger?"

"You know, I'm not sure. Here, I want to try."

"I can hear you," I said between bites, focusing on the scrumptiousness of cheese and sauce as it dripped down my hand. Without thinking, I turned my hand, licking up the ketchup and mayo concoction.

"Why is that so fucking sexy? Fuck. I thought we had her, but then she goes and does something so innocent but hot, and I know we're goners."

"That tongue just might kill me."

I froze, realizing I was practically licking my elbow in front of four hot guys. "Sorry." I cringed. "Sometimes I get hyper-focused on the thing in front of me. I could hear you, but it didn't penetrate that you were at the table with me because all I wanted was food."

I peered up, expecting to find looks of disgust, but instead, I had three guys peering back at me with pure desire. It was the kind of look where I wanted to reach my hand out and check their chins for drool.

"Don't apologize, Rave. That was hot," Porter said, licking his lips.

"Here," Phoenix said, placing a French fry before

my lips. Taking a bite, I paid more attention as the guys ate, remembering I wasn't alone in my room.

"So," Otto said, clearing his throat, "what did you learn tonight?"

"Oh, lots, actually." I wiped my hands and took a drink, replaying the information I'd learned. "It's going to be tougher than we initially believed. There are guards inside and outside, cameras, and nosey staff. The wife checks on him periodically, and his medical condition has to be updated every two hours."

"Shit. Is it worth trying to break in?" Otto asked, thinking through options in his head. It didn't surprise me that he was good at planning things. He'd always been the one to strategize and teach me the best ways to find weaknesses.

"There were a lot of paintings and high-end items, but it would be hard to get them through the gate since they search vehicles upon entry and exit. If he has documents like you think, I might be able to smuggle those out without notice."

"You're not doing this alone," Porter said, his care-free attitude gone. "We'll find a way in. We always do."

I lifted my hands, showing I wouldn't fight him on it. "It was just a thought. There's a way I think I could get Reuben in. The nurse spoke of a guard she had a thing with and how he was trying to get the time off. Maybe you could hack into their system and get Rueben's name sent over to replace him? He was stationed inside the house, so that would be helpful."

"That's brilliant," Phoenix said, kissing me on the cheek before he stood and dumped me into Rueben's arms. He ran off without a backward glance like his feet were on fire. I frowned, not sure I should be offended or flattered.

"He's going to hack. Probably the only thing that would tear him away from you. He gets into zones when he has a good idea," Porter said, softening the dismissal. I could understand his behavior. I often did it myself when playing with my chemicals.

"Any other information?" Otto asked, reaching out to touch me now that I was beside him.

"We have the camera footage to go through, and I can check back to see if the internship has been approved for Porter. It might take a few days before it is because of the background checks."

I didn't add that I was still trying to figure out the best way to kill him without getting caught. Escaping would be difficult, along with the window of opportunity to make it look plausible. Good thing I thrived under pressure. The thought of it being difficult for once made my heart race excitedly.

"If there's nothing else tonight, let's watch a movie or something and relax. The next few days will be intense, so it's our last opportunity to chill until the job is done," Otto suggested.

"Sure. Just let me take a shower and change first. Need to wash the job off me."

Rueben carried me into the shower, setting me on my feet and kissing my lips, my heart pounding as he stole my breath. He stepped out minutes later, smiling as I gawked at him.

"Oh, it's so on like Donkey Kong!"

Now that Little Bird was back with us, I felt calmer. I didn't want to admit I'd been a worried mess the whole time she'd been gone. It had been hard to focus on anything, much less find a strategy that would keep us all safe and out of prison.

"Games or a movie?" I asked Porter after we cleared the kitchen.

"Hmm, maybe—"

"Oh, Porter," Raven called from the bathroom, her head sticking out the door. "I'd like to continue our conversation from earlier about no one losing. Could you help me in the shower?" she asked innocently, batting her eyelashes.

Porter didn't hesitate, rushing to the bathroom, a giggle escaping as the door shut behind them both. I didn't know why I'd instituted a competition earlier. It had seemed fun then, but now that she'd thrown down the first gauntlet, I somewhat hated myself.

Raven was clever and planned to pick us all off one

at a time. I couldn't even blame Porter. If she'd called me in there, I would've gone running as well. Lucky bastard.

I glanced at Rueben, hoping he knew how to get through the rest of the night. He picked up the remote, indicating the TV, so I nodded, joining him on the couch.

"I'm an idiot, aren't I?"

Reuben nodded, grunting in acknowledgment. Sighing, I rubbed my hand over my face as Porter's moan traveled through the walls. My cock instantly hardened as I tried to picture what they were doing. Were they having sex? Was Little Bird on her knees? Were her legs wrapped around his face?

Groaning, I clenched my fists, the urge to rub myself strong. Rueben smirked, not even trying to hide that he was enjoying the free sound show. When the door opened a few minutes later, we both pretended to be watching the TV, but I'd guarantee neither of us could say what was on it. Porter walked out in a towel, a smug grin on his face.

"Looks like I'm out. But I can't say it wasn't worth it."

I gritted my teeth but couldn't find it in me to hate him. It would take a powerful man to deny Raven anything she wanted, and I doubt any of us would've resisted.

Raven emerged a few seconds later wearing a long

sleeve shirt so thin; it was practically see-through. Her nipples were pebbled and stood at attention, ripe for my mouth. The shorts she strutted in were practically indecent, barely covering the curve of her ass. If I wasn't trying to hold out, I'd enjoy them a whole lot more.

"You playing dirty, Little Bird?"

She winked, pausing in the doorway of the twin's room. "I'll be just a moment. I want to check if Phoenix needs any more information. Rueben, would you mind combing my hair again when I return?"

He nodded, shifting his legs again, her grin growing as she entered the other room; the door opened a crack. It didn't take long for another moan to be heard, and I bit my fist to keep mine at bay. I wouldn't make it through the night at this rate.

It felt like forever before she returned, a comb and a bottle of lotion in her hand. She sat on the floor in front of Rueben, handing him the comb.

"What movie did you pick?" she asked, looking back at me. I blinked, glancing up at the screen. Shit, had we picked something? The first thing I saw, I clicked on.

"Um, how about this?"

Little Bird looked at me oddly before shrugging. "I haven't seen it."

The movie started playing, and I tried to relax, but my eyes kept getting pulled to Raven as Rueben brushed her hair. It was such a simple thing, but I felt immensely jealous. The love and care he took with each strand, the way he massaged her neck and scalp. It was clear how much he adored her in that simple action. I'd been banking on our connection and history to carry me through this relationship, but I could see now that I had been misguided.

Porter and Phoenix brought fun into her life, always making her laugh and smile. Rueben took care of her, providing comfort and doting on her. He made her feel like a princess. So, what would I add to the mix? Furrowing my brows, I tried to think about what I had to offer. I'd never been in a relationship before, so it wasn't like I had much experience to draw from either.

I was so deep in thought that when the first moan sounded, I jumped, not expecting it. My eyes landed on Rueben sitting back and Little Bird rubbing lotion on her plump thighs. I licked my lips, having forgotten about the moan, too distracted by the sight of her delicious skin. What I wouldn't give to have her thick thighs wrapped around my head.

The second moan caused me to jump again, but this time, I focused around the room, knowing it wasn't the two beside me. When my eyes landed on the TV, I gulped. Fucking hell. I'd picked a sex movie. And not just a 'roll around in the sheets and keep everything covered' movie, but full-blown nudity.

A guy railed into a woman from behind, her tits swinging with each thrust as she clenched her fingers into the sheet. Her moans were breathy and loud, clearly enjoying what the guy was doing to her from behind. Raven had her head tilted, more like she was studying the angle of the position rather than being turned on by it. I glanced at Rueben, whose face I imagined mirrored my own. Confusion, slightly turned on, and wishing it was actually happening with the girl sitting on the floor.

When it ended, Little Bird stood and moved over to the side, pulling out a yoga mat from her bag. She started to bend and move into positions as she watched the movie, able to do each one from memory, apparently. Another sex scene came on, but Rueben and I were more interested in the girl doing yoga in her tiny shorts and a see-through shirt.

"How come yoga doesn't look like that when you do it?" I asked Rueben. He snorted, shaking his head.

Little Bird bent over to touch her toes, and I about came in my pants. Holy fuck. She wasn't wearing any underwear. Biting my fist, I shifted again, trying to find some relief from my hard as steel cock.

"I think she's trying to kill us," I whispered to Rueben. He nodded, his eyes fixed on her, taking in every inch. Neither of us watched the movie now, our entire focus on her as she twisted. When she bent backward, and her top slid up and exposed her boobs, Rueben couldn't take it any longer.

Standing, he marched over, picked her up, and threw her over his shoulder as he made his way to our room. Little Bird giggled, clearly happy about the turn of events. Rueben stopped at the door, looking back at me and raising his eyebrow. I knew what he was saying without any words.

"You coming? Don't be a tool and keep away just to win a stupid game."

Nodding that I understood, I motioned for him to go on. I needed a moment to myself before I stepped in there. The reality was, I knew once I crossed that line with Raven, my little bird, my whole heart would belong to her.

Turning off the TV, I stood up from the couch, adjusting my erection as I walked around and picked up things. The guys weren't messy, but I needed everything in its place before I could go to sleep. I'd accepted it as a trauma response to my past, the time I'd spent homeless and needed to be able to move at a second's notice. As well as foster care and the group home. If you didn't keep your things safe, they would be taken. So, now, I ensured we were always tidy and ready to go if we needed to make a quick escape.

When there wasn't anything left, I checked all the doors and windows, despite knowing that Rueben had done it earlier the second Raven returned home. Sighing, I rubbed the back of my neck, the tiny hairs soothing my nerves.

"Time to quit delaying and man up, asshole," I mumbled to myself. "She's Little Bird. She's not going to hurt you."

With one more breath, I turned off all the lights and headed for my bedroom. The moans outside the door had me pausing. I gripped my fingers on the doorframe, taking in a deep breath.

"You care that much about winning?"

I jumped, spinning around. Phoenix stood at his door, his face solemn as he watched me. His eyes searched mine, looking for something.

"What?" I croaked, clearing my throat.

"I know it started as something fun, or at least it seemed that way. But you've been holding yourself back all day. Why?"

I started to protest, but Phoenix cut me off with a glance. Deflating, I dropped my head, rubbing my neck. "I was scared, okay? I had a moment where I feared I wouldn't be good enough, or she'd realize I wasn't the version of the boy she remembered."

"That's stupid, and you know it."

"I know, and I already gave myself a stern talking to, and I was about to go in there and place my heart on a platter for her."

Phoenix gave me a smug smile, motioning for me to continue. "Well, then, good. Carry on."

Snorting, I shook my head and pulled Phoenix into a hug. "Thanks for caring about me, Nix."

"Of course. You're my brother."

Releasing Phoenix, I felt more sure of myself, not pausing this time when I opened the door. "Alright, you win, Little Bird. I'm giving in."

The mound of covers in the middle of the bed flew off as Raven jumped up, bouncing on the bed as she pumped her arms into the air.

"I win, I win, I win!"

It took me a moment to realize they were both fully clothed, Rueben sitting back with his legs crossed, a broad grin on his face. Blinking, the image didn't change to one of sexual depravity. My mouth dropped open as it hit me. I'd been played and had fallen for it—hook, line, and sinker.

"Everyone else was in on it? They weren't really giving in to you?" I asked.

Little Bird stopped jumping, placing her hands on her hips as she smirked at me. "A lady doesn't kiss and tell. All that matters is I won. Now, come and snuggle with Ruebear and me."

Shaking my head, a lightness crawled in as I walked toward the firecracker that had returned to me. I wanted to be mad at my brothers for plotting against me, but I couldn't be. I probably would've done the same if it had been reversed. Little Bird was hard to say no to, and I'd been an idiot to make our connection into a game. She was changing us all in so many ways. Softening our sharp edges, brightening our dark souls, and filling our lives with more than the pursuit of justice.

Little Bird had resuscitated us, reminding our group how to breathe again.

Climbing onto the bed, I pulled her into my arms, clinging to the girl I loved. The feelings I had as a child were tenfold now, my heart beating for her.

"I love you, Little Bird. That might be too soon to say, but I don't care. I spent too many years missing you, wishing I could've done things differently, but I didn't have the means to do so. Now that you're here, I don't want to waste time pretending you're not the air I breathe."

She sucked in a breath, her eyes shiny with tears. I took the opportunity to kiss her, to truly feel her lips on mine. To explore her mouth with my tongue and elicit a response to the feelings coursing through me.

Little Bird melted in my arms, her body melding into mine as I held her. Moving back, I placed her against the mattress, not breaking the kiss. Never before had a kiss felt so powerful. It was the life force connecting our two souls, entwining them together for eternity.

My hands caressed her body, warring with pulling her closer or softly touching her all over. It felt like we kissed for hours, months, years, our hearts beating as one as our lips and tongues tangled together. It was both a frenzy and a tranquil meeting as we chased the ultimate high together.

When I couldn't hold off any longer, I pulled back, gasping for air. Raven's hair was a mess, my fingers having run through it. Her cheeks were flushed, her lips puffy, and her eyes dilated so big I could barely see the blue color. Her chest heaved, her breasts moving with the action, capturing my attention. Her fingers moved to the hem of my shirt, moving over my stomach as she pushed it up.

My abs flexed with the motion, her touch sending tingles all over me. When she had it halfway, I raised it and tossed it to the floor. Taking her shirt, I lifted it, staring at her chest momentarily as I committed every detail to memory.

"You're so gorgeous, Little Bird." My voice was awed, amazed I got to hold and touch this beautiful woman.

"So are you, Otto. Is it weird I want to lick all over your chest?" Chuckling, I shook my head.

"Not at all. It's hot. I love that you say whatever you're thinking. Don't ever hold back, Raven."

Descending on her, my hands roamed her body as I explored every inch of her. When her hands did the same, I sucked in a breath, fighting back the urge to explode in my pants. Somehow, the rest of our clothing got removed and tossed to the floor. As we rolled around, laughing at one another, I realized that Rueben had left the room, giving me this moment.

I hadn't mind sharing it with him. We shared everything. But I appreciated the gesture. This memory right here belonged to Little Bird and me only.

"I don't think I'm good at sex, Otto, but I want to try with you if you do."

I blinked, not understanding what she was saying. "There's no way you're bad at sex, Little Bird."

She shrugged, her eyes dropping. "I hope not. I don't want to be. I think I've figured something out about myself, but just in case it's not true, I wanted you to be warned."

"Are you sure you want to?" I asked, leaning over her, our naked bodies pressed together.

"Yes. I want everything with you, Otto. I love you, too."

Sweeter words had never been uttered, so I pressed a kiss to her lips, holding us there. "You've just given me the best gift, Little Bird. I'll cherish it forever."

Grabbing a condom, I rolled it on and lined myself up, bracing my arms on the bed as I peered down at her. Her eyes held mine, love and desire swirling together. Slowly, I pushed in, gritting my teeth to avoid slamming into her. Once I was fully seated, I let out a breath.

"Shit, you feel amazing, Little Bird. You're so tight and wet. Does it feel okay to you?" I asked.

"Mmhmm. More," she whispered, her back arching.

Pulling back, I rocked into her as we gained our rhythm, our breathing hitching up as our bodies got used to one another. I'd been so turned on all day, anticipating the game, that it didn't take long for me to feel the tingle crawling up my back.

"How are you feeling?" I asked, trying to hold back.

"Good. So good. But maybe a little more?"

Moving my hand between us, I circled her clit as I picked up some speed, praying I could hold off until she did. Her eyes widened, her walls clenching tight a second later, as she convulsed around my cock, sending me spiraling over the edge.

We came apart together, our moans filling the room with the smell of sex. Kissing her softly, I dropped next to her and crawled off the bed to toss the condom into the trash and grabbed a towel. After I had taken care of Raven, I pulled her into my arms, kissing her cheek and feeling happier than I'd ever believed I could.

"You were right, Raven. You weren't good at sex," I whispered. Her body tensed up at my words.

"Oh. Sorry." Her eyes closed, and she frowned.

"No, you misunderstand. You weren't good. You

were amazing, mind-blowing, and incredible. Little Bird, you were everything."

Her body relaxed, melting back into mine as she peered up. "Well, um. Okay then. You were great too." She smiled softly.

I huffed like I was offended. "I just said you were mind-blowing, and all I get is 'you were great too'. Seriously, woman. We need to work on your communication skills."

Giggling, she turned in my arms. "I love you, Otto."

Kissing her softly, I snuggled back, my eyes shutting closed. "I love you, Little Bird."

Raven

UNFORTUNATELY, I HADN'T BEEN ABLE TO GET PORTER approved by the time my shift rolled around the following day, and it wasn't something Phoenix could hack without people noticing. So he was still on standby. Thankfully, Rueben had been accepted as a transfer to fill the spot of Rebecca's lover, helping to ease some of the guy's tension that I wouldn't be alone.

"I can't believe I'm relegated to the driver," Porter grumbled from the front. He'd been studying the camera footage all day, looking over the layout and creating likely scenarios of where things were, but he wanted an in-person view to verify.

"I'm sorry, fun guy. I'll keep trying."

Porter scrunched his nose, looking at me like I was nuts. I replayed what I'd said in my head, giggling.

"I'm not a mushroom, Raven." His face was drawn down into a pout, making him cuter than he probably intended.

"Too bad; you will forever be my fungi, now." I grinned, bopping his nose. His eyes shifted to me, his cheeks blushing.

"The only parts of that sentence I like are 'my' and 'forever,'" he muttered behind a smile.

"Ah, poor Fungi. I guess I'll have to kiss and make it better later." I fluttered my eyelashes, propping my chin on my hands. "And there's always the peep show. That's only for my fungi."

Porter shifted in his seat, keeping one hand on the wheel as he rubbed the hard length growing in his pants. Smirking, I leaned closer, placing my hand over his. He sucked in a breath, his hand freezing in place.

"I remember *exactly* how you like it, Fungi. Be a good boy, and I'll reward you later."

I squeezed his hand, cupping his erection in the process, and placed a kiss on his cheek before climbing into the back seat. Porter groaned, the sound sending flutters through my body. While he collected himself, I double-checked my disguise and sat back a moment before he pulled into the gated drive. Porter's eyes were heated as he watched me grab my bag and open the door.

Feeling brave, I blew him a kiss and winked. "And that was a flirt, Fungi. See you later."

Porter licked his lips. "Be safe, Raven. I look forward to the ride home."

Blushing, I stepped away from the car, my mask

falling into place as I approached the guard station. The same man from yesterday stepped out, and I waved, a smile forming.

"Hey, Mark. I hope you don't mind, but I made some extra cookies today and thought you might like some."

I held out the container, his eyes going wide at the gesture. The cookies were an easy way for me to soften him and get him acquainted with accepting things from me without question. Then later, I could add something that would buy time to escape. I didn't want to kill the guards if I didn't have to, so using Harlow's method was out of the question, but a little sleeping or compliance potion would do the trick.

Mark's eyes dropped to cookies, his eyes crinkling at the edges in happiness before he frowned.

"Oh, I shouldn't. I'm trying to watch my figure." He patted his abs, not a hint of fat in sight. Was he fishing for a compliment? Were guys insecure about their figures?

"What? You look great," I said, playing to his ego. He puffed up his chest, confirming my suspicion— time to throw the curveball, making it his choice. "But I'm not one to pressure anyone to eat something they don't want. Would it be okay to leave them here for the other guards, then? I can grab my container on my way out."

"Of course. That's awfully kind of you, Miss Molly."

"It's the least I could do. You guys work so hard to keep it safe here, and I just wanted to share my extras as a thank you." That and the bug Phoenix placed on the container. But we wouldn't mention that.

He cleared his throat, nodding. "I'll be sure and tell the guys. You have a good day now. Sean will be down to give you a ride. I alerted him when you were here."

"Now, who's the sweetest thing ever? Thank you, Mark." I handed him the container, touching his forearm as I spoke, giving him my best smile. Thankfully, it seemed to work as he blinked at me, blushing in response.

That or he had something in his eyes and needed to fart. I could never tell the difference.

Stepping away, I headed toward the iron gate as the sound of the golf cart neared. The gate squeaked as it opened, and I turned to wave one more time at Mark, our last barrier before making it safely out of here. Sean smiled at me, his rosy cheeks round as I climbed onto the golf cart.

"Good evening, Sean. How has your day been?" I asked as the golf cart started to move. I needed to learn more about the guards' outside routines, and I hoped Sean would be my answer.

"Not too shabby so far. Just a normal evening. No

bad guys in sight, Miss Molly. You're safe." He smiled over at me like he alone was ensuring my safety. *Silly boy, I could kill you before you blinked.* "You'll get to meet the new guy. He's taken Nate's place for the week. Not much of a talker, though."

I relaxed at the knowledge Rueben had made it through the first obstacle and had been accepted by the other guards as legitimate.

"I feel so much safer knowing you're out here. These grounds are so pretty. Do you get to walk them or do you have to stay in one place? It would be a shame if you did." I frowned like the thought truly upset me.

"Unfortunately, we're stationary for long bouts, only getting to walk the grounds every four hours. We take turns, so someone is walking every hour. It can get boring at times. As long as I've worked here, there's never been an attempt. I'm not sure why they go to such lengths. But it's a cushy job, so I'm not going to complain."

I smiled inwardly, collecting the data like a sponge. "I'm glad you're not in real danger then. That would be awful!" I gasped. Pleased with how well I was selling this southern belle thing. I couldn't wait to rub it in Royal's face that I'd been able to pull off a character for once. Apparently, I just needed to be in the south to woo the gents.

Sean puffed up his chest, pride blossoming out of him. "I can hold my own if needed. But between you and me," he said, leaning over to whisper, "I'm glad as well. I don't really like guns." A grimace marred his face, a shudder running through him.

I mimed, zipping my lips as the house neared. The same mean-looking guard stood at the front door, his eyes watching us.

"Who's that?" I whispered. "I don't think he likes me."

"That's Commander McDaniels. No one knows his first name. He's in charge, and I don't think he likes anyone. He's like that all the time." Then he cleared his throat, his friendly smile fading away the closer we neared the steps. Neither of us spoke again, the warning clear.

"Thanks for the ride, Sean. I left some cookies with Mark. Make sure to help yourself if you get a chance," I said softly, placing my hand on his forearm. He gulped, nodding.

"Sure thing, Miss Molly. I'll see you at the end of your shift. Have a nice night."

Picking up my bag, I realized that my distraction with the cookies had kept Mark from searching me. I couldn't guarantee it would happen each time, but it was something to take note of.

"Good evening, Commander," I said as I breezed

past the angry man. His eyes darted to me, his face impenetrable as he observed me. I didn't stick around, too worried he'd see beneath my disguise. His eyes were knowledgeable and not like the other guards who were here to do a job and nothing more. This man lived and breathed his post. He would be the hardest hurdle in our escape.

I took my time climbing the stairs, looking in rooms I hadn't been able to do the day before with Rebecca. The house was mostly empty at this time of night, giving me a chance to snoop without notice. Not that I uncovered a lot. Most contained covered furniture, a few were dusty bedrooms, and one supply closet. But what was the oddest was what I didn't discover—a room on the blueprints. Where it should've been was nothing but a smooth wall. Interesting.

Taking a picture to decipher later, I hurried to the third floor before I was noticed. Rounding the corner, I'd forgotten momentarily that Rueben was here, so used to doing it alone. I paused in my steps when his eyes landed on me. They traveled over me from head to toe, calculating every inch as he reassured himself nothing had occurred to me while I'd been out of his purview. I took a second to appreciate him in the guard uniform before continuing my trek toward the patient's room.

"Good evening. I'm Molly, the nurse working here this week."

He tilted his head in greeting, his eyes telling me everything I needed to know.

I'm glad you're here.

Be safe, and I'll be out here watching.

You're not alone.

I brushed past, my hand trailing over his, needing that little bit of contact to settle my nerves. It was odd having to consider others' safety, but as strange as it was, I didn't hate it. In fact, it was nice to have someone supporting me. For the first time, I didn't feel so alone. I'd never realized how lonely these jobs were until now. I'd been moving from a state of aloneness at the mansion to one on jobs. The scenery changed, but that was it.

Before this mission, I thought my life was close to perfect. A house full of sisters, a job I enjoyed, and time to putter around my chemistry set while watching *Phoenix Hospital*. It had been my constant in the past twenty years, and I'd never thought to question it. When Harlow and Ivory had left, I'd thought they were nuts. But now, I could understand the appeal.

Walking over to my patient, I kept my eyes off his face to prevent my hatred for him bubbling to the surface. I had to be here for a few days before I could kill him, so I had to pretend to care about his well-being in the meantime. For now, he was my patient, and I'd only focus on his chart and chest unless otherwise necessary.

I reviewed the notes from the daytime nurse, spotting an error in her calculations. The urge to correct burned in me, but I decided to leave it, knowing it would help me in the long run if she made mistakes.

Going through the motions, I studied his vitals and recorded them. I administered his medications and inspected the machines, ensuring they were functioning properly. Once that was finished, I scanned the documents into the computer and uploaded them where the doctor could view them. The whole process took about thirty minutes.

Now it was time to test the app and the security response time. Sitting down, I pulled a book out of my bag and sat back with it like I was reading before I hit the app on my phone that scrambled the cameras. It would give me a few minutes loop to see how closely they monitored this room. I watched my phone as the timer counted down, waiting for anything to happen. After five minutes, I sighed in relief when no one burst through the doors.

I did the same routine throughout the night, placing myself in different positions around the room. At no point did anyone appear to know what was occurring, giving me confidence the app worked without anyone the wiser.

Around midnight, the door Rebecca had taken me

through opened as a woman wrapped in a silk robe with fur around the hem and sleeves glided into the room. She wore heels and pearls, her hair coiffed to perfection, and even from here, I could smell her floral perfume. She paused when she noticed me, her eyes scrutinizing every inch of me.

I didn't know if she saw me as a threat or just that she didn't recognize me, but her stare unnerved me as she swept it over my frame.

"Who are you?" she asked, the martini glass in her hand swishing. She was the epitome of a bored fifties housewife.

"I'm Molly. I'm filling in for Rebecca while she's on vacation."

Her eyes narrowed, but she nodded like she'd known this but wanted to test me. Her gaze left me, swiveling to who I assumed was her husband since she hadn't introduced herself. But I'd seen her face in photos, and there was no mistaking she was Bethany Mathis, or Bethany Duke as she was called here.

"How is he?" she asked, flicking her eyes to me briefly.

"No changes. I uploaded everything ten minutes ago." She nodded, again like she already knew but wanted to hear me say it.

"You can go on a break. I'll watch him," she murmured, setting her martini down as she sat on the edge of his bed. I froze, not having expected this.

"Go," she said, her voice harder when I hadn't moved.

Placing my stethoscope over the chair, I made a rash decision to leave it so we could record what occurred while I was gone. Maybe she would give away some information. If anything, I'd at least have a better idea of her routine to use later.

Slipping out the side door, I peeked out the side to see if Rueben was still there. His eyes lifted when he spotted me, and I mouthed "break" to him. Nodding, he raised a mouthpiece and mumbled something in it before turning to me and motioning for me to follow. He took us down a few hallways before he opened a door and directed me in before closing it and locking it behind him.

His hands cupped my cheeks, his eyes searching mine. I let him, somehow knowing he needed to after hours apart.

"I'm okay, Ruebear." I patted his hands, his chest releasing a big breath at my words. He nodded, bending down to lift me. My arms wrapped around his neck as my legs circled his waist. "Hi." I giggled, loving how he always wanted me near.

"Better," he whispered, giving me a rare smile that lifted his beard. My hands combed through his hair, soothing some of his anxiety. Rueben's eyes closed at my touch, his shoulders dropping. Suddenly, his pouty lips crashed to mine, their softness shocking as he demanded entrance. My back pressed against the door as I clung to him, his body melding with mine.

I lost track of time as we stood there kissing, exchanging breaths as we twirled our tongues, communicating with one another in a new way. My body rubbed up against Rueben, wanting more from him. His thick hands squeezed my butt, moving me occasionally against him. It was a slow torture. One I knew we didn't have the time for, but I couldn't bring myself to rush him. Everything with him felt like a slow dance, each step placed with perfect precision. I didn't want to step out of line or cause him to stumble, so I'd keep the pace and follow his lead.

When Rueben pulled away, I whimpered, not ready to lose the feel of his lips against mine. He smirked, the look so foreign on his face I almost didn't believe it.

"Later," he whispered, placing one more brief kiss before setting me down.

He put me behind him before he opened the door, peeking his head out. Finding it clear, he opened the door wider and motioned for me to follow. I showed him the back way, waving bye as I returned to the room. I took a quick second to check my disguise in the mirror, smoothing down a few hairs that had come loose. Adjusting my glasses, I took a deep breath as I entered the room, praying I didn't look like I'd been thoroughly kissed for the last half hour.

Halting, I frowned as I scanned the room and found it empty; no phantom wife in sight. Curiosity bubbled up, and I suddenly couldn't wait to watch the footage and discover what Mrs. Duke did.

Now, I just had to survive the rest of my shift without wanting to touch myself. It definitely would make the ride home more interesting.

Porter

THOUGHTS OF RAVEN AND THE FLIRTY THINGS SHE'D SAID ON the drive to the mansion filled my mind for the rest of the evening. I'd been upset when I hadn't gotten clearance. I never thought I had control issues until I wasn't the one with boots on the ground making the decisions.

Though that could be more about Raven than control. I wanted to be with her, and being stuck at the home base wasn't going well for me.

"Porter, I'm about to be the only Hardy in this Crew if you don't stop," my brother hissed, narrowing his eyes at me as I tossed a ball against the wall.

Where I was used to being on the inside, Phoenix preferred his computers and working alone—the introverted weirdo.

"Ugh," I groaned. "How do you do this? I've only been sidelined for one day, and I'm going mad." I leaned back and tossed the ball into the air, forgetting that Phoenix had just threatened me.

"Believe me; I'm not enjoying this either. Your constant chattering is throwing off my rhythm. I feel like I'm missing something, but I can't put my finger on it," he mused, staring at the screen in front of him.

"Argh, leave it for now. You'll see it better if you step away," I encouraged, but really, I just wanted him to talk to me. My brother rubbed his eyes and blinked but eventually nodded and scooted back. "So, it's our turn with Raven tonight. What should we do?" I asked, instantly perking up now that I had an audience.

Phoenix sat up, his interest piqued. "Do you think she'd let me wash her hair? She seemed to really enjoy it when Rueben brushed it. I bet she has the cutest toes. I want to paint them. Yeah. Let's pamper her, Bro."

His idea had merit, as I thought it over. We'd get to touch her and dote on her, two things I enjoyed a lot. Seeing Raven smile because of something I did was the best reward. Phoenix and I hadn't grown up with good parents, only teaching us how to steal and con others before we knew it was wrong. Back then, the only things either of us could give freely were smiles, so we didn't share them with anyone.

Meeting Otto and Rueben in the group home, we'd learned to trust and smile again through their friendship, knowing the true value of their love. And even after all the items we'd stolen over the years—all the riches we'd uncovered—none of it felt as good as earning a smile from our brothers.

And now Raven.

She was like us in many ways, growing up without a real family and relying on herself. She deserved to be catered to and pampered so she'd know how special she was. Raven gave out smiles easily, believing the best in people, but I wanted to earn the ones that reached her eyes and felt like a giant beam of sunshine.

"Do we have any of that stuff?" I scratched my jeans in thought, my body unable to stop moving. Phoenix shrugged his shoulders, lost in thought now. He was either hyper-fixating on the case, trying to solve the thing he missed, or focused on Raven. It could go either way.

"What do you think will happen after this case?" he asked, stopping my movement.

"What do you mean?" My body froze as fear and insecurity rose their ugly heads. Was she going to leave like all the others? How could I prove to her that we'd love her forever? What more did I need to do to show her we were worth it?

"Stop, Port. It's not like that. I just mean, do you think she'll keep taking assassin jobs? Or will she join us? Should we retire? Will we all live together? Raven is with us. I'm just curious about what that will look like. For once, I'm excited about the future. I can see one with her." He smiled softly, the gesture changing his face.

My brother had always been the more subdued twin, careful who he trusted with his heart and kept people at arm's length. I, on the other hand, played the odds game, scooping up as many friends as possible, hoping one of them would work out. To see him confident in our relationship with Raven quelled my fear, trusting his judgment far over my own. I also didn't want to lose that smile on his face.

"Whatever we do, it's going to be a blast. I'm going to grab some things at the store before I pick up our girlfriend. Any requests?"

"Get purple nail polish. I want to see her toes in that color. And lots of snacks. It will be fun to feed them to her."

Chuckling, I stood and patted him on the back. "Will do, Brother. I'll see you in a few hours."

He nodded, returning to his computer and opening a new tab, his fingers flying over the keys before I even stepped foot from the room.

AFTER SPENDING a small fortune at the corner pharmacy on things to share with Raven, I eagerly drove toward the mansion when it was time to retrieve my cutie-pie.

My leg bounced the entire ride, wondering if she meant what she'd said earlier about rewarding me. I'd tried not to think about it too much, worried I'd walk around with a hard-on all night if I had.

But now that I was back in the car with the antici-pated reward hanging in the air, she was all I could think about. Raven had slotted into our life so easily. It sounded insane when I thought about how strongly I felt about her after only a few days, but I couldn't deny my emotions were real. I was falling in love with the girl.

Giddy excitement bubbled in my stomach as I turned into the driveway, getting out to talk to the guard. My friendly demeanor helped to lower defenses, giving me that extra edge to distract someone when I needed to steal something right under their nose.

"How's it going, man?" I asked, waving as I neared with a perfect smile on my face.

"Pretty good. You the only Uber driver in town?" he asked, lifting his eyebrow. I could spot an informa-tion dig a mile away—this guy liked Nurse Molly and wanted to know if I was competition. As much as it killed me, I bit my tongue, knowing for her cover, it worked better. But the words tasted bitter in my mouth.

"Ha. It seems that way, huh? Apparently, I'm the only one willing to drive out here." I shrugged, placing my hands in my back pockets. See, I'm unthreatening and nonintrusive. Just a friendly guy here.

The guard crossed his arms over his barrel chest, his shoulders dropping a millimeter. The sun peeked over the trees, the morning upon us, and coated everything in pinks and purples. I peered around, taking in the place in the daylight. The fences were high and would be impossible to climb without a ladder. I didn't spot any guards this close, but they probably figured the one at the gate would stop most people.

"Who lives here?" I asked, curious what the rumor mill was. I kept my friendly stance, glancing back at the guard.

"Some rich guy. They don't tell us much."

So that's how you're going to play it?

"What do you think someone does to earn this much money? I'm never going to achieve this in my life," I lied, pretending to act impressed. Yeah, no. Blood money didn't interest me.

The guard blew out a breath. "It is pretty insane. They even have gold shitters." He chuckled, warming up to me.

"You're kidding, right?" I asked, lifting my eyebrow in skepticism. "I always assumed people made that stuff up."

"Hand to God. I've seen them for myself. My buddy works during the day and snuck me in when they were out of town. There's a floor only a few people have access to where all their real expensive stuff is."

"Whoa. You have the best job. Much better than driving people around all day. Though, the nurse isn't too bad. She's nice."

"Yeah, she is. I think she has a sweet spot for me," he whispered, grinning like he'd won the lottery. If Raven's affections were true, then he would've. But I knew they were nothing but a role she played; the real girl was all mine and my brothers.

A golf cart neared the gate before I could ask him anything else, waving as I moved back to the car. My heart lightened as she appeared, her eyes glancing at mine before she spoke to both guards, grabbing the container she'd brought earlier. Climbing back into the car, I pulled closer so she could get in. Both of the men waved at her, watching us leave.

"I think Molly has a fan club," I teased, glancing at her. She sagged against the back seat, rubbing her forehead. She snorted at my comment, her eyes meeting mine.

"Good. Means my plan is working. How was your day, Fungi?" she asked, smiling at me as she pulled the pins out. I secretly loved and hated the nickname.

"Boring without you. I annoyed Otto so much that he pawned me off to Phoenix, who only tolerated me for five minutes before he was yelling. By then, I made it a game to see how angry I could get him."

"Poor Phoenix," she mumbled, her head down as she pulled off the wig.

"Poor Porter!" I scoffed. She giggled, and I shifted my legs, my cock liking the sound way too much. "I missed you, Cutie-Pie. Did you discover anything?"

"Maybe. We can look at the footage later. But first, your reward." She smirked at me in the mirror, her shirt disappearing from her body in the next second.

I groaned, my eyes struggling to stay on the empty road and not her luscious curves. "I don't know what's worse. Seeing you topless when I can't touch you, or you covering up your beautiful body and hiding it from me."

"I selfishly like how you sound when you see me naked, Porter. You give me the confidence to show you." Her eyelids fluttered closed, her neck and cheeks flushing pink from her admission.

"God, you're perfect, Raven. I'm glad I can give you that. I'll never stop responding that way, baby." My voice came out huskier, my throat dry.

She finished changing her clothes and climbed up front, her smile radiant as she leaned over and kissed my cheek. Raven rested her head on my shoulder, her hands roaming over my body. I kept my eyes straight ahead, taking deep breaths as my whole body responded to her touch.

"Rave, you're going to make me come in my pants

if you keep that up," I warned, the sound throaty and deep.

"What about in my mouth?"

Before I could respond, she unzipped my jeans and reached into my boxers. Her soft hand slid over my hard cock, and I saw stars. My hands gripped the steering wheel, my knuckles white as I squeezed. If I looked down, I would crash us into something. Breathing deeply, I focused on the deserted road as Raven tried to kill me. When her lips wrapped around the tip, I pressed my foot down on the gas, needing to be home ten minutes ago.

Swerving onto the road, I spun into the driveway and slammed on the brakes as she took me down her throat. My heart pounded in my chest, my muscles so tight that it took no time for my balls to draw up as tiny pinpricks built at the base of my spine. Threading my hands in her hair, I allowed myself to look down, needing to see Raven in action so I could burn it to my memory forever.

"Fuck, Rave. Watching you take me so easy is hot as hell."

Her eyes tilted up, her lashes long against her cheek as she blinked at me, wearing a smile. Fuck. I loved that smile.

"I'm close, baby. If you don't want me to come down your throat, I need you to move."

When she didn't back away, I gave in to my need to

let go as the orgasm rushed over me like an earth-quake and shook my entire body. Groaning, I screamed out my release as I unloaded in her wet mouth, her tongue licking up every drop I spilled.

"How was it?" she asked, some hesitation in her voice.

I mumbled, moving my arms to emphasize how I'd lost the power to think. "You broke my brain. I don't think I've ever come so hard before. Shit, despite the fact you almost killed me, that was hot as hell."

"You promise?" she asked.

"Uh-huh. I'd never lie to you, Raven. Promise."

She climbed into my lap, her core sitting right over my exposed dick. Raven wrapped her arms around me, kissing me as she hugged me tight. I smoothed her hair back, peering into her eyes. She was so confident at times; I didn't notice right away when she needed reassurance.

"Even though it's too soon to say, I'm a jump-all-in type of guy and a hopeless romantic, so just hear me out. I love you, Raven. I just want you to know that. You're perfect just the way you are, Cutie-pie."

Her eyes became shiny as she blinked away tears, her hands moving to cup my jaw. "I love you, Porter, my fungi."

The most effortless smile I ever felt spread across my cheeks, my whole being radiating out as I stared at the girl who owned my heart.

"Phoenix and I want to pamper you. We have stuff to do your toenails, wash your hair, and a face mask. Plus, all the junk food you could possibly want. Will you let us take care of you tonight, baby?"

"You want to do all that for me?" she asked, her hands running through my hair. I closed my eyes, groaning at how good it felt.

"I want to do everything for you, Raven. I want to love you, dote on you, and show you how amazing I think you are. This is my love language."

"What's a love language?" she scrunched her nose, the action so cute I reached out and grabbed it.

"I'll tell you all about it in the bath. Come on, Phoenix's waiting, and I want to get you in before Otto tries to steal you."

"Okay. I'd love to spend the morning with you."

I tapped her leg. "You going to let me go?"

"Nope." She shook her head, her hair tickling my nose. Chuckling, I didn't have it in me to make her move. If my girl wanted to be carried, then I would.

"Okay, but first, I have to put my cockasaurus away."

"Why am I not surprised you named your dick?" she let go, moving back to help me tuck my semi-hard cock back into my pants. She gave it a little pat on its head. "That's a good boy."

"Did you just praise my cock, Rave?"

She shrugged her shoulders, her cheeks blushing as she hid them in my neck.

"I think you just unlocked a new kink for me, baby."

"Oh?" she asked, her brows creasing in thought.

I stepped out of the car, careful not to drop her as I grabbed her bag and the one I had in the trunk. She kept her legs wrapped around me, and I half expected her to be part koala. Raven leaned forward, nipping my earlobe between her teeth. The slight pain sent a jolt through me, and I stopped and sucked in a breath.

"I'm suddenly famished for my favorite type of sandwich. Are you going to be good and stuff me full?"

Holy shit. Raven's dirty talking was hot as fuck. My semi-hard dick thickened at her words, my legs moving before my mind caught up.

Raven

MUCH TO PORTER'S DISMAY—AND MY OWN, IF I WAS honest—Otto intercepted us in the kitchen and insisted we all eat a meal together. It was too cute of a request for me to deny. Plus, I'd missed him too and wanted to know how his day was. Since I'd gotten to spend my day with Rueben, and the twins got me the rest of the "my" evening, Otto stole me so he could be the one to feed me.

"I feel like a baby," I pouted, crossing my arms. Secretly, I loved it, but it felt like I shouldn't, so I wanted to complain a little.

"Oh, well, I guess we could get you a chair," Otto said, moving to place me in the seat next to him. I hadn't expected him to give in, my eyes widening as I clasped his arms.

"Never mind. I'm good here."

Otto chuckled, burrowing his nose into my hair. His laughter vibrated through me, sending goose-bumps across my skin. I couldn't remember ever being this happy before. I loved the other Belladonnas. They had been my family when I didn't have one, giving me a reason to wake up each day. Man taught me how to be strong in every way, giving me the reassurance I'd always be able to take care of myself. For a scared little girl who'd mostly known violence and scary men, it had been a comfort and a promise I'd never be vulnerable again.

I owed a lot to my sisters and Man, but I could see now what I'd been missing. Maybe what we'd all been too scared to truly face—love.

Glancing around the table at the four guys, I watched as they talked with one another, laughed and joked about random things, and shared the details of their day as they ate. The camaraderie and companionship there was authentic, and I knew there would never be anything that compared to the four guys who'd captured my heart.

"Alright, we'll stay the course and keep finding more holes in their defenses. I'll go over the stuff you recorded today with Rueben. Have fun with the twins." Otto kissed me, his hands squeezing my hips before he passed me over to my silent giant. Smiling up at him, I pulled his head down so I could give him a kiss goodnight.

"Sleep well," I whispered a second before Phoenix grabbed me and swung me into his arms.

"You're ours now, Cupcake."

"Cupcake?" I asked with a giggle.

He shrugged his shoulders, pure joy radiating off him as he marched us to the bedroom he shared with his twin. We stepped into their bathroom; the jacuzzi tub filled with bubbles, and a girly squeal left me. Phoenix beamed at me, his eyes shining so bright, I got momentarily lost in them.

"Welcome to Twin Spa, where all your needs will be met with a smile. First, we have a luxurious bubble bath with lavender oil to make your muscles relax and rejoice," Porter said in a game show voice.

"Sounds amazing. You're joining me, right?" I asked with hope.

The twins looked at one another, and I thought I was about to get my wish, but then Porter shook his head. "I've got to set up the last part. Phoenix will take care of you, Cutie-pie."

"You sure?" Phoenix asked, his forehead wrinkling.

"Yep. Don't get too sleepy, though. There are lots of activities planned." Porter winked as he stepped out of view. Phoenix shrugged and helped me undress, his eyes drinking me in with each new inch of skin I uncovered.

"You're absolutely breathtaking, Raven. I'm almost mad at you for hiding your sweet thighs under skirts, but you look too cute in them for me to be that mad." He groaned, his hands squeezing thin air.

"Your brother said almost the same thing." Blushing, I slid into the tub under the warm bubbly water. It sloshed over my skin like a gentle caress, soothing me like they'd said. "This feels amazing."

I leaned back against the side and crooked my finger to get Phoenix to join me. He blinked out of his fog, removing his clothes in a mad rush. My eyes tracked over his golden skin, taking in his abs and the Adonis belt that literally made me drool. He shucked his shorts in one swoop, his meaty cock springing to life once it was free. I'd felt it behind me the other night, but seeing it was different.

He sank into the water, letting out a sigh as it enveloped him. Tugging on my foot, he pulled me closer until my legs wrapped around him and his hard cock nestled under me.

"I'm not sure if I'm going to be able to focus on bathing you, Cupcake. You're too distracting."

My hands explored his chest, running over the tattoos. He shivered beneath my touch, bringing a smile to my face.

"What else is there to do in a bath?" I asked, tilting my head.

"I wanted to wash your hair," he whispered, lifting the heavy strands off my neck. It seemed important to him, so I shrugged and turned around.

"Okay."

With soft and careful hands, Phoenix lifted a cup I hadn't noticed into the water and poured it over my head. His hands were gentle as he took care with each strand, writing me a love letter with his touch. My body quivered with each brush of his fingers, the anticipation of what he'd do ramping up my arousal.

"Have you done this before?" I asked, needing to distract myself.

"A long, long time ago." His voice was sad, and I wished I'd never brought it up. "Has Porter told you anything about our past?"

"No. Just how you met the other two at the group home."

His fingers ran down my back, lifting the hair out of the water as he rinsed it. "We weren't always homeless. We had a home and a family once. They weren't the best parents, but they tried. We were taught early how to steal and con in order to survive. It was fun back then, though Porter probably still feels it is. He's always been more outgoing, more friendly. He likes the adrenaline high of pulling something off, whereas I prefer to uncover information safe behind my computer screen."

"It's not bad to want to be safe," I said, not liking how sad his voice was.

"I know, Cupcake." He kissed my shoulder, his lips warm against my skin. "Thank you for seeing who I am."

I smiled, happy I could give him that.

"Our parents would make stealing a game, giving

us different tasks and objectives. We didn't know they were petty criminals at the time, always looking to score the next big thing. It was their greed that got them killed. Them and our little sister, Penelope."

I gasped, wanting to turn around to comfort him, but Phoenix held me in place. My shoulders sagged, but I accepted he didn't want me to soothe him right then. When I didn't try to move, he released me, his hands returning to washing my hair. He was quiet for a while; the only sound was the water as he scooped it up and poured it over my head.

"She must've been about four at the time, so happy she'd been able to steal some bread. Our parents patted her on the head, telling her to grab something bigger next time. I hated how her face fell. Penny was pure of light, a golden angel, and I wanted to make her happy. So I learned how to fix girls' hair so I could make hers look as pretty as the other kids. After a day of scavenging, Porter and I would bathe her, and I'd wash her hair and fix it. I even stole some ribbons once to give her the pigtails she wanted. We helped her learn how to spot easier marks, teaching her all the tricks that we knew. She was smart and was soon able to pickpockets like a pro."

His words were laced with sadness and pride as he remembered his sister, his movements methodical now as he lathered shampoo in my hair.

"Our parents saw the potential in using a cute

little girl to their advantage, taking her on jobs more and more. They stole from the wrong person, and he came after them, setting our house on fire while they slept. Porter had wanted to scout that night, hoping to earn some favor with our parents. When we returned, the blaze had overtaken the entire house. They had no chance of making it out. We ran then, knowing the cops and social services would be looking for us. Porter became overprotective of me, feeling responsible for Penny's death. But I never blamed him. We were all we had left, and he was the other half of me."

He paused, the silence empty as he collected himself. Tears streamed down my face, heartbroken for him and Porter and the pain they'd lived through. None of us had easy lives, but it bonded us together.

Phoenix finished rinsing my hair and twirled it into one big piece, placing it over my shoulder. His hands squeezed my biceps, his fingers spreading over my skin.

"I hated my parents for being greedy and taking more than they needed. For using us to advance their means. I didn't want to steal anymore after that, but there wasn't much choice living on the streets. Despite my desire to stop, it was a hard habit to break. I often wondered if I purposely got caught by Otto. As good as we were, a ten-year-old boy shouldn't have been able to catch us. I saw something in him, a kindred pain. When we heard your stories about giving back to others, it changed things for me. I wanted to be better than my parents. I wanted to make Penelope proud and help others who needed it. Even before I knew you, you changed my life, Raven."

Phoenix gently turned me around, his eyes boring into mine. Our bodies melded together, my arms wrapping around his neck. I wanted to hold him and take some of his pain, not caring that we were both naked. My fingernails ran up the back of his neck, his body shuddering in my arms.

"Finding you now, you've managed to save me and Porter again."

"What do you mean?" I asked.

"We had a purpose but no real joy. Your lightness and purity permeate into all of us, changing us into something new. Every single one of us has softened, smiled, and laughed more since we found you. You showed a bunch of thieves the one thing they could never steal but had to earn—your heart."

"You guys do the same for me, you know? Show me it's okay to be vulnerable and depend on others. You might have earned my heart, but you brought mine back to life, resuscitating it from the hollow lump it had become. So, I'll be your heart, but you're my reason to beat Phoenix."

"Leave it to you two to make a confession of love medical," Porter interjected from the doorway.

Phoenix groaned, his forehead meeting mine. "Bro. I hadn't gotten there yet. Way to ruin the mood."

"Nonsense. I came to rescue you both from becoming prunes and tempt you to the next section of Twin Spa, filled with all the girlie products anyone could ever need. Time to test your facial skills, Cutie-Pie."

Phoenix coughed under me, his cock twitching against me as his hands gripped me tighter. "Not cool, Bro," he groaned. Porter snickered, walking toward me with a towel.

"My turn, baby."

I couldn't help but glance at Phoenix's dick as I stood, finding it growing hard in the water. He fisted it once, and I licked my lips, wondering if he tasted like his brother.

"On second thought, let's circle back to that. It's time to give our girl the sandwich she's been craving."

Porter dried me off, lingering over my private areas with his touches. My nipples pebbled, heat enveloping my body as desire rose back up. A moan escaped me as his hands moved to my breasts, abandoning the towel.

"She's dripping, brother. Time to test out your tongue skills."

My legs were spread a second later, my ass parted by Phoenix as he licked up my center from behind. Porter sucked a nipple into his mouth, my hands gripping his forearms as my legs shook. I glanced down, watching Phoenix's tongue peek out from my folds before one of his fingers plunged into me.

"Ahh," I whimpered, my pussy gushing at his touch.

"She likes what you're doing, Nix. She's close."

Porter pinched my nipples, massaging my breasts as he took my mouth with his lips. I lost my surroundings as the twins pleasured me, sending my body into overload. My orgasm slammed into me, my cries swallowed by Porter as my legs gave out on me. Someone picked me up, carrying me a few feet before placing me on something soft.

The cold air kissed my flushed skin, tiny droplets of water still pebbled on me. Phoenix came into view a second later as his body covered mine. His hands roamed over me, my body convulsing under his touch, still sensitive from my orgasm. His arms wrapped around me, turning so we rolled over, my body on top of his.

"I want to watch you ride me, Raven. Will you?"

I nodded, willing to give this sweet boy anything he wanted. He lifted up on his elbows, rolling on a condom his brother threw at him. My eyes trailed over his cock, taking it in fully now that it was right before me.

Different hands ran down my arms from behind, a naked body pressing against me. "You're not ready for us both to take you at once. So, tonight, I'll wait my turn until I can fill you up."

I whimpered, his words making me aroused. I didn't know what he meant about being unable to take them both, but I trusted he knew better than I did. Porter lifted my hips, spreading my pussy as he directed me over Phoenix, helping me to lower onto his brother.

My head fell back, my toes curling as my walls stretched over him. I was panting by the time I was fully seated. Bracing my hands on his abs, I took a few seconds to get my breathing under control. The video I'd watched the other day returned to my mind, and I moved my hips, twirling them as I jerked forward. Phoenix groaned, his hands gripping my thighs. Porter covered my back, one hand fondling my breast as the other plucked at my clit, urging me on in my movements.

"Holy fuck, you're so wet, Raven. My cock is gliding in and out of you so easily. I love that we turn you on this much. Each little noise and response you give us is a gift."

Leaning my head on Porter's shoulder, I rocked forward, keeping my hips moving as I pushed on. I found a good rhythm, the three of us working together as I chased my next orgasm. This one crawled up my back, spidering like fireworks as it detonated.

"Ahhh, I'm coming." My muscles convulsed as my

pussy clenched around Phoenix. Porter pinched my nipple, sucking on my neck as I screamed. Phoenix reared up, slamming into me one more time before he stilled, grunting out his release.

Before I could recover, my ass was lifted off Phoenix, and my body pushed down onto him. Phoenix cupped my face, staring at me fondly as he gathered my wet hair off my forehead. Porter lined himself up, pushing into me, sending me crashing into Phoenix's lips. My nipples brushed against his chest, their pebbled peaks sensitive to the motion and sending tendrils of desire through me.

Phoenix kept kissing me as Porter pistoned into me from behind; their actions were in sync, and it felt like they were one person. Phoenix dropped one hand between us, rubbing my clit as my orgasm built again. Whimpering, I squeezed his shoulders as my body prepared to crash. My eyes closed as stars appeared, my body boneless as I came down from the high.

When I opened my eyes, I was between the twins; their bodies pressed into me. It was the best kind of hug.

"You back with us, Cupcake?" Phoenix asked.

Nodding, I smiled, kissing his lips. "Yeah. I think I'm ruined for any other sandwiches, though."

The twins chuckled, their hands caressing me.

"I love you, Raven. I wanted to say it earlier, but butthead interrupted."

"I love you too, Phoenix. I love you both, actually." Turning my head to catch Porter's face. Happiness peered back at me. "I love you, Porter."

"I love you too, beautiful girl." He placed a kiss on my lips, pulling back as he smiled.

"Come on. The night isn't over. It's time for the rest of Twin Spa. And the best part, no clothing required."

Laughing, I let them pull me up as we piled onto the blankets Porter had set up on the ground. He hit play on the TV, and a movie started. Phoenix sprayed some detangler in my hair, taking his time as he combed through the semi-dry locks. Porter and I did face masks while he did that, laughing at one another and trying to get the goop onto other parts of our bodies.

"Your pec needs a face mask." I giggled, rubbing some on him.

"Hmm, I think yours does too."

Once Phoenix had my hair combed out, he eagerly moved down to my feet and placed them on his lap. I watched him as he painted my toenails, so focused on his task. Porter leaned into me, his lips brushing against my ear.

"Thank you for bringing my brother back. He never got over Penny's death. You've given him a reason to smile again, to step away from his computer."

Blushing, I nodded, not sure what to say. As much

as they believed I'd given them, they'd given me just as much.

The three of us finished the movie in a cuddle pile, eating junk food. "I think Twin Spa is my favorite place," I sighed. Porter and Phoenix grinned, their happiness my favorite part.

Raven

THE NEXT FEW DAYS FELL INTO AN EASY PATTERN. PORTER took me to work, Rueben kissed me within an inch of my life during lunch, and I slowly altered the meds to show a decline in our patient. When we returned home, we'd have a meal as a family and discuss the case until I'd go off to spend time with someone. They never seemed jealous, just eager for their friend and brother to connect with me.

Otto had gone through the camera footage but hadn't uncovered anything from Mrs. Duke's daily visits. She'd sit with him in his bed, holding his hand, as she spoke with him about things from the past. Then she'd silently cry against his chest for ten minutes before wiping her eyes and kissing his cheek. I felt sorry for her despite my initial thoughts about her and hoped my actions would give her peace.

Thankfully, my alterations were enough to get clearance for a doctor to attend with me on the second to last day on the job. We'd agreed that if it hadn't come through, I would still proceed with our plan, knowing we were running out of time. So we all sighed in relief at the approval—especially Porter. He was ready for action.

"You ready, Dr. Romano?" I teased.

Phoenix snorted from the front as he drove us to the mansion today. He had to pretend to be Porter since the guards had gotten used to seeing him drive me daily. We'd picked the name from *Phoenix Hospital* as an inside joke since he was our favorite doctor, despite the show doing him dirty.

Porter pulled at the top of his scrubs, not liking how the material felt against his skin. We'd given him a brown wig, a pair of glasses and added some weight around his middle, hoping it would distract anyone from recognizing him—especially since Phoenix would be fulfilling the driver role. He wore a long sleeve shirt under the scrub top to cover his tattoos, using thick concealer on his hands. Once we made it into the house, it wouldn't be as necessary, but getting past the gate would be the first hurdle.

"I'm just glad I finally get to do something. I've felt useless on this case."

"Nonsense. I've enjoyed our drives to and from work." I winked at him, causing his cheeks to flush as he wiggled in his seat.

"Those have been good," he said, clearing his throat. "Don't forget you gotta be friendly to Mark. Ask him about the game last night. We talked about it yesterday."

"I can be friendly," Phoenix mumbled, frowning. "What game?"

Porter sighed, slouching down in the seat so he looked shorter. "It's basketball season, bro. You know what, just pretend you have to take a shit or something and leave. You'll give yourself away."

A giggle escaped me as I remembered a story Harlow had told me about her last mission. She'd been cornered by her new bestie in the bathroom, so she used farting sounds to distract her while she snuck out the window.

"I can do it, Bro. Have some faith. You don't have to protect me anymore," Phoenix gritted out, his voice stern and hurt.

"It's not that, Nix—" Porter started but was cut off as the car pulled into the driveway. "Good luck. I love you, man." Porter squeezed his shoulder before sliding out of the door. I did the same, fighting the urge to kiss his cheek. Phoenix gave me a grateful nod in the rearview, a determined look on his face.

"Hey, Mark. How's your day been?" I asked as we walked up. He smiled at me, his eyes shifting to Porter.

"It's better now. Who's your friend?" he asked, assessing Porter, his eyes narrowing. Crap. I guess we hadn't made Porter non-threatening enough.

"Oh, this is Dr. Romano. He's here to run some

extra tests on Mr. Duke." I leaned forward conspiratorially. "Between you and me, I'm more of a doctor than this guy." I rolled my eyes, scoffing. Mark smiled at that, dropping his protective stance.

"Guess what I made today?" I shook the box of laced brownies, opening the lid to let the addictive chocolate aroma escape.

"It's no use saying no, is it?" He chuckled and took the box, setting it inside. So far, our plan was off to a great start.

"Will we be let in anytime soon? I have a patient to see," Porter drawled, sighing loudly. Mark gave me a look, rolling his eyes as he grabbed his wand and scanned it over him. I sucked in a breath as he patted him down but didn't seem to think anything was off about the extra poundage around his waist. Phew.

The golf cart neared on time, and Phoenix swooped in to distract Mark from checking me. Not that he had in a few days, but we definitely didn't want him to today. We'd sewn Porter's tools into my bag, knowing we'd need them to get into the safe.

Mark spotted the golf cart hitting the gate as he chatted with Phoenix. I had to admit, I'd also been a little nervous, wondering if Phoenix could pull off Porter's carefree spirit, but as I walked to the golf cart, I knew I'd been wrong to doubt him. Porter seemed to think the same, his shoulders relaxing as he climbed onto the back of the cart.

"Hey, Sean. This is Dr. Romano." I leaned in to whisper, Sean's cheeks turning rosier than usual at my nearness. "I told them I play a doctor on TV, and he wasn't needed, but they didn't believe me."

Sean chuckled, shaking his head at me. I grinned, settling into the seat as the cart took off. I didn't usually get to interact with people on a job for this long and, therefore, never thought about them after it ended. But this job had been different. Both with my guys working with me and getting to know the people here. If this had been my real life, I'd garner to say I'd made friends.

It was an odd thing to realize. That it had taken me until I was twenty-six to make friends, but it was true. Being a Belladonna was isolating in a lot of ways. At first, I'd been excited to meet the other girls and train with them, hoping to make my treehouse of friends a reality.

But a bunch of broken girls living in a mansion, a treehouse of friends it did not make.

I knew Man had the best of intentions, rescuing us from worse fates. But for the first time, since I'd met him, I wondered what it would've been like if I hadn't gotten into his car that day.

But I guess in the end, it didn't matter. I did get in that car and traveled down the assassin path that led me to my guys. And that wasn't something I'd ever regret. What it did do, though, was make me reconsider some preconceived notions I held about myself. Maybe I could do something different after all this? Perhaps I didn't have to be an assassin for the rest of my life if I didn't want to. The desire to get this job done doubled with an unknown future to look forward to.

"Any new gossip today?" I asked Sean, remembering I needed to focus on the now before I got lost in the future.

"Nothing exciting. Commander has been coming down on some of the guys more. He's suspicious of someone. I'm not sure why. He grilled that new guy for an hour earlier. But he's tougher than me; didn't say a thing, just watched the Commander as he ranted at him."

Fear sank in my stomach, and I glanced back at Porter. Shit. Was Rueben okay? I'd blow up this whole house before I left without him.

"He needs one of my brownies," I teased, hoping it sounded light. Sean chuckled, rubbing his stomach. But seriously, he did.

"I'm going to miss your treats, Miss Molly. Have a good day."

I smiled at him as we stepped off the golf cart and headed toward the door. The Commander was in place, his eyes trailing over me as I neared.

"Good evening, Commander. I brought some brownies today. Make sure you get one," I greeted, just like I'd done all week. He didn't reply as per usual, his eyes watching me the entire time. He was still our biggest hindrance, and I prayed our plan worked.

Once inside, I breathed a small sigh of relief we'd passed through but hurried to the room, needing to see Rueben was there. His giant frame came into view as I crested the top of the stairs, my heart slowing at his presence.

"You're okay," I breathed, stopping short when I saw his face. Rage burned through my blood as hot as the coals of Kilauea, the hottest volcano in the world.

"Who. Did. This?" My words were clipped, my hands clenched so tight my nails dug into my palms, and I was about to blow a gasket and start killing everyone in this house. With. My. Bare. Hands.

Rueben stared at me, shaking his head. "Doesn't matter," he croaked.

"It was him, wasn't it? Sean said he questioned you. That's it. I'm taking him out now." I turned on my heels, the need to punish the brooding asshole down-stairs my only focus. Arms wrapped around my waist and lifted me, my feet running in the air like a puppy trying to swim.

"Let me down," I hissed, barely containing myself from throwing him to the ground.

"Angel, I'm fine. Focus. Then we leave," Rueben whispered in my ear, his words and use of a pet name quelling some of my anger. "I love you, Raven." He kissed my cheek before setting me down on my feet and pushed me into Porter, who quickly ushered me into the room.

I took a few minutes to take deep breaths, needing to calm myself before I blew everything. Though each time I thought about the black eye and cut on his lip, the anger returned, and I had to start over. After an hour, I felt calmer and focused on where I was. Blinking, I cursed when I realized I needed to start preparations.

"You're not late yet. I've been watching the time," Porter said, reminding me he was there. Shoulders sagging, I walked into his arms, needing a hug. A beeping sound started, and Porter reached into his pants to turn off an alarm.

"You ready?" he asked. Nodding, I grabbed my phone as we took seats, so the loop would show us sitting down. Scrambling the cameras, I nodded to Porter when it was clear. He got to work scanning for the safe and removing a picture on the wall. I watched him work, intrigued by his skill as he spun a dial on the safe, opening it a few seconds later.

In the few times Mrs. Duke wasn't crying, she would open this safe and take things out and put things in. We hadn't been able to see the combination or where it had been precisely on the wall from the stethoscope camera, but it had been enough to convince us there was something worth looking into here.

Porter cleared the safe, bringing over the contents and hiding them in Mr. Duke's bed. I glanced at the timer, seeing we only had two minutes left.

"Time to wrap up," I whispered, bouncing on my toes. Porter nodded, placing the painting back and taking his seat. The alarm went off, and I got up, pretending it was for my patient. As I reviewed his vitals, Porter slipped out the side hallway, using the shadows and dark corridors to sneak into a few other rooms to grab anything he discovered. He had ten minutes before he needed to be back, and the next part of our plan would come into effect.

My heart raced as I waited, hoping he was being careful. I busied myself with the patient and showed a more significant decline on his chart as I uploaded it. Just as I expected, the phone rang on the bedside table.

"Hello?"

"Molly, are you sure these readings are correct?" Mrs. Duke asked.

"Yes. I checked them three times. I think we need to call an ambulance. I'm worried."

She sucked in a breath. "What does the doctor say? I'll be right there to talk to him."

Porter slid into the room, adding some things to my bag and under the patient's bed. I nodded that Mrs. Duke was on the way. Rueben opened the door a second later, and I kept my eyes off his face so I didn't go feral again. He stayed inside as Mrs. Duke rushed over to her husband.

"Is there anything you can do, Doctor?" she asked, taking her husband's hand. If this man hadn't been responsible for countless deaths, I'd feel bad about the condition he was in now. But as it was, I only felt sorry for his wife.

"No. I think it's time, Mrs. Duke. We need to call an ambulance."

After strategizing for hours, I'd concluded the best way for us to get out of here with everything was an ambulance. It doubled as the perfect cover to kill him without being on camera. Otto and Phoenix would pose as paramedics in the borrowed ambulance, ready to intercept our call.

Mrs. Duke cried harder but nodded. I pulled out my phone and called Otto, nerves racing through me. There were so many moving pieces in this plan, and too many people I cared about were at risk.

"911, we need an ambulance at the Duke estate." I pretended to answer other questions, handing the phone off to Porter as I unplugged the machines to move him. Grabbing my bag, I scanned the room to ensure we had everything. Rueben came over and helped us push the bed toward the stairs. He and Porter lifted it as we descended, my pulse racing a mile a minute. We were almost free and clear.

I could hear the sirens in the distance, hoping that in their shocked states, no one asked questions about how it got here so quickly. I pulled open the front doors, barking at the Commander to move. He sneered at me, jumping back a second later as the gurney appeared.

The lights flashed down the driveway, and I sighed in relief that Mark had let them through, the pot brownies helping to lower his defenses.

So close. We were almost scot-free.

The ambulance stopped, and Otto and Phoenix hopped out as they rushed to open the doors. The gurney was loaded with the loot; again, no one questioned why there hadn't been one inside the ambulance. The Commander's eyes bounced back and forth as he tried to figure something out. But it was too late.

Porter jumped into the back of the ambulance as Otto raced around to the front. Mrs. Duke pulled Phoenix aside as she asked questions, demanding to ride in the ambulance. We'd prepared for this, so I stepped outside and touched her arm.

"Rueben will follow along and bring you to the hospital, Mrs. Duke. Okay?"

She started to protest, but my gentle giant took her hand to lead her away. The Commander came into view, his gaze assessing. He knew something was going on, but not what. I stared down the Commander, my eyes wishing death on him.

A pop sounded out in the night a second before Phoenix jumped in front of me, his body slamming into mine. My head bounced off the door as I crashed back. Screams and shouts rang out, my head buzzing with all the noise. Something wet dripped on me, and I reached down to touch it. My hand lifted to my face, red covering it.

"Raven! Raven!" Porter shouted at me as arms pulled me into the ambulance. A second later, Phoenix was shoved on me, the doors slamming shut before the ambulance took off. Porter kept shouting at me, but I couldn't focus.

I stared at the liquid, trying to figure out what it was, as my senses returned to me, and the smell of copper filled my nose. Sucking in a breath, my heart pounded in my chest as my vision blurred. *Blood*. There was blood on me.

Hands gripped my face, yanking me toward them. "Raven. It's Phoenix. He's been shot. You have to save him. *Please*."

Raven

PANIC AND FEAR GRIPPED ME; THE PAST FIGHTING WITH THE present to take hold. My heart pumped hard in my chest, the sound echoing in my ears as the world around me blurred. The smell of copper threatened to overwhelm me, the slick substance becoming sticky with each passing minute.

"Raven!"

Porter's cry shook me loose, and I pushed my panic aside. I'd trained for this. I'd learned everything I could, so I'd never have to be in the situation again where I couldn't save someone. I could curl up in a ball and cry, passing out from the memories. Or I could use the strength I'd been developing, proving I was more than I believed.

Taking a deep breath, I instantly regretted the action when the smell threatened to send my body back to my freakout state, not caring what I'd mentally prepared for. Grabbing some cotton out of the bags, I shoved it up my nose, hoping it would keep the smell at bay. Snapping on gloves next, I tuned out everything else and zeroed in on Phoenix. If I just focused on fixing him, maybe it wouldn't be so bad.

I scanned his body as I crouched on the ground, noticing that Porter pressed something to his shoulder. Red soaked the material, making it impossible to tell what it had been.

"It's just paint," I whispered, trying to trick my mind. "On three, lift his shoulder. I need to check if the bullet went all the way through."

I concentrated on the procedure, the steps falling into place in my mind.

Find the wound.

Check for the bullet.

Clean the area.

Stop the bleeding.

Lifting his shoulder, I found an exit wound and sighed in relief. Grabbing a bottle of saline, I counted out loud to three and had Porter remove his shirt as I squirted the saline over the bullet hole. I cleaned the area thoroughly, removing debris and germs from the wound. Once cleared, I used the blood clotting agent to slow the bleeding.

"Just like on *Phoenix Hospital*," I chanted, grabbing the staple gun and sealing the wound shut. I hadn't let myself look at Phoenix's face, too worried I wouldn't be able to compartmentalize if I saw him. Now that my steps were done, I glanced at his face, not liking how pale it was. My fingers found his pulse, the steady rhythm a welcoming beat.

"I think he's going to be okay," I whispered, too scared to look at Porter now.

He apparently didn't have the same feelings, wrapping his arms around me as he squeezed tight.

"Thank you, Raven. You saved him."

The numbness I'd been in faded at his touch, and the panic returned. Squeezing my eyes shut, I blocked out the horror of the back of the ambulance and the knowledge I had almost lost someone I loved.

The ambulance slowed, my eyes flashing open in fear. Why were we stopping? Was the bad guy still after us?

Which I knew was funny to think since we were technically the bad guys in this situation, but anyone who came after the people I loved was the villain. It might be messed up logic, but it was my logic.

The doors flew open, and I lifted my butterfly knife, ready to take down whoever threatened us. Sagging in relief at the sight of Otto, I held back the tears that wanted to fall.

"What happened?" he shouted, his fear covering his face as he scanned us.

"Someone shot Phoenix."

"No. Someone was trying to shoot *you*, and

Phoenix stepped in, Raven. I think it was your nemesis," Porter corrected.

My mind went red with rage as a feeling unlike anything I had ever felt before filled me. I thought I'd been angry earlier at what that dick had done to Rueben, but this was ten times more.

"Steel Strike just signed her death certificate," I hissed, moving to go after them.

"As hot as seeing you go all stabby is, Little Bird. We don't have time right now. We need to get Phoenix out of here along with the stolen goods. Rueben won't be far behind."

The three of us sprung into action, adrenaline kicking into gear. Porter and Otto moved Phoenix to the back seat of the car while I grabbed my bag and the items stashed under the bed. I slipped on the blood and knew I'd need to clean it up before the ER asked questions. In under two minutes, we had the twins in the car and Otto and me back in the ambulance.

Grabbing the vial of potassium chloride, I quickly injected it under Mr. Duke's tongue to hide the injection site. In the frenzy of everything, I'd almost forgotten to kill my mark. What a rookie mistake! Geesh.

While the formula entered his bloodstream, sending him into cardiac arrest, I grabbed the bleach and scrubbed the floors, walls, doors, and gurney. I gathered everything I used and shoved it into a plastic bag, then stripped out of my scrubs, which were also covered in blood. Pulling on an extra pair, I fell back into the wall when Otto took a sharp turn.

"Suffering succotash!" I yelled, despite the fact Otto couldn't hear me.

Righting myself, I moved closer to the patient and pressed my hands to his chest. I scowled at the man who'd killed so many people for his own greed. I felt nothing for his death, already moving on to the last one on my list. This man deserved no more of my time or thoughts.

The ambulance slowed, but I was ready, counting out loud as I began chest compressions. The doors swung open as the hospital nurses and doctors converged on the ambulance.

"John Duke, age 65. Coma patient went into cardiac arrest two minutes ago, has a history of liver disease. Wife is following," I rambled off, the thrill of being part of the medical action exciting me.

The nurses took over, shouting orders as they pushed the gurney into the hospital. Slamming the doors, I raced around to the front and climbed in, my ass barely on the seat before Otto pulled away. My breathing calmed the further away we drove, our plan succeeding despite my nemesis interfering.

"We did it, Little Bird. And you saved Phoenix. You overcame your aversion."

"I don't know if I'm fully healed, but it was a good place to start. I'd do anything for you all."

Otto beamed at me, turning the ambulance into a parking garage. We jumped out after he parked on the top floor and wiped down the interior one more time, ridding it of any DNA. Once that was resolved, we moved to the stairwell and grabbed the bag we'd stuffed back there earlier with spare clothes.

Changing our appearance, we headed down the stairs to the street and walked a few blocks before we spotted Porter. My heart rate spiked, and I nearly yanked the door off to climb into the backseat where Phoenix was resting. His green eyes met mine, and all the oxygen left me as I collapsed onto him.

"You're okay," I cried, finally letting out all my emotions.

"Thanks to you, Dr. Raven."

Wiping my eyes, I chuckled, the sound wet and deep, but there was no mistaking my relief at discovering I hadn't lost someone.

"Any word from Rueben?" Otto asked, turning back around to face the road.

"No. I'm not sure what happened after the shot. I pulled them into the back to get out of there, but I saw the Commander cornering Rueben."

"Shit," Otto cursed, pulling out his phone. He tapped onto an app and pulled up Rueben's location. "It shows him moving, so we have to hope that means he got away. Stay back when we get to the airfield just in case it's the Commander."

Porter nodded, the tension in the car ramping up again as we slowed and pulled off the road a few blocks down from the airfield. I scanned the cars but didn't spot the SUV Rueben had been driving. The following five minutes felt the longest as the four of us waited to see if the last member of our family would be returning. If he didn't, I'd hold true to my claim and burn down that house, not caring who I injured in the process. I'd liked Mark and Sean, but I loved Rueben and wouldn't blink to take them out for him.

"There's the SUV," Otto whispered, all of us on edge as we waited for it to turn into the lot and park. When my silent giant stepped out, our car breathed a collective sigh of relief.

"Okay, let's go. The plane is ready."

In the next ten minutes, we unloaded the cars and gave them the same treatment as the ambulance. We'd hired someone to pick them up later and return them to the rental company. Phillip greeted us as we rushed onto the plane, not batting an eye at Phoenix's ragged appearance.

"We'll be taking off in five minutes. Are we still heading toward Canada?" he asked, one foot in the cockpit, one foot out.

"Actually, could we make a detour to New York instead?" Otto asked, looking at me for confirmation.

"What's in New York?" I asked, wrinkling my nose.

"Our place. I think we should take time to recoup and plan where your nemesis won't know."

My eyes widened, nodding before I could process. Why hadn't I thought of that? Oh yeah, because I wasn't used to having a team or depending on others. It was nice not having to make all the decisions.

"Yes, good plan."

Otto smiled, giving Phillip the new coordinates, and I rechecked Phoenix. He didn't have a fever or anything, so I prayed that meant I'd done a good job of cleaning the wound. Maybe we could take him to a doctor off books once we were in town to verify I hadn't fucked up his shoulder. Yeah. That would be good.

Once the seatbelt sign went off, Rueben scooped me up, holding me close. I soothed my hands over his arms and beard, running my fingers through the short hairs.

"I thought you'd been shot," he whispered, his voice pained. "Then that douchebag tried to stop me, so I went feral on him. I don't think he'll be peeing standing up for a while."

Gasping, I leaned back and assessed him as I peered into his eyes, seeing every emotion he felt. I ran my fingers over his face, his eyelids closing at my touch. I loved that Rueben spoke more to me, even if it was in whispers. I knew it meant he trusted me with his words.

"I'm sorry you were scared. It all happened so fast. I had to focus on Phoenix so I didn't crumble. I hated that you weren't with us, but I'm glad you kicked him in the nuts. That jerk deserved it. I would've done worse. So, he's lucky he can still pee, even if it is sitting down."

Rueben smiled, his big paws cupping my face as he tilted me back and forth like he was scanning every inch of me. When he was satisfied, I curled up in his arms and laid my head on his chest. This mission had been draining, and I was glad it was over. Having some downtime to prepare for the last one would be just what we all needed.

GENTLE ROUSING WOKE me later as I was moved to a seat and my lap belt buckled into place. Blinking, I rubbed my eyes, noticing we were landing. Bright lights of the city flashed around us, and excitement bubbled in my belly. I was going to see where the guys lived and where Loxley Crew stayed during their off time.

Rueben carried Phoenix off the plane and placed him in a waiting SUV. I crawled in, wanting to be close in case he needed me. Porter scooted in next to me, his arms going around my middle as he looked at his brother.

"I'll never be able to thank you enough for what you did," he whispered, his chin resting on my shoulder.

"I'd do it for any of you. It was the fear of losing him that pushed me past the trauma of my past. I don't know if I'm cured, but it felt like a giant step in the right direction."

"I was so proud of you, Cutie-Pie. You were so brave at that moment." Porter kissed my cheek, his lips warm against my cool skin. Settling back into his arms, I held Phoenix's hand as we drove to the guy's place. I had no clue what to expect, so when we pulled up to a tall building in the heart of the city, I turned my head, convinced we were stopped behind something. The door opened, and I jumped, causing Porter and Otto to laugh.

Scowling, I climbed out behind Porter and stared up at the tall structure. People passed by on the street, the city still bustling this late at night. A man in a black suit opened the door for us as we neared, another one stepping out to retrieve the keys from Otto and walking toward the vehicle.

"Where is he taking it?" I asked, covering my mouth with my hand as I yawned.

"The parking garage."

"Oh." For some reason, that hadn't occurred to me.

The guys snickered, directing me to the elevator. Rueben had Phoenix in his arms again, the staff ignoring the odd display as we passed. The elevator opened, and Porter inserted a black card into a slot, hitting the top floor. I raised my eyebrows, continuing to be impressed.

"I can't wait to show you the view," Porter said, bouncing on his feet. "We only keep a small percentage of the money from the loot we steal, but times that by four, and it's still a lot of money. We share everything, so using it for a secure place in the city seemed like the best investment."

I nodded, understanding what he meant. Sometimes it was easier to blend around a billion people. No one would notice them, and they could come and go as they pleased without curious neighbors. Man had chosen to live in seclusion instead, keeping us on the outskirts of a town. Though, perhaps adopting a bunch of small girls required more secrecy. That wasn't something that would go unnoticed.

The elevator doors opened into their condo, showcasing the dark hardwood floor and floor-to-ceiling windows that looked out onto the city. The walls were a mixture of brick, soft grays, and blues, giving the place a warm feeling. It wasn't designed by an interior decorator but had been done by four men who wanted a true home. Pictures of them throughout the years hung on the wall, mixed in with some famous art pieces.

A giant TV hung from the far wall, a stand with a million game and movie consoles. I walked into the kitchen, my mouth dropping open at how big it was. White cabinets and white marble filled the space with a massive island in the middle with six barstools. An oversized stainless steel refrigerator stood off to the side, not a single fingerprint in sight. The kitchen opened up to a small breakfast nook with another floor-to-ceiling window.

My mind glazed over as I took in the different rooms, finding six bedrooms, five bathrooms, an office, a workout room, another TV room, and a supply room. Their place had to be 4,000 square feet, covering the entire top floor of the building.

"This place is bananas."

"We're glad you like it. Come on. Let's show you which room you can use and hit the hay. I think we could all sleep for a week."

Nodding, I followed Otto to an empty room and set my belongings down. After a shower and changing into a shirt I believed belonged to Rueben since it practically touched my shins, I went in search of Phoenix, needing to be close. The other guys appeared to have the same idea, a separate mattress placed on the floor next to the huge one.

Once I was satisfied with his vitals, I climbed into

the bed and curled up beside him as plans of revenge filtered through my head. Steel Strike wouldn't get away with this. I'd make her murder hurt for causing Phoenix pain. I'd be so quiet she wouldn't even see me coming and would have no choice but to call me the Silent Blade.

Roeben

THE PAST TWO DAYS AT OUR HOME WITH RAVEN HAD BEEN bliss. After how the last job ended, we'd all needed time to recuperate and recharge. Phoenix had been shot, something none of us had ever encountered on a job before. The knowledge we could've lost him or Raven—who the bullet had been intended for—had been sobering. The four of us had become even more possessive and clingy, barely letting her out of our arms since we'd arrived.

"Need air," Raven hissed, making me smile. I loosened my grip but didn't set her down. My arms didn't feel complete anymore unless she was in them.

"Okay, how about I need to pee? You're not going to come in there with me, are you?" she asked, tilting her chin in what I assumed she meant to be stubborn determination but only made her cuter.

I lifted my eyebrow in jest, wanting to see how she'd react.

Raven's jaw dropped as she sputtered, at a loss for

words. "But... um... privacy," she finally said, crossing her arms.

Chuckling, I stood from the couch we'd been snuggling on and deposited her at the bathroom door. I pushed her in, making sure to latch the door behind her. Her bodily functions wouldn't bother me, but I could let her have this if she needed it.

While she did her thing, I wandered back to the kitchen and spotted Phoenix standing at the stove with his arm in a sling. Our doctor had cleared him, stating that the "EMT" had performed perfect care and execution and should become a surgeon. We'd opted to leave Raven's name out of it, hoping it would be easier to dismiss an EMT. Raven's reaction to the comment had been adorable, her cheeks blushing so hard I momentarily thought she wasn't breathing.

"Morning," I grunted, walking to the coffee maker. Phoenix lifted the spatula in greeting, humming to himself as he danced to some song on his phone.

"What should we do today?" he asked after placing the French toast onto a plate. Outside of the sling, you'd never guess he'd been shot. The normally reserved and gloomy Phoenix had been replaced with a version that was more similar to his twin—upbeat, optimistic, and smiles for days. Though, I couldn't deny my own personality hadn't changed either since a little bird had swooped into our lives.

The Raven effect was a powerful thing.

Leaning back against the counter, I sipped my coffee as I thought about his question. The only thing I truly wanted to do was spend the day with Raven, naked in my bed. I'd been holding back, waiting until she had her time with the others, knowing she needed to be stretched a little, or I'd hurt her. Hearing her moans as the others pleasured her and spending countless days with her body pressed against mine as I kissed her had driven me to a state of profound need.

"Alone time," I muttered, my eyes meeting his. A knowing grin spread across his face, and he nodded.

"Okay, Rueb. I'll make it happen." I nodded in thanks, appreciating that he'd understood what I meant.

Raven skipped into the kitchen, now dressed in a black skirt and Spiderman shirt, which made my cock twitch at the sight of her bare legs. I couldn't wait to have them wrapped around my head. My eyes zoned in on her, the rest of the room disappearing as I watched her. Raven jumped up on the island, her height closer to Phoenix's now. They flirted back and forth, making one another laugh. I loved hearing the sound. It was my second favorite sound—the first being her moans.

Otto and Porter trailed into the kitchen, rubbing their eyes a few moments later. Porter immediately plastered himself to Raven's other side while Otto grabbed a mug of coffee and joined me against the counter.

"Have you?" he asked, lifting his eyebrows. I shook my head no, then took another sip.

"Today," I whispered, his nod letting me know he understood. He clapped my shoulder before walking over to grab a plate of food.

"Porter and Phoenix, I need your help today," Otto said, shoving the fluffy French toast into his mouth. Porter opened his mouth to protest, but Phoenix cut him off, motioning with his eyes toward me.

"Sounds good, boss man," Phoenix chirped, kissing Raven's lips before taking his plate to sit down.

Porter grumbled but took his own food, snagging Raven to sit in his lap in the process. He'd been the clingiest since we'd arrived home; the gunshot affected him the hardest. While the four of us were as close as brothers, Phoenix was his twin, and their bond was inseparable. I didn't know who the twins would be without one another.

Picking up the last plate, I joined my family at the island and listened to their conversation. The sound was pleasant, their teasing laughter a soothing background to the noise in my head. Once everyone had eaten, I eyed Raven as she pretended to wash the dishes. I didn't think the girl had ever done one in her life.

"Angel," I said, stepping up behind her. "Spend the day with me?" I asked, my voice soft. The disuse of it over the years made it hard to speak for long periods. My brothers never demanded anything of me, so I quit trying, only speaking a few words most days. Raven made me want to try, though. To share more of my voice with her. Some things were still too hard to say, but I had another way in mind.

My hands captured hers in the water, stopping her from scrubbing. She peeked at me from behind her, resting her head on my chest.

"Of course. I just want to do... this." Smiling, I shook my head, drying her hands and picking her up off the step stool she used to reach the cabinets. "But..." she turned, frowning at the dishes.

"Leave it, Little Bird. We'll finish it later. Have fun with Rueben." Otto kissed her lips, leaving her slightly breathless as he walked away. The twins took turns next, making Raven a swooning mess as they departed.

Phoenix winked at me, and I shook my head. I didn't need their help getting her aroused, but I'd take it for now. Directing her down the hall, I led her to my bedroom. Her small hand fit in mine perfectly, and I grew excited at sharing this part of myself with her.

My bedroom wasn't much to look at. The walls were dark and calming as I entered, helping to ease some of my tension. The carpet beneath our feet was soft to the touch, soothing me more with each step. My room was smaller than the other guys, my big bed taking up most of the space, with a simple bucket chair and dresser off to the side. I had nothing on my walls or any personal effects in here. I found them too distracting when I needed to sleep, preferring the simple luxury of silence.

"I have to be honest. This isn't what I expected your room to be like. It's nice and comforting, so I get that part, but it doesn't scream *you* at all," Raven said, her head swiveling around to take in everything like she thought it was an optical illusion and I was hiding something in plain sight.

Smiling, I shook my head and led her to a door most people assumed was my closet. It wasn't. Wearing only black clothing made my wardrobe easy, and it all fit into the one dresser.

The main reason my bedroom was smaller was because we'd converted the room next to mine and a good portion of my original room into my sanctuary. Opening the door, I sucked in a breath as I prepared to show her the room that was more me.

I didn't have a red room of pain or anything like that. No, what I'd discovered due to my past abuse was I needed a gentle approach. It wasn't about control for me in the bedroom but submission in every sense of the word.

Submitting to my past and letting go of the screams that echoed in my head on a constant loop.

Relinquishing my body to the experience and using my other senses to keep me out of my head.

Trusting in someone else to understand and give me comfort and gentleness in their touch.

It had taken me a while to get to a place where I felt ready for sex; the pain and scars from my mother had taught me not to trust females. I thought I might be gay at one point, but after a failed experience, I knew that wasn't the case either.

Due to my size and looks, most of the girls I met wanted me to control them and be rough. Again, I tried it, but when I broke down crying with a girl because the idea of hurting her reminded me too much of my mother, I knew sex that way wouldn't work for me.

I almost gave up at that point as feelings of failing at something else in my life bombarded me, especially for something that had yet to yield any enjoyment.

Raven gasped as she stepped in, her hands covering her mouth, her eyes widening. Where my other room was simple, this one was not.

Silk drapes hung from the ceiling, creating a bohemian vibe. Plush rugs covered the floor, making the space a tactile experience with the hardwood and rugs. Multiple speakers had been placed in the ceiling, floor, and walls. Twinkle lights hung around the room in various colors, intertwining with the silk in places. Other spotlights placed throughout the ceiling could be selected for different lighting options. However, my favorite was the fiber optic lights in the ceiling that resembled stars.

The walls were black and soundproofed, with one wall a mural of the beach at sunset. Several oversized bean bags, chairs, and loungers were placed around the room, with copious pillows and blankets. A dark wood cabinet stood in one section of the room filled with toys and objects. There was also a fridge, sink, and microwave. When I needed solace, I came in here and could spend days before I needed to leave. A door to the bathroom was the only thing that marred the walls, and even it was painted black, blending into the scene.

The last section of the room and my personal favorite. The center of the room had tray flooring with two steps down to a large mattress that covered the entire space. More drapes circled it, providing a canopy effect if pulled closed with an opening at the top so the lights could shine in if desired. The sheets were silk with velvet and faux fur covers, providing the ultimate sensory explosion.

Everything in the room was designed to enhance sexual pleasure through sensory play and safety.

After breaking down into sobs, the woman I'd been with sat with me and talked me through my feelings. She introduced me to a club where I met someone who showed me what I needed and how sex could be with trust. And now I wanted to share that with Raven.

Pulling her to me, I lifted her and held her close. My body vibrated both from fear and desire. I didn't believe she'd laugh at me, but I couldn't squelch the small kernel from experiences past that hadn't gone well.

"I need something different from sex," I whispered. "Not every time, but I get the most pleasure from this and wanted to share it with you."

Raven's hands rubbed over my head, her nails digging into my scalp and beard. That small kernel of doubt was vanquished at her touch. I should've known she'd understand. She'd already been giving me so much without realizing it.

"Whatever you need, Ruebear. Just show me."

A groan escaped me, my arms trembling with need. Walking forward, I took the steps to the bed and placed her on it. Her body sunk into the covers, her trilling giggle a balm to my heart.

Pointing to stay, I swallowed as she complied. My words had dried up already from too many emotions, so I walked over to the cabinet to gather what I needed. Once I had the items I wanted to start with, I hit the remote to activate the lights and music I'd selected.

Raven kneeled on the bed, her eyes curious as she watched me. I placed everything on the bed and removed my shirt, watching as she inhaled and licked her lips at my strip tease. Smirking, my movements grew more confident as I shucked my pants, my cock now on display.

"Oh, fanny flutters," Raven hissed, her eyes growing comically large. She looked down her body, then back to my cock as it thickened against my leg, then back down. "You're gonna have to rally, girl. This is the ultimate challenge. Time to shine!"

Snorting, I realized she was talking to her vagina. Shaking my head, I held my hand for her to take and brought her to stand. I took my time removing her clothes, letting my fingers caress her skin with each pass. Goosebumps dotted her flesh, and I knew she'd love sensory play. She was already so responsive.

Picking up a silk blindfold, I held it up to her to ask if she was okay with it. She bit her lip but nodded, letting me tie it around her eyes. Pushing on her shoulders, I directed her to lie down on the soft sheets. I wanted to show her the best of sensory play so, in turn, she could do it for me. The room itself provided sensory stimulation from the colored lights, soft music, aromatherapy, and soothing fabrics; it created an environment to entice your hearing, sight, smell, and touch without even undressing.

Now that I had her completely bare, I could ramp everything up, sending her over the edge with just a touch. Taking the feather, I traced it over her skin, going over the peaks and valleys of her curves as I watched her inhale and move against the silk sheets. Moving some oil under her nose first, I let her get a whiff of the sandalwood before I touched a little to my fingers and smoothed it over her nipples. Raven gasped, her legs moving more. I drew on her stomach, going up and down her arms and legs, watching it absorb into her skin.

Needing to engage her sense of taste now, I grabbed a strawberry and parted her lips with it. Her tongue peeked out to taste the sweet juice, a moan sounding. Placing it into her mouth, I watched as she ate it, licking up the juices with her tongue, and I had to squeeze my eyes shut so I didn't get too excited yet.

Raven whimpered, the sensations having ramped up her arousal, and I knew she was ready for step one. Dropping down between her legs, I licked up her folds, her legs squeezing my head. She tasted so sweet I couldn't get enough of her. Her moans filled my ears, surrounding me, so she was the only thing I heard, tasted, and smelled. Plunging one finger in, I watched as she trembled around the digit. Her walls stretched as I added more, showing me she'd take me just fine once I got her ready.

Moving up her body, I grabbed one of the toys I'd gotten just for her and placed it at her entrance, rubbing her wetness over it. Her head thrashed back and forth as she moaned, her back arching in anticipation. It was beautiful. Gathering her up, I placed her between my legs and rested her back to my front. I grabbed her hands and put them on my thighs, pressing down to show I wanted them to stay.

She squirmed against me, her ass rubbing against my cock. It was a delicious and torturous experience, but I wouldn't move her if my life depended on it. With one hand, I brushed my fingers over her nipple as I fucked her with the dildo. Raven screamed at the move, her legs draping over my thick thighs as she rode it for me. Her wetness dripped over my fingers, coating my hand in her arousal. When she was ready, I pulled out the dildo and removed the blindfold. She blinked at me, her pupils blown with lust and her cheeks rosy.

She glanced down at the rainbow suction cup dildo, her eyebrows rising when she saw the shape and size. She pointed at it, her face shocked.

"That thing was in me?"

I nodded, chuckling. *Yeah, Angel. You'd take me just fine.*

Lifting the blindfold, I wrapped it around my eyes

and moved down to lay flat on the bed. I gestured that it was her turn to use the things on me like I'd done to her.

"Oh, this is going to be fun."

Smiling, I relaxed back into the soft mattress and silky smooth sheets. The music was a soft and seductive melody that filled my ears. I inhaled the aroma of her sex and sandalwood, groaning at how arousing it was. I relished in the sensations already present, shoving everything else out of my mind as I grounded myself in this moment. My cock felt heavy against my leg, desire coursing through my body as I waited for Raven.

With gentle hands, she went about the same routine I'd done for her. First, she moved the feather over my skin, eliciting goosebumps just as I'd done. My breathing increased as I waited for each step, moaning as her fingers touched me with the oil, my nipples extra sensitive from the build-up. By the time she brought the strawberry to my lips, I was about to explode, my cock harder than it had ever felt. When her lips touched my skin, I sucked in a breath as she moved across me. It took me a minute to realize what she was doing.

My body trembled, emotion vibrating through every inch of my six-foot-four frame as Raven kissed each of the scars that marred my skin. I'd covered most of them with tattoos, but they were still there, showcasing the trauma and pain I'd been through at the hands of my mother. And yet, Raven soothed away the residual pain that always lingered and replaced it with her touch and love. Her fingers caressed my dick, the sensation too much after everything else.

"Fuck," I cursed, sitting up and ripping off the blindfold. I needed to see Raven. Her blue eyes peered at me, her smile the sexiest thing about her. "Come here," I whispered, dragging her to my lap.

She looked down again at my cock, now at full mast. "I don't think it's going to fit," she whimpered.

"It will fit," I promised, spreading her pussy lips and running my cock through her folds. Her heat felt divine against me, and I almost forgot to put on a condom. Grunting, I rolled it over myself, quickly, and positioned her at my tip. "Breathe."

Raven nodded, her eyes focused on mine as I helped her sink onto me. I remember the other toy I had gotten and grabbed it, turning it on to pulse and placing it over her clit. The vibrations traveled from her to me, giving me another sensation to focus on outside of how good she felt. Raven groaned, sinking further as she gave into the pleasure, not the fear.

"So. Wet."

Raven's head fell to my shoulder, her arms wrapped around my neck. Moving my hands to her ass, I spread my fingers over the back of her thighs as my thumb pressed into the line between her pelvis and leg. Together we moved, taking it slow until she adjusted to me.

Once she felt confident, I let her take the lead, moving to a comfortable speed. She pushed off my shoulders, her head thrown back as she took her pleasure. Her pussy gripped me like a vise, her heat and wetness making the perfect home for my cock.

When her nails scraped against my scalp again, I didn't have the willpower to hold back any longer. Grabbing the bullet vibrator, I placed it on her clit as I pinched her nipple, needing her to come more than anything I wanted in my entire life. Watching Raven fall apart on me was the most beautiful and glorious thing I'd ever witnessed. My orgasm froze, the need to watch every second of hers was more urgent.

Her hair brushed my thighs as she screamed out her release, her walls squeezing me tight. Her nails dug into my back as she convulsed, and I couldn't hold off any longer. With a growl, I surged up in her, bringing her lips to mine, my cock emptying itself as I came hard.

Sounds of heavy breathing greeted me when I returned to my body; my orgasm having sent me flying through time and space. Brushing back Raven's hair, she smiled at me.

"I love you," I said, ensuring my words were heard.

"I love you, Reuben. And any time you need that,

just let me know. It was amazing. I didn't know sex could be that sensual."

Smiling, my body sagged, knowing she hadn't hated it, and this wouldn't be the only time I experienced the best orgasm of my life. Taking care to clean her up in the bath, I brought her to a few more orgasms before snuggling under the heavy blankets, looking up at the stars, and saying more with our hearts than words would ever convey.

Raven

Over the next week, the guys and I grew closer as we spent time relaxing and caring for one another. It almost seemed like Phoenix had never been shot, but then I'd catch sight of his sling, or he'd grimace when he moved a certain way, and the memory would flood back.

I still couldn't believe I'd been able to perform the necessary steps to save him. The twins had volunteered to help me test my fainting problem to see if I was fully cured with an episode of *Phoenix Hospital*. But after waking up between the twins with no knowledge of how I'd gotten there, I knew I wasn't. It was at least a comfort to know when faced with a crisis for someone I loved, I could push past my own fear and do what was necessary.

As the days wore on, I avoided planning the kill more and more. Typically I thrived on this part of the process, enjoying learning and devising plans. But I knew we weren't out of the woods yet with my nemesis. They would continue trying to stop me, and I wouldn't put it past Steel Strike to use the guys against me again, now that they knew I wasn't alone. Which in turn only amped my anxiety up a million degrees.

It didn't help that the fallout from their strike against us at the Duke residence had called into question Millicent's death, along with the nursing and security agency the Dukes used. Guilt flooded me for the first time after a job that I might've screwed something up for the people who worked there, except for Fern. That dude had been a creep, constantly popping by like he expected to catch me doing something. It was only Rueben's stare that kept him away most days.

The only positive from the whole cluster was that I wouldn't have to be as stealthy like I'd been with the other two. I didn't need to make it look like an accident. No, Jerome Fulton would die knowing his sins had killed him. It allowed our plan to be bolder since we wouldn't need to cover our tracks, but I didn't like that one bit. It had been a topic of contention between Loxley Crew and myself all morning.

"Little Bird, you need to focus. What information did you obtain?" Otto asked, nudging my leg with his sock-covered foot.

"It's tighter in some ways because of his system but less in others because he only has two guards, and the building is easier to access. It's still too dangerous for you guys to break into. I'll have an easier chance nabbing him than you will getting in and out," I said, finally deciding I was done playing with their lives.

I'd been trying to find a solution that would be safe, and there wasn't one. Therefore, they just needed to drop this. Robbing one more person wouldn't change anything, but one of them dying would break me.

"Did you forget who we are? We're not giving up because it's dangerous, Little Bird."

Throwing my head back, I let out a loud groan as I rubbed my temples. Otto and I had been locked in this debate all morning. I hated being at odds with him, but I couldn't shake the feeling something terrible would happen.

Tattooed hands lifted me from my chair and sat me on their lap. Rueben's arms wrapped around me tightly, holding me close to his chest. His beard tickled my neck as he leaned closer.

"Help us make it safe," he whispered, the plea thick in his voice.

Sagging in defeat, I debated the best way to finish the job without any of us dying. I needed to hear their idea again instead of completely dismissing it.

"Fine. Go over your plan from the top. I wasn't listening the first time," I grumbled, crossing my arms and ignoring the fact I was being held.

"Phoenix can't hack their system unless he's

closer, and then it's only about twenty seconds before he has to back out and wait. There's a building on the opposite block that should give him enough range and keep him safely out of harm's way." Otto lifted his eyebrow, giving me a chance to argue my points.

"Okay. Carry on." I motioned with my hand, turning it over in the air for him to continue. I narrowed my eyes at him when he smirked, getting way too much enjoyment out of my pout.

"Porter and Rueben will access the maintenance elevator and use the shaft to reach the floor below the penthouse. From there, they'll use these stairs once Phoenix disengages the locks."

"The first guard will be at the top," I interrupted, remembering why I'd tuned out the first time. "They'll have to incapacitate him before they reach the next locked door."

Otto smiled reassuringly, and I wanted to smack it off his face. At this moment, I didn't care that they were Loxley Crew. They were my boyfriends—my family—and I didn't want them in harm's way; end of discussion.

"Which Phoenix will be able to unlock. I'm assuming the other guard will be stationed at the vault?" he asked, looking down at his notes.

"Yes," I mumbled, irritated he hadn't taken my cue to back off.

"This is where we could use some of your mad

scientist skills, Cutie-pie," Porter said, perking up. The twins had been silent on the other side of the table to the point I'd forgotten they were in here. I'd zoned everyone else out as I stared daggers at Otto for not agreeing with me.

"Fine. I'll see what I have on me. What's the plan from there? Doesn't Jerome have one of the toughest locks to crack?" I asked, hope they would leave it alone brimming.

Porter cracked his knuckles, sitting up as he stretched his arms behind his head. "I've been waiting my whole life to take a crack at one of these, pun intended." He winked, but instead of my usual smile for him, I frowned, not liking that they weren't taking the threat seriously. Porter sighed and stood up, kneeling in front of me.

"I know you're scared, Raven. I am too." He let the fun guy persona I teased him about drop, his green eyes swirling with deep emotions as he grabbed my hand. His fingers were soft as they held it, his thumb sweeping back and forth. "It's not easy for us to let *you* enter that place. We want to protect you and lock you up, but we're trusting in your skills like you've asked us to. *Please* do the same for us."

His words struck me, and I slumped forward as all the fight left me. I knew he was right. I didn't want to be treated like a bird with a broken wing; so, I couldn't do the exact same to them. Fair was fair.

But it didn't mean I couldn't level the playing field. They needed a better plan, and I had a pesky nemesis to dispose of. With Steel Strike out of the way, it would be one less thing for us to worry about.

"Okay, point taken. It just means we need the absolute best and unbreakable plan ever. How are you guys with heights?" I asked, cocking my head.

Porter glanced behind me to Rueben, gulping as he returned to my face. "Um. Depends."

"So, here's my plan."

Loxley Crew eagerly listened as I laid out each step for me to break into the penthouse and kill my mark and how they could piggyback off my entrance and exit. It took forever to go over, but by the end, we'd devised every contingency plan known to man until we were all satisfied.

"Mm, I could live off these tacos." I shoved another in my mouth, bouncing around as I happily ate. After our planning session, we'd ordered food and moved to the kitchen.

"What about you, Otto?" Porter teased, and I stopped, remembering I'd been sitting in Otto's lap and had just given him a lap dance. The hard length beneath my butt confirming it.

"Don't stop on my account, Little Bird. Watching you enjoy what you're eating, along with the sounds you make and how excited you get about it are the best types of foreplay. My dick might be hard, but I'd take it as payment to have you sitting with me."

I swooned and panted simultaneously. Otto had a way of being sweet and hot at the same time. He kissed my neck, moving the taco suspended in the air closer to my mouth, encouraging me to keep eating. I did, but I was more mindful of the lap dance portion this time. Mainly because now that I could feel him beneath me, I had to restrain myself from turning and pulling out his dick and licking it like there was no tomorrow.

"I think I'm going to take a bath," I blurted once everyone was done, an idea coming to me. I needed to do more research to make a dream I had the other night a reality. The guys glanced at me oddly but let me go once I gave them all kisses.

I skipped down the hallway and headed for Rueben's room. His bathroom had the soaker tub, and I wanted to use it again. Plus, it was the closest to the items I needed. And hopefully, it would put me the furthest from prying eyes. I didn't have much alone time—not that I minded since I loved being with my guys—but for this, I wanted to explore without interruption.

Walking into Rueben's serenity room, I instantly

calmed as I absorbed the energy of the room. This had easily become one of my favorite places, and I spent a lot of time reading and relaxing in his cloud pillow corner.

Opening his magic cabinet, I found the sex toy tray. My face blushed as I looked at all the different types he'd bought me. I was learning to accept my increased sexual desire as part of loving my guys, but it was still a change for me to think about sex all the time and be comfortable with it. Hopefully, this experiment would help my confidence even more.

Once I had the suction cup dildo, butt plug, and lube, I hurried to the bathroom and set my items on the counter as I started the bath. While the water filled the tub, I pulled up the video I'd saved earlier on double penetration. It had finally clicked what Phoenix and Porter had meant about not being ready. Now that I had been with all my guys, I wanted to be with all four at once. And to do that, I needed to be able to take two of them together.

Gulping, I picked up the plug and lube as I watched the woman on the screen show me how to prep and insert it. Following along, I bent and twisted my body in a million directions as I tried to do precisely as she did. After a few minutes, I was sweating and huffing, and the butt plug was still in my hand.

"I'm not going to be owned by a butt plug. I can do this."

Lifting my leg on the counter, I bent the other one and reached between my legs from the front, finding that marginally easier. The tightness shocked me as I pushed it in, my eyes bulging at the slightest inch.

"Shit. Were there beginner butt plugs, and I'd gone with the masters?" I gasped.

Never one to quit, I gritted my teeth and kept pushing. My legs shook from being in this position, my muscles screaming at me to move. Letting go of the plug, I held my breath for a second to see if it would fall out. When it stayed put, I brushed off my hands.

"That'll do for now. An inch is better than nothing," I consoled myself. The video kept playing, the woman more efficient than I was at inserting her butt plug. Now she rode the dildo she'd attached to a mirror, showing off the plug and how she rotated her hips for maximum pleasure.

"Oh, hers is so pretty. I want one with a diamond on it!" Giggling, I thought about asking the guys for a diamond, not for my finger, but my ass and the faces they would make. Knowing Rueben and Porter, they'd leave right then and steal me one to make it happen.

"Okay, so this part seems easier, at least." I focused back on my task, lubed up the dildo, and suctioned it to the side of the tub, figuring it was a better height for my short legs than the sink.

Bracing myself backward, I held onto the counter as I sank onto the dildo, the shape and size similar to the twins. Even with the butt plug in just an inch, I could feel how much tighter everything was. Every little move sent shivers through me, and I panted this time from pleasure instead of exertion.

"Oh, my, geez!"

Squeezing my eyes closed, I mimicked how I imagined the woman was moving, rotating my hips and thrusting as a slow orgasm built inside me. A tiny moan escaped me as I impaled myself, the dildo stretching me more with each thrust. It wasn't as good as sex. I didn't have my guys talking to me, or their hands roaming over me, their bodies pressed against mine as their heat warmed me. But I could see how, in a pinch, this would be an acceptable alternative.

"Holy fuck," a voice whispered, and my eyes flew open.

The twins stood in the doorway, their jaws unhinged as they took in the scene. My orgasm was so close I didn't stop but kept riding my fake ding dong. The fact they were watching me with heat in their eyes and the sight of their growing erections spurred me on, making it hotter than it had been before.

Porter was the first to move, pulling his shirt over his head as he neared. I wasn't surprised in the least by that. The boy was horny twenty hours out of the day and always up for any type of play. His cock greeted me as he neared, hard as steel and already leaking some pre-cum.

Hands gripped my face, and he bent down to kiss me, moaning into my mouth. "Just when I think you can't get any hotter, you do, Rave."

His hands moved over me, his thumb finding my clit and circling it. It was the last push I needed as I let go and came, shuddering in his arms.

"If that weren't so hot to watch, I'd almost be offended," Phoenix said from the doorway. He'd stripped down to his boxers, stroking his dick through the material.

"Why would you be offended?" I asked, slowly moving off the dildo. I pulled it free and added it to the sink to wash.

"That you'd want a dildo when you have four dicks to use."

"Oh." I turned, realizing how it might look. "I wasn't. That wasn't." Groaning, I rubbed my face as I tried to find the words. My phone made a noise, and the twins looked at it, their eyes growing larger. "It's research. I wasn't horny, or I was, but for what was to come. So, I wanted to be ready for more with you guys, so I was doing research and then practicing. But I couldn't even get this stupid, ugly butt plug in all the way."

Porter's eyes sparkled as he neared, taking my face between his hands. "I love how your brain works, babe. Don't ever feel bad. Okay?" I nodded, closing my eyes as I rested my naked body against his. "It's sexy that you were doing this for us. Want some help with the plug? Then we can see about making whatever you were practicing a reality."

"Really?" I asked, my eyes flying open as hope bloomed in my chest. Porter kissed me, his tongue swirling with mine as my desire returned.

Phoenix pressed up behind me, his hands warm against my butt. They smoothed over my cheeks as he kissed my neck and spread them. Porter took the opportunity to reach behind me and push in the plug, my breath catching as he got it in further.

"Whoa."

Porter laughed before picking me up and carrying me out, his twin following. The plug shifted with each step, and I suddenly wondered if I was ready for what would occur.

As we neared where Rueben and Otto were, their heads swiveled to me and took in my naked body. Heat filled their gazes, and Otto shifted, his erection still present from earlier. They didn't even bat an eye at Porter's nakedness.

"Our girlfriend requires all of us. You guys up for it?" Porter teased, wiggling his eyebrows.

"My room," Rueben bellowed, his voice the loudest I'd ever heard. The twins didn't waste a minute, turning and carrying me back to my crime scene.

"Arrest me, officer. I'm guilty!" I giggled at my joke.

Porter chuckled, tossing me onto the bed, the plug making me moan as I shifted. Porter smirked, joining me on his side. His hand spread across my belly, sending tingles through me.

"What are you guilty of, Cutie-Pie?"

"Loving you all and keeping you to myself."

The four men around me smiled, their eyes molten as they neared. Yeah, I would never give them up. They were mine.

Phoenix

Climbing onto the bed, I glanced over my shoulder at my other two brothers. The four of us had been close since we'd met in the group home, bridging a bond beyond blood and societal norms. We'd left all the toxic masculinity crap behind us, being whatever we needed for one another—platonically speaking.

But with that bond, outside of Porter and I, the rest of us had never shared a sexual partner together. This would forge us closer as a unit with Raven as our center... or push us apart. As usual, Porter had jumped all in, not worried about any potential fallout, so I had to think for both of us and consider all the options.

The intimacy it could bring excited me, and I wanted it—for me, my brothers, and us.

But would it be *too* much?

"Quit thinking about it, Brother," Porter chided, narrowing his eyes at me. I glanced at Rueben and Otto, taking in their expressions.

Otto removed his clothes, watching the scene

before him without blinking. Once he was naked, he joined Porter and Raven on the bed.

Rueben lifted an eyebrow at me, the question clear on his face. *Are you backing down? I thought you were braver than that.*

If the giant was comfortable with this, I had nothing else to fret over. Rueben had always been the most closed off about sex, keeping his bed partners secret from the rest of us. We knew he had this room, but until I saw the open cabinet, I never knew it was used for sexual purposes.

Taking a deep breath, I pushed down my boxers and walked toward the bed. Rueben grabbed a few items from the cabinet and sat them on a step. I spotted lube, condoms, a small vibrator, and a silk piece of fabric.

Raven moaned between Porter and Otto, and I sat at the bottom, watching as their hands roamed over her. It was the best kind of show, seeing her pleasure firsthand and hearing it as she moaned. Porter's hands were deep in her pussy, his mouth tongue fucking hers. Otto held one of her legs over his hip, his mouth licking her nipple as he sucked and tweaked it. Slowly, I rubbed my cock to the scene, noticing every little movement Raven made.

Rueben kneeled down on the bed and tapped Porter on the shoulder, motioning for him to move lower. Porter laid flat on his stomach as he licked up her center, sucking her clit into his mouth. Otto had moved to Raven's head, his cock now in her mouth. Seeing an opening, I moved across the bed and took over loving her breasts.

Smoothing my hands over the mounds, I rolled my thumbs over her nipples as they hardened into stiff peaks. Their deep pink color called to me, and I bent down to swirl my tongue around them, moaning into her skin. Raven smelled of cotton candy, and I licked her up like she was the sweet treat. I kept at my task, loving on each of her nipples, squeezing her tits in my hands, and losing focus on everything else.

"Nix, you front or back?" Porter asked, pulling me from my job. I blinked, not understanding him, until he smirked, his eyes dropping to Raven. Oh, right. When my brain realized what he was asking, I swallowed.

"Back."

Rueben handed me a condom and the lube, giving me a look like I better prepare her well, or I'd hear about it. Nodding in understanding, I moved Raven between my legs and held her for a few seconds to kiss her.

"Hey, Nix," she sighed, her hand brushing against my cheek.

"You enjoying yourself, Cupcake?"

Her smile couldn't have gotten bigger if she'd tried, nodding as she moved her legs languidly.

"You ready for me to take the plug out?" I asked, smoothing my hands over her.

"Out?" She blinked, not understanding.

"Yeah. So I can take its place."

"Oh." Her cheeks flushed redder. "Yes, please."

"So polite, Little Bird, for a dirty girl," Otto cooed, snagging her attention. He pulled her to her knees and used the vibrator I'd noticed earlier to distract her. Taking my time, I pulled the butt plug out, watching as she responded. Once it was free, I slicked it with more lube and pushed it back in and out a few times to get her used to the motion and lube her inside. She squirmed on her knees, her head tossed back, her dark hair falling everywhere.

Rolling on the condom, I squirted more lube around me, stroking it up and down. Taking Raven's ass, I stretched her cheeks wide and nudged the opening with my tip. She felt tighter than I thought possible, squeezing me like a baby with a strand of hair you'll never see again.

"Shit," I cursed, focusing on foot fungus to rein in my orgasm.

"How does she feel, Brother?" Porter asked. I couldn't tell where he was anymore; I only noticed where Raven and I began and ended.

"So good," I wheezed. Raven whimpered, her ass squirming as I paused. I had a few more inches to push and didn't want to rush it.

"More," she begged, spurring me on.

"Patience," Otto soothed. He moved, and a second later, I could feel something pressed against me, only separated by a thin wall. His fingers plunged into her, moving against my cock.

"Holy fuck, I can feel you."

After a grueling few minutes of testing my willpower, I finally got the last few inches in. I held Raven to me, our bodies panting together as we caught our breath. Each little twitch of her walls had me seeing stars.

"So full," she moaned.

"You can take some more, babe," Porter encouraged, moving some of her hair off her neck. My knees ached, my thigh muscles burning, and I knew I couldn't hold this pose much longer.

"Need to move," I wheezed. Porter nodded, helping us both lay down. He wrapped Raven's legs around his waist as he kneeled between my legs. Porter and I had always been close, but even this was a new level.

The moment he entered, I felt him, the walls around me clenching harder. Raven moaned, wiggling as she tried to find some relief. I reached down and flicked her clit, the action helping to ease some of her arousal. Once Porter was seated, he nodded at me over Raven's shoulder, and we moved together. With every thrust up, he pulled back as we see-sawed our girl-friend between us.

Rueben and Otto moved closer, Raven's hands moving to stroke their hard dicks as she moaned. In that moment, the four of us connected through our girl, giving and receiving pleasure from her. It was a beautiful representation of our group, and I prayed we'd always have this bond.

It didn't take much longer for my orgasm to crash back into me; not happy it had been denied for so long. I came hard, my balls drawing up and my muscles tensing. Raven clenched around me, squeezing every last drop from my dick. My body shook as I came back down; the love and emotion I felt for this group was overwhelming. There wasn't anything we couldn't do together. I firmly believed that now.

Porter and I moved out of the way as Rueben and Otto took turns with Raven. We both climbed off the bed and disposed of the condoms. The bathtub full of water caught my eye, so I checked the temperature. It had grown cold since she'd filled it, so I emptied and turned the water back on. She would probably want one after her time with the others.

Adding salt and bubbles, I waited until it was ready to return to the sex room. Rueben could call it all he wanted, but it would forever be known as the sex room to me.

Reuben had a blindfold over his eyes as Raven

moved a feather over him. Otto thrusted into her from behind, so I was amazed she could focus on him. She started to cum again; her face beautiful as she found her release.

I ignored Otto's cry of pleasure, not wanting to see his O-face. I guess there were some boundaries I didn't want to cross—my brothers' O-faces and their poop ones. Some things needed to stay sacred.

The big man sat up and pulled Raven on top of him, helping her sink onto his massive dick. I'd always been amazed he hadn't split anyone in half with that monster. It made sense why he'd gone last, letting us warm her up. Otto gathered his breath on the side, so I joined him. Running my fingers through his hair to soothe him.

He'd been running himself ragged this past week, and I was worried about him. He hadn't been sleeping or keeping his schedule like he needed. While he pretended to let Raven help him devise a plan, the truth was he'd been up for days crafting the perfect one. When he would get into these cycles, it always took one of us to pull him out of it, or he'd have an episode. I'd been laid up myself and distracted by the black-and-blue-haired beauty. It was no excuse, though. We'd need to tell Raven and all do better.

Otto's body relaxed at my ministrations. I massaged his scalp and temples, the only area I could touch without bumping him with my dick. After a few minutes, he sat up and nodded to me.

"You need to tell her," I whispered.

"I know. I will. We've just been busy."

Lifting my brow, I crossed my arms over my chest. He knew that was just an excuse. He didn't like people knowing, thinking it made him appear weaker.

"You're going to sleep tonight even if I have to cuddle your ass."

Otto's face tightened, but I didn't drop my stare, and he nodded, relenting to the order. We had the plan memorized, so he had nothing else to focus on other than taking care of himself. I knew once Raven became aware, she'd be on his ass more than the three of us had been, which was probably why he was holding off letting her know until this job was completed.

"I just care about you, Brother," I said softly. There was nothing like almost dying to make you think about the people who truly mattered. I already knew that, having learned that lesson way too early, but now it felt even more important. That or our invincibility no longer existed with even more at stake—our heart, Raven.

"I know, and I appreciate it. I'll do better. I promise." I reached out and squeezed his shoulder before he stumbled up the stairs and out the door. Raven and Rueben had already finished, lying in one another's arms as they caught their breath.

She looked beautiful and sated, a soft smile crossing her lips. Bending down, I picked her up and ignored the pain in my shoulder. I wanted to be able to carry her, so I'd deal with a little bit of discomfort if I had to. Raven didn't realize I was holding her until I stepped into the bathroom, and she immediately tried to get out of my arms.

"Phoenix, no! I can walk."

"Already here, Cupcake."

She huffed but smiled when she saw the full tub. Placing her into it, I climbed in behind her and sank with her against my chest and enjoyed the quiet as we lay together. My fingers ran up and down her arm, luxuriating over touching her whenever I wanted.

"What were you and Otto talking about?" she asked. It didn't surprise me she'd caught that. She might be oblivious to social cues at times and had just had half a dozen orgasms, but Raven was a trained killer, constantly soaking in her surroundings.

"I told him he needed to sleep tonight, and if he didn't, I would cuddle his ass."

Raven giggled, and I moved her up so I could wash her hair. "Do you do that often?" she asked.

"More than you'd think. Sometimes Porter and I will sandwich him. He just doesn't get the extra ingredients," I teased, making her giggle.

"I'm glad you all had each other. A little jealous of the bonds you guys created but happy all the same."

"It wasn't like that with the other girls?"

She shook her head, picking water up and pouring it through her fingers.

"No. We liked one another and would protect each other at all costs if it came down to it. But probably due to how Man found us all, we were skittish and wary of too much bonding. Then once we understood the risks of being an assassin, it became natural to hold each other at arm's length. If they died, it wouldn't hurt as much, you know?" she asked, lifting her shoulder.

"Sounds lonely."

"It can be. But not always. Darcy's the oldest and like a big sister. We play pranks on each other; even if she doesn't realize we're in a prank war, we are. One time she got me with a drone that exploded pink, tiny dick glitter all over me. I still find those suckers in my room. Then there's Karma, who bakes the most delicious treats ever. Harlow and Royal are both OCD and disagree on where things go, and so are constantly moving them to piss one another off." She laughed, and I joined her.

"Tell me more," I begged, wanting to hear more about her time there.

"Hmm, well, Selena can be quite the slob but will hack our phones to leave funny screensavers. Ivory and Naomi are twins. You don't mess with Ivory though; when she gets in the zone, she can be a little unhinged. Tabitha is very much like a cat. She doesn't say much and spends most of her time tinkering in her workshop. She tried to teach me how to drive once, and I was so bad that she threatened to blow up any car I got in because it would be better for the world. I didn't like driving anyway because I'm so short, so I took it as my excuse to never try again, and just bought a plane."

Raven laughed, the love for the other girls evident as she spoke about them. She might not believe they were close, but it was obvious they cared for one another. For the first time, I worried she wouldn't want to stay with us.

"Will I get to meet any of them?" I asked instead of the question I wanted.

"You'd want to?" She turned and looked over her shoulder.

"Of course, Raven. They're your sisters."

"Okay. That would be kind of cool, I suppose. Selena just got married, and Harlow no longer lives at the house. But after this job, we can go back to get my stuff, and I'll introduce you to whoever is there."

Inwardly, I sighed in relief. "Will there be any secret handshake I need to know? A vow of silence I need to take?" I asked as I finished rinsing her hair.

Raven giggled and shook her head. "No. None of that. Though, don't look Tabitha in the eyes. She takes offense to that."

"Duly noted." I nodded as I helped her out and dried us both. I wasn't sure if she was messing with me after hearing about her prank war or not, but I'd take it seriously.

The house was quiet as we left Rueben's room and went to Otto's, where we'd all taken to sleeping most nights. When I spotted him in bed, I nudged Raven toward him, spooning behind her and doubling our chances of keeping him there. Kissing Raven on the cheek goodnight, I relaxed in the knowledge this was our forever—together.

THE NEXT DAY, WE MADE OUR TRAVEL PLANS AND LANDED IN the city at midnight. The guys enjoyed the luxury of having a plane on standby, eliminating finding flights and being on the grid. It was my favorite investment, and with how Phillip didn't bat an eyelash at my latest travel buddies, I would definitely be giving him a raise.

"Why do you guys always stay in a rental?" I asked around a yawn. "Hotels have room service."

"It's more private, for one," Otto said, squeezing my thigh. "And we like not being on the radar. Four guys traveling together raise a lot of flags."

"Hmm, I guess that makes sense. I do miss my 2am cheesecake."

"I have a cheesecake you can have, Cutie-Pie," Porter quipped.

"Really? And you're just now telling me. Give me!" I demanded, twisting in the seat.

Phoenix smacked his brother, narrowing his eyes at him. "That was mean, asshat."

"You don't have cheesecake?" I asked, knowing I was missing something but not sure what. I frowned, the thought of not getting it upsetting me.

"No, he doesn't. He meant his dick, but he should know better than to joke about food with you. I think you should make him watch us next time without allowing him to touch himself. Lord knows he could do with some impulse control. Better yet, lock him out altogether. Punish him, Cupcake," Phoenix grumbled as he shifted his sling. Porter's eyes grew comically large, a pout transforming his face as he stared at me, begging not to.

I didn't have the same reaction. A dark shudder ran through my body at the idea of punishing Porter. His eyes changed as he watched me, and he shifted in his seat as he rubbed his jeans, which seemed a lot tighter than a second ago.

"See! Point for me," Phoenix grumbled.

"You okay, Nix?" I asked, picking up on the anger running underneath his comments.

"I'm fine," he mumbled, shuffling lower in his seat. The lust I'd seen earlier in Porter's eyes vanished as he became concerned about his twin. Porter assured him, but Phoenix brushed him off. I turned back around, wanting to let them work it out.

Rueben pulled up to a two-story house a few minutes later, the neighborhood quiet this late at night. Light poles dotted the streets every few feet, cars parked in driveways with perfect lawns, and not a piece of trash littered the streets. I didn't know if it was idealistic or a bit Stepford, but it would work for now. We only planned to be here one night, anyway.

My phone vibrated, and I fought the urge to check it, hoping it was Darcy coming through with where I could find Steel Strike. I was determined to take my nemesis out tonight before we struck the mark tomorrow. It would be one less thing for me to worry about, and that eased my mind. I felt terrible for not telling the guys, but they'd only interfere, and I needed to do this quickly.

We settled into the house, going to bed shortly after. Time dragged on as the hours ticked by until I could leave without anyone noticing. Darcy had sent the location where my nemesis was staying, proving my theory right, they were tailing us. I wouldn't be able to rest now until they were eliminated. I wouldn't let Steel Strike near the guys ever again.

In the early hours before dawn, the house finally felt settled as the snores of the guys filled the room. I'd chosen to stay with the twins, knowing they were deeper sleepers, and I'd be able to sneak out and be back before anyone was ever the wiser.

Lifting Porter's arm, I slid out of bed and crept to my bag. Silently, I pulled on my black pants and shirt before stuffing my feet into my boots. Once I had my pack together, I stepped toward the balcony doors and opened them slowly. I'd practiced earlier, ensuring they wouldn't make a heinous screech when opened. Taking the front door seemed too risky, so I opted for the balcony. There was a tree nearby I could swing to and then jump down.

Taking a deep breath, I jumped and caught my hands on the branch, swinging my body weight a few seconds before vaulting to the next branch. Two more jumps and I touched the ground, the house as dark and silent as I'd left it. Smiling, I let the adrenaline rush through me as I took off down the street. I didn't want to risk anyone hearing a car pull up, so I'd wait until I was out of the neighborhood to find a ride.

I was two blocks over when high beams came to life, blinding me. Crouching down, I covered my eyes and blinked to regain my vision. The car door slammed, and I reached for my knockout spray. Footsteps louder than what Steel Strike should have sounded in the dark night.

Stepping out of the beams, I glanced around to pinpoint where the attacker was coming from. When they stepped into the stream of light, I lifted my hand to spray, my finger on the nozzle.

"Little Bird," Otto cooed, my finger a nanosecond away from spraying him. My heart beat in my chest as I tried to regain my breathing.

"Strawberry Shortcake, Otto! I nearly knocked you

out." I placed my hand on my chest, holstering my spray.

"Maybe you shouldn't sneak out in the middle of the night then," he admonished, his tone more hurt than accusatory.

"You snuck out first," I pointed out, motioning to the fact he'd been waiting for me.

"Only because I knew you would. I've been sitting out here for hours. I almost thought you were going to prove me wrong." He stepped closer, his hands going to my hips. I tilted my head back to look at him. "Why, Raven?"

Using my name shouldn't have hurt as badly as it did.

"It's my business, and I didn't want any of you to get stuck in the crossfire." I stuck my chin out, my stubbornness in full force.

Otto moved one hand to my face, brushing my hair back before resting it on my neck.

"You're part of a team now, baby. We don't do things alone. That's how you get killed."

"I'm doing this," I gritted, ignoring how my body wanted to cave to the sweetness. Otto smirked, and I knew I wouldn't like what he was about to say.

"Fine. But I'm coming with you."

"No." I didn't have to think about it. He wasn't coming. He'd only get in the way.

"Then we're going back." He shrugged his shoulders like we were debating that peanut butter and chocolate weren't the world's greatest combination. It was—if you thought otherwise, you were clearly wrong, like Otto.

"There is no way I'm doing the job tomorrow until Steel Strike is taken care of."

"I love how you say taken care of like you're talking about taking out the trash. It's cute, Little Bird."

"It's not cute. It's badass. I'm the trained killer, so get out of my way, or I'll make you."

"You might be able to take me; I'll give you that Little Bird. But I doubt you could take Rueben *and* me."

My face heated as I clenched my jaw. The man in question stepped into my line of sight, proving he'd been here just as long. Guess I could've just taken the front door since no one else was in the darn house.

The events that occurred over the next minute weren't my finest, but instinct and stubborn pride overruled me.

Slamming my foot into Otto's, I kicked him in the groin as I spun out and twisted his arm. He didn't even put up a fight, going down instantly. I dropped him and took off running, hoping I was quicker.

I was not.

Reuben's arms snaked around me within a second, pulling me back to his chest. He tossed me into the truck and shut the door quicker than what should've been possible. He didn't even look at me as he stomped over to his friend, his shoulders tight with tension. I yanked open the handle, only to fall back from the force as the door stayed locked tightly.

"Freaking child locks. I'm not a child!" I banged on the window, ignoring how much it hurt that Rueben had tossed me in here, his usual soft touch and care gone.

He didn't even look over as he picked up his friend and helped him return to the truck. As I watched Otto limp, guilt swarmed me, and I locked down all my emotions. There wasn't time for feelings when I had someone to kill.

Reuben stood in front of the other door, blocking it, so I couldn't try to force my way out when it opened. Sitting back, I crossed my arms and legs as I stared out the window. If they could be pissed, so could I. I once went an entire month not talking to Harlow. Granted, I didn't think she noticed, but I'd done it. This would be a piece of cake.

"Don't look like that, Little Bird. We're still going to do it. Just together. Now, will you give us the address, or should we drive around this Canadian town until we run out of gas and hope we stumble upon another person dressed like you?"

Gritting my teeth, I debated the pros and cons. The faster I got this over with, the faster I could return with my guys and the girl *they* loved—not the killer version of myself.

"The Oceanside Hotel," I muttered, turning and looking out the window.

Rueben reached across Otto and buckled me in, squeezing my leg twice before he put the truck into gear. I didn't want to read too much into the gesture, but it softened me, and I dropped my arms from my chest.

The ride was quiet as we made our way there; the GPS giving off the directions. When Rueben pulled into the back parking lot, I said nothing as the three of us sat there.

"I have to go in alone."

"No," Rueben said, using his words to slice my heart open more.

Pressing my eyelids closed, I took a few deep breaths. "You'll be a distraction."

"No," he said again.

Bending over, I pressed my head between my legs as I screamed. Sitting up, I turned and gave him my death glare. Rueben didn't flinch; he just held my eyes as he tried to tell me everything he couldn't say.

I love you. This is what we do. No one goes alone. I got you. Let us help you.

I love you, Angel.

Otto sat back, a smile on his face despite how pained he seemed. Sweat beaded along his brow, and I worried I'd done more damage than I'd realized. Guilt swarmed me as I realized I'd actually hurt him.

"I'm fine. Go in, and then we can grab some fatty food," he encouraged.

"Stay out of my way. I take the lead. Don't play hero," I commanded. Rueben nodded as he opened the door and walked around to open mine.

Taking a second to recenter myself, I pushed them both out of my mind as I got back into my killer mindset. Slinking along the building, I held my phone up to the door and hit the button to disengage it. When it beeped green, I slid inside and climbed the stairs. I didn't glance back to see if he made it in. It would serve him right if he didn't. Instead, I focused on keeping my breathing steady as I climbed.

"Stupid stairs," I grumbled on the eighth floor. Wiping my brow, I took a second to bend at the waist and catch my breath. "With all the sex cardio, I thought I'd be in better shape."

A chuckle behind me had me spinning, my knockout spray raised again before I remembered Rueben had followed. Placing my hand back on my chest, I rolled my eyes to the ceiling as I tried to calm down.

"Don't do that. I have to pretend you're not here, or I won't be able to focus. Please. Just do this for me so I can return to being the fun girl you love."

I dropped my head as I rubbed my temples. Large hands gripped my face, tilting it back up.

"I love every version," he whispered, bending down to kiss me.

The walls I'd constructed fell at his soft touch and words. Reuben pulled me to his chest and carried me up the rest of the stairs. I didn't know how he knew which floor, but I was a puddle of goo with shaky legs, so I'd let him carry me for now.

Rueben stopped on the fifteenth floor, proving he knew all along where we were going. He sat me down on my feet and kissed my forehead before patting my hair. It felt like the equivalent of a coach telling the next player they had this.

Or at least that was what I assumed organized sports were like since I'd never played any. Unless assassin relay counted? Yeah. I didn't think so.

Taking a deep breath, I nodded as I opened the door and crept down the hall. The closet I needed loomed ahead, and I hurried to it, using my phone to gain entry. Once inside, I pushed all thoughts of everyone else out as I made quick work of climbing the shelves and opening the panel in the ceiling for the air vent. Squeezing in, I had to suck in a big breath to push through, as my oversized hips didn't want to fit. Again.

"Why do I always try to go through the smallest spaces? It's like I forget the size of the junk in my trunk since I can't see it. I'm going to need a 'big caboose' sign so I can warn people so I don't accidentally knock them out with it," I mumbled as I army crawled through the vent. "Though, that would be hilarious at the next assassin retreat. How did you take down your last mark? I knocked them out with my ass."

Chuckling, I focused on my insane conversation to ignore the sensation of being too enclosed. Never thought I was claustrophobic until right at this moment. It took me a few tries until I had the right room, and I hoped I hadn't scared the family of four too badly when I dropped down on them. Oops.

Carefully, I slid the tile over the bathroom this time and eased my way onto the counter. I stalled every few seconds to ensure no sound came from the room. Once clear, I returned the tile and pulled my mask over my face. With a knife in one hand and the spray in the other, I stepped out of the bathroom.

A shape was curled in the bed, but I knew better than to trust it. Scanning the room, I took my time as my eyes adjusted to ensure Steel Strike wasn't hiding and using pillows as a decoy.

The body turned, the red hair of Steel Strike spread over the pillow, and I knew I had her. Holding the spray over her face, I pressed the blade to her throat. Immediately, her eyes opened as she reached for her weapon, but it was already too late.

"You should've stayed away, Steel Strike," I seethed, emotion thick in my voice.

"I never thought I'd see the day the Peppermint

Killer used a blade. I thought you were too good for all that," she sneered, trying to buy time to distract me.

Smirking, I pressed on the nozzle and watched as they fell asleep and their body relaxed into the bed. Only then did I remove my blade. I'd been prepared to use it if I had to, knowing Steel Strike couldn't leave this room alive.

Pulling out my syringe, I lifted the tongue and injected the same solution I'd given my last mark—potassium chloride. It would be a painful two minutes as their body went into immediate cardiac arrest. Steel Strike's eyes popped open a second later, the knockout potion having worn off as the other chemicals spread through her bloodstream. I waited by her bedside and watched her die, finally able to take a breath when she quit convulsing. I headed to the door and stopped before I opened it, turning my head back.

"And it's *Silent Blade*, bitch. You don't warrant a peppermint!"

With those parting words, I slipped out of the room and down the hall without being seen. My hands shook as I neared the stairwell, the adrenaline leaving my body and the knowledge that my family was safer.

Rueben grabbed me the second I stepped through and held me close. His arms felt so nice; I melted into him and let out my sobs. I hadn't realized how hard it would be to kill someone I'd known. Someone I'd trained with and respected.

Someone just like me.

Tears fell before Rueben even made it one flight, and I clung to him like a baby koala as he soothed me, taking each step slowly as I cried out my feelings.

"I didn't know," I murmured, hoping it would assuage my guilt. It didn't. "I'm sorry I tried to do it alone. Thank you."

Rueben didn't respond; he just kept holding me and rubbing my back as he descended the fifteen flights of steps.

My tears dried up by the fifth floor, and I wiped my eyes and nose on my sleeve. Yeah, it was gross, but I didn't have anywhere else to do it.

Rueben peered out the backdoor before he stepped out and headed toward the truck. I'd turned in his arms so I could see, wanting to assess the scene now that we were in the open. The truck came into view, and I smiled, the feeling of safety flooding me. I needed to apologize to Otto too, but I couldn't see him.

"Did he follow you?" I asked, glancing up at Rueben. He shook his head, frowning as he picked up his pace. Fear slid up my throat, something feeling off now.

Reuben barely had time to set me down before yanking the door open. Otto had fallen between the seats and the floor, his body constricting and seizing. Rueben jumped into action as he ran around to the other side to brace Otto's head and turn him on his side.

My feet froze in place as I stared open-mouthed, this scene feeling too familiar for my liking as I tried to remember what to do. I needed to do something. I couldn't lose Otto.

"Drive?" Rueben yelled, his voice breaking me out of my fog. The sound was pain-filled and hoarse. I shook my head and climbed into the seat, clocking the time as I counted. We'd missed a good portion of this episode, but I could at least help with the time we were here.

Seizure, my mind said. *Otto was having a seizure.*

It took a few minutes, but Otto finally stopped, his body sagging to the seat. Rueben wasted no time turning on the truck and driving out of there like a bat out of hell. I pulled Otto's head into my lap, gently brushing his hair off his forehead, and hoped he was okay.

Was this new? No, Rueben hadn't been shocked.

How long had it been happening? How bad was it?

Little pieces of information connected in my mind, anger growing out of the fear as we drove. It was much easier to blame them than myself because I had a feeling I'd caused a lot of this. And that wasn't something I wanted to look too closely at just yet.

I HADN'T LEFT OTTO'S SIDE SINCE WE'D RETURNED TO THE house. The guys had jumped into action and helped him shower before giving him meds and putting him to bed. Once again proving they were familiar with his ailment and how to help him. I'd never felt more outside of a group than I did right then.

Even with the Belladonnas, I'd never felt this excluded. With them, it was a mutual protection we offered one another, keeping each other at arm's length so it wouldn't hurt as much if something happened. A pain we were all too familiar with. We were united in our quest as assassins, and that bond held us together. Enough that you didn't feel like an outsider in the mansion and belonged to something bigger than yourself.

I'd honestly thought it was as close as you could feel to someone. That was, until I met my guys.

To feel on the outside now after being taken in left

a gaping hole in my heart—one I wasn't sure could heal.

The twins had been upset with me for sneaking out. So, I added it to the pile of shame I felt already, the hole in my heart growing as I questioned everything in my life. I was hemorrhaging on the inside, and I'd soon be a husk of the person I was as every ounce of life bled out of me.

I killed people and didn't even blink an eye.

I hurt the ones around me to further my own selfish gains, not caring how my actions would affect them.

I'd been alone for so long that it was the only way I knew how to be. I never had to consider a team before, which was probably why assassins worked alone.

It was an excuse, but I would eagerly use it because I didn't deserve to be loved, cherished, or adored. Nothing was more obvious now than that. I wasn't wired like the others. My life would be solitary, and I'd have to accept that. This had been a nice vacation, but it was all it could be.

Assassins didn't get happy endings.

I'd finish this job, and then I'd disappear. Though I couldn't go back to the mansion just yet. I didn't think I'd mentioned where it was, but I couldn't take the chance. Phoenix would find me with the smallest breadcrumb. There was no telling what I'd let slip when I'd been love drunk. I'd need to add that to the list of things to avoid on a job—drugs, alcohol, and copious amounts of dick.

Otto stirred on the bed, and my eyes flew to him as I checked him over. Someone had called a doctor to run tests since we didn't know how long he'd been seizing before we'd arrived. The doctor hadn't been worried, stating there weren't any signs of brain damage, but to keep an eye on him for the next ten hours. I'd already been sitting here for eight, and this had been the first time he'd moved. My body had become stiff long ago, but it felt justified, like I didn't deserve to be comfortable when he was in pain.

"Hey," he whispered, his eyes landing on my face. I searched them, looking for the hate I knew he'd feel.

I swallowed, not understanding what I saw reflected back. Licking my lips, I moved off the bed and held in my groan as my muscles yelled at me.

"I'll grab one of the guys," I rasped out, parched from not talking or drinking in hours.

"Wait." Otto reached out and grabbed my arm. "I'm sorry I didn't tell you sooner. I just didn't want you to think of me differently... as weak."

I shook my head. His words didn't compute. His hand was warm on my arm and thawed the frozen layer I'd erected around myself.

"Little Bird, look at me... *please*." The pleading tone killed me, but I couldn't face him. I'd crumble and give in to comfort I didn't deserve.

"She's beating herself up and taking on the blame. She's been withdrawing slowly each hour you've been asleep. We've been waiting for her to bolt," a voice said from the darkened doorway.

My eyes snapped up; green orbs seared into me and threatened to demolish all the shame and self-hatred I'd piled on.

"Don't," I warned, my voice shaky as I shook my head.

The figure moved forward, and Porter came into view. However, it wasn't *my* Porter. This version was hard, his usual smile replaced with a frown. There was no laughter, no light or joy. This Porter was covered in darkness, and I hated myself even more for ruining him.

"*Don't* what, Raven? Don't care about you? Don't call you out on your shit when you're being dumb? Don't remind you that we love you? That we're a family? Don't stop you from sabotaging the best thing any of us has ever had. Which '*don't*' is it?" Dark Porter asked.

Despite the hardness of his words, there was no anger on his face, just sadness. Tears I'd been able to shove down and ignore reared their ugly head and filled my eyes. My lip trembled as his words slashed through the barrier, piercing my soul.

"Loving someone means accepting their flaws and imperfections. You're perfect in many ways, Raven, but you do have flaws. It doesn't make us love you any less, though," Phoenix said, stepping into the room and standing shoulder-to-shoulder with his twin.

"Love is working on the hard things and fighting together to find a solution. Not running off to sacrifice yourself," Porter added, his voice softening some.

"Love is never giving up," Rueben whispered, his eyes boring into mine as he joined them, making a hot guy wall.

"Loving someone isn't always easy, but it's worth it, Little Bird. Are you willing to be with us for the hard stuff or only the good?" Otto asked, finishing their love monologue.

My body shook as emotions threatened to spill out, my heart pounding in my ears as I tried to align what they were saying with what I'd thought and felt.

Had I been giving up when it got hard? Was I sabotaging because I didn't feel worthy? Looking for any excuse to run away?

Otto tugged on my arm, and I fell back to the bed as all the fight and the need to run escaped me. He pulled me into his arms, and I went willingly, too weak to push away his comforting embrace. The tears I'd been holding fell in silent rivers down my face as I nuzzled into his chest. The bed dipped on both sides, and more bodies pressed into me, cocooning me in their warmth and presence.

"I'm sorry. I didn't know."

I sucked in a breath, wiping my eyes as I pulled away and sat up. I glanced around at the four men who owned my heart and were far more competent than me in this area. It was odd to feel dumb about something but refreshing at the same time because it meant I could learn. And I was an excellent student. I could learn anything if I tried.

"I've never been in love before. I thought I knew what it meant to love someone, but when my only examples were *Phoenix Hospital* and the memories of a six-year-old, my database was lacking. While I love my sisters, and they love me, it's different." I shrugged one shoulder, playing with the string on the comforter. Someone squeezed my foot, reminding me I needed to face the people I hurt and not hide. "I'm sorry I got scared and withdrew. I just thought you'd all be better without me. All this mess was my fault, and I couldn't face that." My lip trembled as I accepted all the emotions I'd been feeling—confusion, fear, loneliness, shame, and guilt.

"Is it wrong that I get a little excited about being smarter than you in something?" Phoenix asked, his eyes sparkling. Porter smacked him, and his smile returned. "Ow, Bro. That one hurt. Gunshot, remember?" Phoenix pouted, putting on a fake grimace and making Porter feel guilty as he started to hover and apologize.

"Wasn't it the other shoulder?" I asked, winking.

Porter immediately stopped and realized I was right, smacking Phoenix again for good measure. Phoenix doubled over, laughing at his brother. Porter shook his head and crossed his arms, but the darkness I'd seen earlier had lifted, and he was back to being the sunshine boy I knew.

"We're all learning how to navigate a relationship, Little Bird," Otto said from behind me. He sat up, wrapped his arms around me, and kissed my cheek. "You're not the odd one out. We might know how to work as a group, but we're new to being in a relationship. We're all going to make mistakes. Just like I should've told you about my seizures sooner. I'm sorry about that. Each day we're together, we're learning more and more about how to love and trust one another. It's only going to get better with time. So, are you with us? No more running off?"

"Yes, I'm with you. I don't want to be anywhere else. I love you guys."

"We love you," rang out around me, and I relaxed fully, my body catching up to the sleep deprivation and agony I'd put it through.

"Sleep. We'll figure the rest out in the morning."

With that, I closed my eyes as I settled back against the bed and vowed to be just as good at loving them as they were to me.

I HAD no idea how long I'd been asleep when I woke up. The light had shifted in the room, but that didn't mean anything since I had no clue what time it had been to start with. The bed was empty, the sheets cold next to me, so I sat up and pushed the covers off. My body ached, and I'd need to do some yoga to stretch before we headed to the job.

The job!

With Otto's seizure and my vigil at his bedside and subsequent sleep, we would've missed our original time window. Sugar toast!

Jumping up, I raced out of the room and down the steps. I skidded to a halt in the living room as I took in my four guys laughing as they played some game on the TV.

"Cutie-pie! Flash Rueben for me so he crashes his car."

I blinked, trying to connect his request and the fact we weren't on the job. "Huh?"

A second later, Porter cursed as a crashing sound came from the TV, and he dropped his hands as he fell back onto the couch. Rueben smirked, chuckling as he kept his focus.

"Fucker," Porter grumbled, punching Rueben in the arm. Now that his arms were free, he reached out and pulled me into his lap. The controller poked me in the leg, and I cringed, reaching down to pull it free. "How are you feeling, Cutie-pie?"

"Better." My cheeks flushed as I recalled my earlier reaction. "I thought we had a job?" I bit my lip, hoping I hadn't screwed it up.

"We rearranged some things and added a few nights to the rental. We're going tonight if you're up to it."

I glanced at Otto, sitting on the other sofa with Phoenix. He turned at my stare, giving me a reassuring smile. "I'm fine, Little Bird. Promise."

Sighing, I snuggled back into Porter's arms. "Then let's hunt us a bad guy. It's time for Jerome to pay for his crimes."

"Am I the only one who goes half-chub at her murderous ways?" Porter groaned.

The other guys said nothing, but if the casual shift they all did was any indication, then I'd say they agreed with Porter.

Huh. And here I thought my darkness would push them away.

Feeling fully accepted and like things were back on track, I watched them play the silly game as I planned all the ways I could use this new knowledge.

"You've got your plotting smile on," Porter whispered, his breath tickling my neck.

I glanced up, shrugging one shoulder, not denying

or confirming his assessment. Internally, I loved the fact he knew my different smiles.

"I want in. Please?" His begging lit a fire in me, and I remembered what I'd discovered on our drives. I pulled his head lower to whisper in his ear.

"Will you be a good boy and do exactly as your mistress commands?"

Porter shivered underneath me, his dick twitching at my words.

"Yes, mistress. I'll do whatever you ask. Please command me."

Smirking, I trailed my fingers up his neck and to the nape of his head. "Very well. When we finish this mission, here's what I want to do."

As I explained my plans to Porter, his cock pressed harder into my ass, and his hands tightened on me. His body trembled with need, and his breathing became labored. Porter's arousal was liquid fire, lighting me up inside. Kissing his cheek, I stood and retreated to the bedroom to prepare. I'd never been more ready to finish a job than I was right now.

On the other side of punishing Jerome was living the dream with my guys, and nothing would take that from me.

Nothing.

I DOUBLE-CHECKED THE LINE I'D CONNECTED FROM THE rooftop of the building Phoenix was stationed in to the one Jerome inhabited. Satisfied everything was secure, I moved to the escape hatch I'd discovered. The hatch hadn't been on any blueprints, but I'd had a hunch after finding invoices and parts ordered after Jerome had moved in. With Phoenix's help, we'd been able to track down the construction company and access their plans.

Now I had a secret way in and insurance that Jerome couldn't escape since we'd blocked the rest of it shut. If he tried to use it, he'd find himself with compound fractures on both legs. Falling feet first into concrete would end with him at the least in a full-body cast, or at the most... dead. Win-win if you asked me.

Using the drill, I removed the lid and set it off to the side. I secured a second rope in case we needed to use this as a way out. My arms grimaced in thought, hoping it wouldn't be required. I still hadn't gotten around to doing that extra cardio or weight training I kept saying I needed.

Oh, well. Nothing I could do about it now. I was pretty sure hand jobs weren't included in the training regiment. Bummer.

I sat on the edge, my feet swinging into the open space. My pack was secured onto my back, and I'd successfully completed all my tasks. It was go time.

"LB in position. PR?" I asked over the comms Phoenix had set up.

"We've made it to the top floor. That elevator shaft was hardcore," Porter said, breathing heavily over the earpiece.

"OP?" I asked.

"Secure. We've got our eyes on you. On your go, I'll deactivate the security system. You'll have intervals of twenty seconds to get in before it resets."

"I'm ready. Sound off," I whispered, my hands gripping the edge as I braced myself inside the chute.

"Ready," Porter said.

"On my mark," Phoenix started. "One, two, go!"

At his command, I let go and slid down the chute, keeping my arms close to my side as I counted in my head. I needed to stop fifteen feet down, or I'd go too far and miss my window.

"Twelve, thirteen, fourteen, fifteen." My hands and legs shot out as I stopped myself, my body moving down a few extra feet. I quickly kicked out the panel on the left, swung my body through the opening, and landed on the four-inch beam. I steadied myself just as Phoenix shouted the alarm was back.

"Everyone good?" I asked, my breathing labored from the move. I hadn't had to do it that quickly in all the times I'd practiced this. So I'd been confident I could do it, but there had been an ounce of fear I wouldn't make it in time.

"First guard is down, and we've made it through the stairwell door. What did you put in that dart, Rave?" Porter asked, choking back his laughter.

"I'll tell you later," I said, smiling at my newest invention—knockout with a side of molly. He'd be humping the floor in his dreams, too blissed out to do anything if he did wake up before we were gone. I was thinking of calling it dreamscape.

"We're almost through our window, and then I can jump back in. On my mark," Phoenix said, his business voice sending shivers through me.

"Now is not the time to get turned on," I whispered.

When a choked snort sounded through my ear, I remembered too late that everyone could hear me over the comms this time.

"Jolly green giant," I cursed as my face heated.

"One, two, go!" Phoenix said, his voice lighter.

Not wasting time, I ran across the beam and jumped, swinging to the one closer to the wall. I'd landed in the private gym, figuring it would be empty at two in the morning and the easiest to access. The only hindrance was the ceiling was twelve feet high. Once I reached the wall, I hooked my rope line and jumped, sliding down it. I didn't have time to rappel.

"Stop!" Phoenix shouted just as my feet hit the ground. Taking in lungfuls of air, I didn't move. Jerome's security system included motion-censored plates, making it difficult to get far twenty seconds at a time, but I was patient and would play this game of hopscotch as long as it took to get to the end.

On and on we went, waiting a minute between the twenty-second intervals as we made our way into the penthouse from two directions. Since we had different destinations, we'd opted to split up to give the other group better odds. The guys hadn't liked it but couldn't argue my reasoning. Plus, if anyone was going to get caught, it would be them. Their task was longer and required more diligence than mine.

Plus, once I made it to Jerome, I'd use his biometrics to turn off the alarm and give us a better chance of escaping.

"I'm outside the bedroom," I whispered. In the next bout, I'd be inside and my last victim in sight.

"We're almost to the safe room and the last guard," Porter said.

"You're all doing great. Stay focused, and we'll be out of here soon," Otto encouraged.

"On three," Phoenix said, bringing us back to task. "One, two, go!"

I grumbled how he always said "on three" but actually meant "go" as I turned the knob and slid through a crack in the door, flattening myself against the wall. I could hear soft laughter, but I focused on the room and took in the layout as my eyes adjusted. The voice that spoke into the darkness sent a chill through me.

"I've been expecting you, Peppermint."

"I'm not a fucking Care Bear or My Little Pony," I grumbled.

A light flicked on, showcasing the face of the man I'd had nightmares about since I was five years old—Jerome Fulton, aka Carlos Ramirez.

The scientist who'd created Artevac.

The president of Good Meds Pharma who'd killed thousands for profit.

The man who'd murdered my parents in cold blood after they'd become addicted to the drug he'd created and hadn't been able to fulfill their agreement.

When it had come time for my first kill, I'd asked Man to find the man responsible for my parents' death. It had taken a while for him to locate who I'd described. Carlos hadn't been a regular street drug dealer like I'd always believed. Nope, Carlos here was a brilliant scientist who'd been denied test subjects for his latest drug trial. So when he needed people, he sought out the desperate; promising them a fortune beyond their wildest imagination. And all they had to do was take some medication and report back the side effects.

My parents hadn't been drug addicts, making those few early memories of them being kind and loving harder to ignore. This man had offered them a way out of poverty, only to sentence them to a life of addiction. And when they couldn't physically continue his trials, he'd killed them.

In my opinion, he was the worst of the worst—preying on people's weaknesses and exploiting them for his own gain.

But not anymore. Now he was *my* prey.

I took out my knife and flipped it over my fingers, hoping I created a menacing picture in my black leather. I'd made a special concoction for him, and I couldn't wait to use it. Carlos didn't get to die peacefully in his sleep. Not even a heartache was horrific enough for this man. I wanted him to hurt and regret everything he'd ever done.

"You sure about that?" he taunted, taking me a second to figure out what he meant.

Snorting, I gave my best sadistic smile. Try calling me a Care Bear now, asshole.

"Oh, I'm sure. And you will be, too, once you meet the end of my blade."

"Now, Cindy, there's no reason to lie. We both

know you're not going to kill me with that." He smirked as he folded his hands together, the epitome of calm and collected.

That just wouldn't do.

Shrugging, I stopped flipping the blade, moving to put it back on my belt. Quicker than he could track, I threw it toward his shoulder. My eyes stayed on his face the whole time, but I knew the second it made contact. His eyes flashed with surprise as he grimaced, the chemical taking effect the second it pierced his skin.

His arrogance would cost him. Carlos thought he was safe in his penthouse with his high-tech security and armed guards. But he hadn't dealt with me or my team before.

Yeah, *my team*.

It had been Otto who'd given me the idea. Using components from his medication, I extracted the tropane alkaloid and made it more robust. It wouldn't kill him, but it would make him compliant with anything I asked.

"What did you do?" he hissed, his pupils large as the chemical took effect. His muscles tightened next, and the complete loss of free will followed.

"You might have heard of a version called Devil's Breath," I said as I stalked forward. I'd barely heard Phoenix in my ear telling me it was clear. Now that I had him subdued, it was time to eliminate the alarm.

Carlos tried to fight the drug, but with each second it coursed through his bloodstream, the less control he had.

I slapped my hands down on the desk when I neared, making Carlos jump at the noise. His eyes met mine, half a sneer on his face as he tried to fight the effects.

"You're mine to command now, Carlos. Deactivate the alarm."

His face screamed how much he wanted to ignore me, but his mind and body were under my control. With sluggish movements, he picked up the phone next to him and lifted it to his face and did as I asked. I moved around the desk to watch, ensuring he didn't try to alert anyone.

The alarm beeped as a disembodied voice spoke over the speakers, "Alarm disengaged."

"That wasn't so hard. Now, I want you to record yourself saying the following." I pulled out a piece of paper and sat it on his desk. He scanned over it, his cheeks puffing out as he tried to hiss at me.

"Anytime now. The countdown has begun." I tapped my wrist, twirling my finger in the air.

"You won't get away with this."

"That's where you're wrong. Not only will I get away with this, but I'll live better knowing you're gone from this world. And all the families you robbed loved ones from will have some compensation for the lies you sold them. *I'm* stopping the cycle. Little ol' me."

He sneered at me as best he could, his fingers twitching to do something, but he couldn't unless I told him. My grin spread wider as I hopped up on the desk. I could hear Porter and Rueben taking out the last guard and working on the safe. Pretending to file my fingernails, I waved at him to carry on.

"Chop, chop. We're killing time here, Carlos. Record. Read. Be sincere. Go."

He lifted the phone and hit record, sitting it on the tripod I'd unfolded and set up. Smiling at him, I motioned for him to keep going.

"Dear viewers, I've realized my life no longer has value due to the countless people I've murdered. Yes, *murdered*. Either through physical violence or my drugs, I'm responsible for thousands, if not millions, of deaths. I've sent my lawyer a document with all the families affected by my misdeeds and bequeath 75% of my fortune to be divided between them. The remaining portion is to be used to set up recovery centers, so I can leave a legacy that will actually make a difference and not just the memory of the piece of shit person I am. The center shall be named Hopevale, so all that enter do so in the name of hope and recovery. My life is over, and I fully admit to taking my own life. Please respect my wishes. Again, I'm sorry I was such a scumbag."

I mouthed the words along with him, smiling at the end.

"Stop recording." He did as I said; the fight drained out of him now.

Picking up his phone, I uploaded the video to the drive Phoenix had set up and then wiped all traces of our entrance from the cameras, looping them for an hour before we came. With that taken care of, I pulled the blade out of his arm, keeping my eyes on his face. *Don't look at the blood. It's not real.*

"Not only are you dying at the hands of a little girl you vowed to kill twenty years ago, but all your millions and research will be given to those you've harmed. You have nothing left. Your name is mud. Your legacy is gone. You're done, and it was me and my team who did it. I'm the predator, and you're the prey. Now, say it with me. *Silent Blade.*"

"Sil-ent Bl-ade," he bit out. I tapped his head mockingly.

"Good asshole. Enjoy Hell."

Pulling out the syringe, I jabbed it into his arm, leaving it lying on the desk. It was all the drugs he made combined. It felt fitting he should die by his own creations.

Hopping off the desk, I didn't even look back as I left the room. This man had stolen my past. I wouldn't let him take my future too.

Once I was free of the room, sound returned to me,

my mind able to focus on something other than the asshole who'd killed my family.

"Raven!"

"I'm here. I'm clear of the room and headed to the roof. Everyone else?"

Arms wrapped around me before I heard a response, and I went into reflex mode, flipping the person over my shoulder. I froze when Porter's face stared up at me, a look of amazement on his perfect golden skin.

"Marry me, Cutie-pie," he gasped as he caught the breath I'd just knocked out of him.

"Idiot," Rueben grumbled, winking at me. I suspected Rueben had seen me but had let Porter touch me first, knowing how I'd respond.

"You think you would've learned after the first time, Fungi!" I teased, reaching down to help him up.

"Nah. It's more fun to run head first," he countered, making me shake my head as I smiled. Porter was too cute for his own good most of the time.

"Everything grabbed?" I asked, glancing at their packs. I had no clue what they'd been aiming to steal other than the evidence. Rueben nodded to two duffles on his shoulders and the one Porter had dropped.

"We're good. Let's go before the guards wake up."

I giggled. "That's going to be a while. I'm sure they're having the time of their life right now."

Porter and Rueben chuckled as we headed toward

the back staircase. The trek was easier now that we didn't have to wait on Phoenix to disengage the alarm. Hooking the bags to the zip line, we sent them through the air onto the other roof.

"You sure you don't want to take it across?" I asked, glancing at the thin wire connecting the skyscrapers.

Porter gulped, moving backward toward the door as he held up his hands, afraid I'd somehow be able to hook him up without his consent and shove him across. Reuben also swallowed and shook his head no.

"Spoilsports," I teased.

Releasing the wire, it flew back toward the other end. Quickly, the three of us changed into regular clothes and shoved everything into a backpack that Rueben would carry.

They'd insisted that Porter and I leave first, pretending to be a couple in love. Though, with the way Porter's hands roamed my body as we rode down the elevator, there wasn't any pretending on my part. No one paid attention to us as we walked out of the lobby; our eyes focused solely on one another.

Reuben emerged five minutes later, and the three of us walked to the van parked a few blocks over, where the other two had converged once they'd grabbed the bags. The doors flew open, and Otto jumped out, checking me over before pulling me into a tight hug.

"You did it, Little Bird. It's over."

Those words broke the last bit of restraint I held as I grieved for the little girl who'd lost her parents and had subsequently been thrust into this life. I loved where I'd ended up and all the people I'd met along the way, but I couldn't say the same for every family Carlos had messed with. And now, no one else would have to.

It had taken me twenty years, but I'd finally avenged George and Laura Hopevale. *Their* legacy would live on, giving genuine hope to families.

I knew it wasn't the end of villains. There would be others; bad guys were like bed bugs—burrowing in places and impossible to kill outright. But it didn't mean I would stop taking them down; however, that looked in the future.

"Come on. Let's head home. Phillip is waiting for us."

Words had never sounded as sweet as those right then.

Raven

Stepping off the plane back in Colorado felt different this time than any of the other times I'd returned to the Belladonna mansion. It wasn't because I had four men with me who owned my heart, bringing me alive in so many new ways. But more how I didn't feel the same eagerness I typically did to return to the mansion.

Most often after completing a mission, I'd hide away in my room with as many of Karma's creations as I could gather from the kitchen and binge *Phoenix Hospital*. I'd occasionally come up for air to shower, but it wasn't a top priority. I needed that time to decompress before I jumped back into the fray, my search for Otto and retribution powering me.

Except now I had Otto, and I'd avenged my parents. Where did I exactly go from here?

"Wow. This place is beautiful. Maybe we should purchase a house here!" Porter said as he peered around at the mountains and clusters of trees off in the distance.

"How many houses do you have?" I asked curiously. "I thought your base was in NYC?"

"That's our main residence, but we have places worldwide. You never know when you need to get away," Otto said as he grabbed my hand and drew me near the car.

I waved at Pierce, who had the good grace not to lift his eyebrows too high at my new companions. He'd seen a lot working at the Belladonna mansion in his short time, so I doubted this even registered as the weirdest.

"Hey, Pierce. Tabby give into your charm yet?" I teased. He huffed, shaking his head as he smiled and opened the doors. The poor sap was obsessed, and she had no idea.

"Welcome, Ms. Raven. I take it *your* trip was good?" he asked, his teasing more polite and covert than my own had been.

"Very."

I grinned as the four guys followed me into the car. It was a tight squeeze, but no one wanted to sit up front. I ended up across a few laps, my head resting on Rueben's chest. The drive was quiet as the guys observed the scenery as it passed by, taking in my world and where I'd lived for twenty years.

I knew the second the mansion came into view as they sat up straighter, peering out the window. The fountain at the front was bubbling as we neared, driving down the cobbled drive. The white columns stood out brightly against the tan color of the house. I tried to remember what it had been like the first time I saw it. It was the biggest house I'd ever seen back then. It had become my home, my place of refuge and comfort. I'd grown into the killer I was today inside this house.

Though that didn't fit quite right either. I had become a killer, an assassin. But I'd also become more confident, funny, strong, and educated. Perhaps more importantly, I'd become a sister, a friend, and a protector.

As it turned out, my biggest flaw was not perceiving myself for all the parts I was. The time to embrace every aspect of myself was now. I couldn't keep living and only think of myself as a killer. That wasn't even the coolest part of me, and I needed to drop all my shields to live out the life I'd dreamed up in my stories.

"You guys ready to meet my sisters?" I asked, excited at the idea.

"They're not going to kill us on sight, right?" Porter asked, gulping.

I shrugged and headed toward the door. "Depends on who we run into first." The guys shared a look, their faces going pale at my words. Giggling, I couldn't hold it in anymore. "Relax. You're with me. You'll be fine."

Rueben was the first to step forward, followed by Otto and then the twins. I opened the heavy door and took a few minutes to inhale all the different smells that were unique to the Belladonnas.

Gasoline and oil from Tabitha's tinkering in her workshop.

Chocolate and sugar from Karma's latest baking creation.

Roses and hydrangeas that Royal cut, probably after conversing with them.

And the faintest whiff of Man's cologne, letting me know he probably had retreated to his office hours ago and hadn't been out in a while.

Darcy stumbled around the corner eating a piece of pizza, stopping in her tracks when she spotted me. Her blonde hair was piled high on her head with her panda headphones visible. As usual, she wore her favorite sweatshirt and leggings. She blinked owlishly at the guys behind me. I looked around, ensuring I didn't spot any dick-spraying drones. I didn't need the glitter bomb today.

"I think I'm hallucinating," she mumbled as she took another bite.

"I thought that too. But there's actually two of them." I nodded, pointing at the twins. Darcy blinked, her face twitching like she wanted to smile at me but wasn't quite sure if I was joking or not. "Oh! Remember that search we set up to find my friend?"

"Brown hair, gray eyes, cute smile one?" she asked, glancing from me again back to the guys.

"Yes! Ta-da!" I did my best *Wheel of Fortune* impression as I showcased Otto.

Darcy seemed to regain some of her consciousness now; my theatrics confirming she wasn't hallucinating, and nodded as she finished her pizza. "Cool. Have fun with all that." She gave me a wink as she twirled her hand around at the four guys behind me.

"Wait!" I shouted, rushing her and body-slamming her in a hug as much as my five-foot frame could muster. Darcy let out an "oof" but accepted the embrace. Out of all my sisters, she was the most open to touch and had given me many hugs over the years. This time, I gave her one.

"I'll miss you, Darcy. But don't think this means our war is over. We'll just have to be more creative," I mumbled into her sweatshirt.

"Whatever, dork." I could hear the smile in her voice as she paused. "I'll miss you too."

With that, I disentangled our bodies and let her return to battling monsters.

"So, that's Darcy," I said, spinning to face the guys. They had varying degrees of amusement on their faces.

Smiling, I took off up the stairs, suddenly very

excited to show them my room and pack. I'd miss the house and living with the girls, but it wasn't like I wouldn't ever see them again. I understood that now. We were never all here anyway, someone was always off on a mission, yet it didn't take away from our bond. So, this wouldn't either.

The guys followed me into my room, and I watched as they took in all my possessions. Porter flopped onto the bed, cuddling with my pillow and burrowing his nose into it.

"It smells like you." He sighed, not blinking when Phoenix slapped him as he sat beside him. He stared at my collection of *Phoenix Hospital* merch, from the figurines to the signed photos I'd gotten. Otto looked over my chemistry table, reading off some of the labels. Rueben went to my closet and opened the door. I didn't take him for fashion, but you learned something new every day.

When he emerged, he had a suitcase under his arm, a duffle on his back, and a pile of clothes on hangers under his other arm. My eyes bulged as I watched him dump it on the bed, pointing at the twins to start packing.

"In a rush, Ruebear?" I asked, a warm feeling spreading through me. Rueben gave me a look that could melt ice in a blizzard.

He handed me the duffle and pointed toward the bookcase along the far wall. Jumping up on my chair, I kissed his cheek before hopping down and doing as he asked. Once all the clothes were packed, the twins started in the bathroom while Otto helped me with the books. Rueben had left at one point, returning with some boxes. I didn't know where he found them, but I was glad for them all the same. Occasionally he'd point at something, asking if I wanted to take it or leave it.

With the five of us working together, we had everything I wanted to take boxed up in no time. I stared at the nearly vacant room; my bedding and a few things on the shelves were the only items remaining outside my chemistry lab. I'd decided to take a few of my sprays but left most, knowing if the girls needed them, they could grab some until I had time to make more. Plus, it would give me a second lab whenever I visited. If Man adopted a new girl, I'd move it, but it could stay for now.

"Wow. I thought it would feel different when I left here, but it doesn't. I guess it was time."

"Your home is with us now, Little Bird. But we don't expect you to forget who you are. We'll be right next to you on the plane whenever you need to return."

Snuggling into Otto's chest, I nodded. I took the guys through a house tour as I said goodbye to the staff and each of my sisters I found along the way. The guys had loaded everything into a truck that Pierce had brought around, making it easier to haul all my stuff back to the airport. Now, we all sat around the kitchen island, snacking on Karma's chocolate chip cookies.

"Seriously, these are the best things ever," Phoenix said, groaning around another mouthful.

"You can thank Karma for my hips. I keep saying I'll do more cardio, but it never sounds as fun as enjoying these heavenly creations."

The guys chuckled at me, and I wiped my mouth, knowing I had one more stop to make. "I'll be right back. You guys okay here?"

They nodded, and I slipped off the stool and headed to the secret basement. I knew Man wouldn't care that I was leaving, but it wasn't easy to put my feelings into words. He'd been a father figure to me in many ways, though that wasn't how he liked to be perceived. Man kept his distance, knowing someday we'd either venture out on our own or be taken from him. I couldn't imagine it was easy knowing that. Yet, he kept rescuing girls who needed him, showing them how to be strong and fight. He gave us all a chance to survive in this world, and that was a gift I didn't know how to repay.

His office door was cracked, so I knocked gently. Knowing Man, he left it like that, expecting me to stop by once I was home. Despite not leaving the house often, he knew everything that happened with the

Belladonnas' comings and goings. It made this conversation slightly easier on me knowing he wouldn't be surprised.

I stepped into the pristine office, the floors shining up at me as I approached his dark mahogany desk. The bookcases behind it were filled with volumes, tomes, and artifacts I had to believe he collected before becoming a recluse. There weren't any personal mementos or pictures. That just wasn't Man's style.

His white head of hair was bent as he worked on something, his hand flying across the paper at a speed I didn't know he was capable of. He didn't glance up, but that wasn't uncommon. His free hand motioned for me to take the chair, letting me know he'd heard my entrance.

"I'm back from my mission. Every mark was taken out despite some hiccups. I also had to decommission Steel Strike as they threatened the successful completion." I took a deep breath, my heart rate pounding against my chest. "I want to thank you for helping me become the person I am. Taking out Carlos after all these years and ending the pain and suffering he caused. His death feels worthy. When you found me, I was a broken little bird needing a home. You gave me that and taught me to fly. Now, I think it's time for me to leave the safety of the mansion and venture out on my own. I found my friend and a few others who make me happy."

"Are you stepping away only from the mansion or the Belladonnas, too?" he asked, his pen stopping.

"Just the mansion for now. I love being a Belladonna and the work I do. I'm not sure I'd know how to do anything else," I admitted.

"Don't underestimate yourself, Raven."

It was short and to the point but the sweetest thing Man had ever said to me. I nodded that I'd heard him, pivoting to leave before I embarrassed myself and tried to hug the man.

"I'll be in touch," he volleyed as I stepped through the door. Smiling, I took that as his goodbye and blessing as I returned to my guys.

Their eyes caressed me from head to toe, acting like I'd been gone longer than the five minutes it had taken. But I wouldn't complain. Having their attention and love was a reward all in and of itself.

"You ready?" Otto asked, his words holding more than one meaning.

"Yeah. I am."

The four guys stood, surrounding me as we walked out together—a life full of possibilities, laughter, and love ahead of us.

I couldn't help but look back at the mansion, something I typically avoided at all costs, too scared the bad guy would be right there to grab me. I wasn't afraid anymore. If anything, *I'd* become the boogeyman—the one bad guys were terrified of, murmuring my name into the shadows.

"Who's next?" I whispered, the adrenaline already spiking at the thought. "The—"

"—peppermint?"

"What?" I shrieked, spinning to glare at the guy who dared call me Peppermint Killer.

"I asked if you had a peppermint. Don't you carry them with you?" Porter asked, his eyes twinkling.

Narrowing my eyes, I pulled one out of my bag and handed it to him. He popped it into his mouth, swirling it around with his tongue in deliberate motions before chomping on the candy, making me wince.

"Your poor teeth," I hissed.

Porter winked as his hands gripped my hips and lifted me into the truck. At this height, we were eye level, and Porter didn't waste the opportunity, kissing me and letting the peppermint flavor roll over my tongue. Phoenix pulled Porter away, tilting my head back and kissing me next. The angle of his kiss made my head fuzzy as his tongue swept across mine.

The body in front of me moved, and my head was again pulled toward someone new. My eyes fluttered, taking in my silent giant, who had to bend down to reach me. His large hands cupped my cheeks, belying his size as usual with his gentleness. Rueben's lips landed on mine next, the kiss slower as he devoured me like I was the best-tasting chocolate he'd ever had.

All too soon, I was yanked back again, meeting Otto's lips as he twisted my body so my lips landed on his. A dizzy feeling encompassed my body as I panted, breathless from their kisses.

"What was that for?" I asked a few minutes later after I'd regained my bearings. The twins chuckled from the back, Rueben driving on my left side and Otto on my right. I hadn't even felt us take off.

"Just loving you, Little Bird. Every new adventure should start with a kiss."

"Yeah, it's for good luck," Porter said.

"Sign me up then." I giggled, settling back into the seat, my four guys cocooning me like they often did, placing me at the heart of them.

I might not have grown up to be Robin Hood with her merry men, but I'd become something better— even more than the assassin Silent Blade, Raven the Belladonna, homeless Little Bird, and innocent Cindy.

I'd become me.

Raven

A FEW MONTHS LATER

THE KID'S LAUGHTER FILLED THE SPACE AS THEY RAN AROUND the expansive ballroom, hopping from one attraction to the next. The families affected by Good Meds Pharma were spread throughout the room, enjoying the charity function. Thanks to the evidence we recovered, the families had been able to refile their lawsuits and get the closure they needed. To celebrate, PROP held a function in their honor.

I'd been shocked when I learned about Loxley Crew's charitable foundation and how they used PROP. For some reason, I pictured them dropping off bags of cash on people's front porches, ringing the doorbell, and running away as they watched from the bushes.

"Better than hiding in the bushes?" Otto asked, draping his arm around my shoulder.

"I guess so. Though, it would be cool to do it once."

Phoenix laughed as he came up to my other side. "These families operate on the legal side of things, so they need to be able to access help in a way that doesn't get them in trouble with the IRS."

"I guess that makes sense. Doesn't mean I don't want to do it still," I grumbled, pretending to pout. In all honesty, though, I enjoyed getting to see the kids and families have fun. They all deserved the chance to be carefree and spoiled for a few hours.

"Just got word back from Phillip, and we're all set to fly out in the morning. Barcelona, here we come!" Porter cheered, doing a little hip dance as he neared me. I smiled, a giggle escaping at his antics. He grabbed me and spun me, my aqua blue dress spinning out. It matched the blue in my hair perfectly, and I'd had to have it the second I'd spotted it. It glittered like the stars, swooping out at the slit up one leg as Porter twirled me. The front had a deep V that went down practically to my belly button.

"Should I be jealous you've got a bromance going on with Phillip?" I teased.

Porter chuckled, dipping me as he kissed me. "Definitely. The dude can fly a plane!"

Rolling my eyes, I spun out into the arms of Rueben. He lifted me under my butt, bringing my face closer to his. I laid my head on his shoulder as he swayed, my fingers running along the back of his neck. We didn't need words as we danced, our hearts communicating for us. When his turn was done, he kissed my lips and set me back down as Otto took my hands.

I was the closest to his height in my heels, so we swayed like we would at a middle-school dance with my arms looped around his neck, his on the base of my back.

"Has life been everything you thought it would be out of the mansion?" he asked, his lips brushing my ear.

"Better," I cooed. While there had been some bumps as we all navigated living together full-time, it had been the best time of my life. That could be down to the fact the orgasms had muddled my brain, but I wasn't going to question it.

"I love you, Little Bird. I thank the stars every day for bringing you back to me."

"I love you too, Otto."

My gray-eyed boy smiled, twirling and watching my hair fly out behind me. Phoenix was waiting for me, picking me up and wrapping my legs around his waist.

"Not one for dancing?" I asked.

"I prefer to do the horizontal tango, Cupcake. You look so divine in this dress that I can't decide if I want to fuck you in it while it drapes around you or if it will be better on the floor."

Groaning, I rocked forward, my clit making contact

with his hard cock. Phoenix slammed his lips into mine, his hands threading through my hair as he kissed me like no one else was in the room.

"I take it that's our cue to leave." Porter chuckled from behind me, nipping my neck. "I have your requests completed, mistress," he purred, his hands skating over my behind.

My body shivered at his declaration, my pussy dripping at his use of 'mistress.' Porter and I had discovered his love of praise, adding a fun new layer to our intimacy.

"Good boy," I exalted, my hand trailing over his face. His body vibrated at my touch, his cock visible beneath his suit pants. "Lead the way."

Porter nodded, spinning on his feet as he took off. In these moments that he gave me control, he was more subdued and focused, like he could relax for the first time all day.

We'd gotten a room for the night, so we didn't have to go too far, just an elevator ride up thirty floors. The tension in the small space was thick as we all shifted, trying not to look at one another so we didn't give the security guard watching the monitors a show.

"I'm pretty sure I can hack into the feed and delete anything," Phoenix muttered, moving his hand down the front between my breasts. Goosebumps littered my skin, my thighs shifting together as all brain function flew out the window.

Rueben growled, the sound not helping my situation below, but the next second instead of contemplating moving Phoenix's hand lower, I was pulled over Rueben's shoulder as he exited the elevator.

"Is that why the British call them lifts? Because of all the people getting lifted out of them for sexy times? If so, I'm here for it."

The twins chuckled, now used to my weird mutterings. I hadn't stopped talking to myself; there just happened to be someone else to hear it now.

The door was pushed open before us, Rueben's stride not breaking as he sat me down on my wobbly feet. "Right, these need to go," I said, kicking off the high heels. The guys appeared disappointed for two seconds until I turned and lifted my dress.

"Holy pajamas! She hasn't been wearing underwear all night," Porter cursed.

"I've never seen anything look so pretty before," Phoenix added as I bent over slightly to reveal the plug I'd been wearing. Thankfully, the guys had taken me seriously, getting me several cute ones to wear. This one flashed, vibrated, and sparkled. It was a regular night at the club in my asshole.

"I call dibs," Otto said, making the twins groan.

"But first, I need to take care of Porter," I said, spinning around. He gulped but took my hand and led me to the bedroom. It looked exactly as I'd wanted. I knew sexual activity was challenging for Rueben away from his sanctuary, so I'd brought some of it with us.

Porter had plugged in a soothing oil mister, having learned our lesson with candles. Soft lights lit the room as music played. Velvet and silk were tossed against the bed. I moved to the silk blindfold and handed it to Rueben. His body relaxed, and he kissed me, doing as I requested.

"Otto, you watch from there. You may undress but do not touch yourself yet. I want to watch how hard you get."

I glanced at Porter, double checking he still wanted Phoenix involved. He nodded as he removed his clothes and dropped to his knees.

"Phoenix, undress and get on the bed. Porter's requested you join in. Are you cool with that?"

Phoenix looked at his brother briefly but nodded, willing to do whatever his twin needed. Rueben sat against the other side of the bed, listening to us as he waited. The sound of our pleasure would drive him wild, as would the sight for Otto. After exploring more of my sexuality, I discovered more and more about my men and myself. And tonight, I got to be in charge.

Leaving my dress on like Phoenix had wished, I sat on the edge of the bed and draped the fabric over my thighs so my pussy was visible. The two in front of me groaned, increasing my arousal.

"Porter, be a good boy and use your mouth to show me how much you love me."

"Yes, Mistress," he purred, bolting forward to do as I requested. I leaned back on my elbows as his tongue licked up my folds before he flicked my clit. Over and over, he did this, slowly ramping my desire up.

"More," I demanded, motioning for Phoenix to move closer. His legs wrapped around me, his chest hitting my back. Phoenix pulled my hair to the side, placing soft kisses down my throat and collarbone as his hands roamed. I hadn't found what Phoenix liked best yet, other than being included. He was the epitome of a team player.

I soon lost myself to the pleasure the twins bestowed upon me, forgetting I needed to direct them so I didn't lose track.

"Porter, coat yourself in me, but do not enter." He nodded, moving forward to drag his cock between my glistening pussy lips. I glanced over at Otto; his hands braced on his thighs as he watched. His dick stood straight at attention, heavy and thick as it leaked pre-cum.

"Phoenix, time to take the dress off."

He nodded into my neck, lifting the material over my head and placing it beside us. His hands moved over me easier now, his dick bumping into my back as he pressed forward. Porter stood, and I crooked my finger at him. He vibrated with need with each step, licking his lips in anticipation.

"On the bed," I directed, standing and taking Phoenix with me. Bending over Porter, I stroked him once before pressing him between my breasts. His abs flexed as he watched before he tossed his head back and gripped the sheets. Phoenix moved in behind me, his hands rubbing over my ass, dipping into my center, and eliciting a moan out of me.

"Shit, Raven. You're dripping wet. You need my dick bad, baby."

"Yes, please," I begged, letting him take control. Phoenix didn't waste time; thrusting into me and pushing me forward onto Porter. My tongue reached out and licked the tip of Porter's cock, his eyes darting to me as I did it again. He moaned, his thighs flexing beneath me.

"You're such a good cockasauras," I whispered. "You get so hard for your mistress and look perfect between my breasts. You want nothing more than to cum all over them, don't you?" I purred.

Porter nodded, his voice a groan. "Yes. Yes."

Phoenix plowed into me, hitting me just right with the added sensation of the plug, my orgasm quickly approaching. The sound of his balls slapping against my clit had Rueben stroking himself as he listened. I glanced back at Otto to see if he'd listened and hadn't touched himself yet. He panted, his fingers digging into his thighs, his cock dripping more as he watched.

"Come here, Otto." He bolted up, joining me on the bed. "Touch my clit and bring me to orgasm and then you can get yours," I promised. His hand reached down, finding my swollen nub.

"Porter, are you going to obey me? Are you going to give me your cum like I want?" I prodded.

"Yes."

"Then give it to me. Cum for me."

I stroked his cock between my breasts faster, his breathing increasing as he let himself go. Thick white streaks of cum spurted out, landing on my tits as he came. My orgasm crashed into me, and I threw my head back as I let out a breathy moan.

"Ah, yes, yes!"

When I came down, Porter looked more relaxed than I'd seen him for months, his body languid as he basked in the afterglow. I didn't have time to focus on him too much as Phoenix plunged in hard, his pelvic bone rubbing against the plug and activating the vibration.

"Shit," I moaned, my eyes rolling back as I came quickly again.

From there, I didn't know what occurred as my body became limp. I was moved onto Rueben's chest, his hands roaming over me. Once I had my bearings, I took the silk blindfold and used it to stroke his hard-as-steel cock. Rueben's thighs shook as I ran my nails up and down one. Otto came up behind me, a bottle of lube in his hand.

"Ready, Little Bird?" nodding, I sucked in a breath as he pulled out the plug. My eyes rolled back in my head as emptiness encompassed me. I whimpered, wanting the full feeling returned.

"You're so needy for our cocks, Little Bird. You make us all feel good. You don't ever have to worry about not getting it."

Otto soothed me with his words, brushing his fingers through my hair and running his hand up and down my spine. When he was ready, he pushed in, filling me whole again. I panted once he was fully seated, wondering if I could take him and Rueben together.

"I might die, but what a way to go," I wheezed. Rueben chuckled, lifting me so I straddled him.

"You can take it, Angel," he promised.

Nodding, I sank on his cock; my walls stretched tight, and I wondered if I'd ever be able to walk the same again.

"Great balls of fire," I hissed, my hands resting on Rueben's abs. "Don't even think of moving." The guys cursed, the vibrations making me moan. "That's moving."

Despite my request, they alternated their thrusts and pushed me toward the other. My head rested on

Rueben's chest, his hands brushing my hair as he caressed my cheek.

"You're so fucking beautiful, Little Bird. Taking both of us like this. Shit. I'm not going to last long. You had me primed to go from the second you dropped your dress," Otto cursed.

I whimpered, nodding that I agreed. I bet it was sexy. Part of me wished I could see it, but I didn't trust cameras to not send it to someone I didn't want it to go to, so I'd have to take their word for it.

Another orgasm rose, tingling up my spine as it took over, shooting through my body to my toes. Forget seeing stars or fireworks; my body erupted like the Big Bang. Once I returned back to my body, I opened my eyes to find my four men gazing at me.

"Let us take care of you now, Rave," Porter whispered.

I nodded, too boneless to do anything else.

Soft hands washed me as the warm water ran over me, the soap smooth against my skin. Gentle hands lathered shampoo in my hair, soothing my scalp as they massaged it. My body started to wake up as the water turned off, a colossal towel waiting for me to step into. From there, Porter rubbed lotion over my body as Phoenix and Rueben combed my hair. Otto painted my toes blue, placing kisses on my soles every few seconds.

"I love Twin Spa plus two," I sighed. The guys laughed, snuggling closer under the sheets.

"Tell us a story, Little Bird."

Smiling, I closed my eyes as I thought of the perfect one.

"Once upon a time, there was a girl with blue streaks in her hair, and she had four dashing boys. They sought out the bad guys, taking back what wasn't theirs and giving to those in need. They laughed and loved one another, never fearing anything because they had each other."

"What happened next?"

"Whatever they wanted. Together forever."

"Sounds perfect, Raven."

And it was.

DRESSED TO KILL SERIES

Don't forget to check out the rest of the Belladonnas.

Each book can be read as a standalone as part of the shared universe.

Harlow by Katie May and R.A. Smyth

Selena by May Dawson

Ivory by Kira Roman

Royal by Ann Denton

Raven by Kris Butler

Naomi by Alisha Williams

Karma by Amber Nicole

Darcy by Marie Mistry

Tabitha by Stacey Brutger

AUTHOR'S NOTE

Awww! I hope this book made you feel as good as I did writing it. It's like a warm hug from Rueben while the twins pamper you and Otto feeds you cake. Or, at least that's my wish. It's weird to think an assassin book could feel so warm and light, but that's Raven for you. She's complex and makes no apologies.

I truly loved writing this book and being part of this shared universe. Talking about cameos and working together to create this world with the other authors has been a blast. The other Dressed to Kill books I've read so far have all been amazing too, so make sure to check them out if you haven't. With it being a shared world, this will be all you get from these characters. I might do a bonus scene at some point for funsies, so there's at least that to look forward to. Raven has been such a fun character, and I truly love the guys and their relationship.

As always, I couldn't do this without my wonderful team behind me. Emma your support and love is unmeasurable, and I'll never quit saying thank you!

Heather, Megan, and Lindsay, thank you for dedication and devotion to making this book the best. I think this was the first book where all three of you licked Ruebear, even if Heather conceded in the end, I'm glad that you loved the character so much. He's such a gentle soul and I'm glad he has such fans.

To my arc team and all the readers who pick this up, thank you for your continued support. Some days it can be hard to be a writer, but your love and encouragement remind me that there's someone who wants to read my words.

To any new readers, welcome to my crazy brain and I hope you pick up some of my other books.

ALSO BY KRIS BUTLER

For the most up to date look at my releases. Check out all my books here: https://authorkrisbutler.com/my-books

LUX BRUMALIS

Penalty Box

Dead Lift

Breakaway

THE COUNCIL SERIES

(completed series)

Damaged Dreams

Shattered Secrets

Fractured Futures

Bosh Bells & Epic Fails

The Council Boxset

THE ORDER DUET (COUNCIL SPINOFF)

Stiletto Sins

Lipstick Lies

DRESSED TO KILL SHARED WORLD (STANDALONE)

Raven

F*CK STEAL KILL

F*ck Steal Kill

DARK CONFESSIONS

Dangerous Truths

Dangerous Lies

Dangerous Vows

Reckless (Cami's Novella)

Relentless (Nat's Novella)

Dangerous Love

TATTOOED HEARTS DUET

Riddled Deceit (Part 1)

Smudged Lines (Part 2)

Open Road (Road trip Novella)

Tattooed Hearts Completed Duet

MUSIC CITY DIARIES

Beautiful Agony

Beautiful Envy

Beautiful Unity

VACATION ROMCOM

Vibing

SINNERS FAIRYTALES

(standalone)

Pride

ABOUT THE AUTHOR

Kris Butler writes under a pen name to have some separation from her everyday life. Writing has become her second love, providing a safe place to normalize mental health through her characters. Kris enjoys writing emotional books with flawed characters, sassy heroines, and all the book boyfriends she loves to drool over. You can find her at home most nights reading with her husband and furbaby, trying to maintain her nerdy sock collection, or playing tabletop games with her friends. Kris loves to talk with readers about her books, even if it's just them yelling at her for that cliffhanger. If you enjoyed her book, please consider leaving a review. You can find her in her reader group or on social media.

Join my newsletter
Join my fan group
Check out my website

Printed in Great Britain
by Amazon